LINTANG
AND THE
PIRATE QUEEN

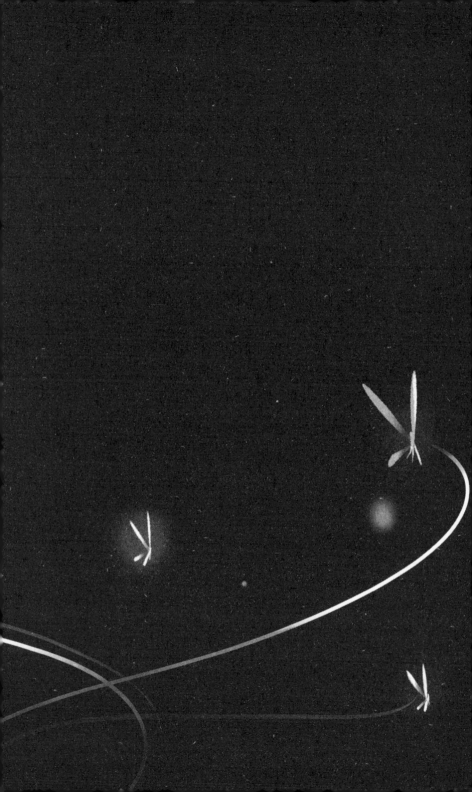

LINTANG
AND THE
PIRATE QUEEN

TAMARA MOSS

CLARION BOOKS

HOUGHTON MIFFLIN HARCOURT

BOSTON   NEW YORK

Clarion Books
3 Park Avenue
New York, New York 10016

Copyright © 2017 by Tamara Moss
First published by Penguin Random House Australia. This edition published
by arrangement with Penguin Random House Australia Pty Ltd.
First U.S. edition, 2019

Clarion Books is an imprint of Houghton Mifflin Harcourt Publishing Company.

hmhbooks.com

The text was set in Bembo Std.

Library of Congress Cataloging-in-Publication Data
Names: Moss, Tamara, author.
Title: Lintang and the pirate queen / Tamara Moss.
Description: First U.S. edition. | Boston ; New York : Clarion Books,
Houghton Mifflin Harcourt, 2019. | Originally published: Australia :
Random House Australia Pty Ltd., c2017. | Summary: Lintang's dream of
adventure on the high seas comes true when Captain Shafira invites her to
join her pirate crew, but Lintang's best friend, Bayani, has stowed away
and is keeping secrets.
Identifiers: LCCN 2018052488 | ISBN 9781328460301 (hardcover)
Subjects: | CYAC: Adventure and adventurers—Fiction. | Pirates—Fiction. |
Seafaring life—Fiction. | Imaginary creatures—Fiction. | Best
friends—Fiction. | Friendship—Fiction. | Stowaways—Fiction.
Classification: LCC PZ7.1.M6778 Lin 2019 | DDC [Fic]—dc23
LC record available at https://lccn.loc.gov/2018052488

Printed in the United States of America

DOC 10 9 8 7 6 5 4 3 2 1

4500774076

For Marguerite

The Mythie Guidebook Entry #38:
Fey [Twin Islands]

~~~~~~~~~~

The Twin Island fey (pixie) is a sky mythie and the smallest of the humanoids, at barely the height of an adult thumb. It has the wings of a dragonfly and wears a dress of friol petals.

Diet: Berries, nectar, and kitchen scraps. When visiting the islands of Tolus and Thelkin, food should be stored securely.

Habitat: Populated areas in the Twin Islands.

Frequency: Common.

Behavior: These mythies are considered pests. Missing items, spoiled food, and broken possessions are often the work of Twin Island fey. They enjoy provoking angry responses from humans and animals alike.

Eradication: Twin Island fey are too clever for traps and too fast to be squashed. The best thing to do is ignore their behavior until they get bored and go away.

Did you know? Each fey has a unique glow that distinguishes it from others.

Danger level: 1

The Uninvited Pixie

THERE WAS A PIXIE in the larder, and Lintang was going to be in so much trouble.

"Shoo," she said, waving her flaming wooden torch at it.

The pixie darted away and poked its tongue out at her.

Lintang waved her torch again. "Go! Mother will feed me to a river monster if you ruin anything."

The pixie zipped between the dangling panna leaves and a ham. Its white glow made it easy to spot. Lintang jabbed the fire at it and almost ignited the hanging herbs.

She shouldn't have left the larder door open. She knew better, but she'd come home for lunch and Mother wasn't here, so she thought she'd peek inside to see how everything was arranged. There were rules for how food had to be stored, and considering she was turning thirteen in less than a year—and would be a true adult —she'd figured it wouldn't be so bad if she had a closer look.

Except it *was* bad, because now there was a pixie inside.

The pixie didn't care that Lintang would get in trouble. It buzzed around pots of grains, dancing out of the way when Lintang tried to singe its petal dress.

This was the cheekiest pixie in the village. Whenever food disappeared, or the gaya paddocks were open, or the fishermen's nets down at the bay were untied, its little white glow could be seen bobbing cheerfully away from the crime.

The pixie wiggled its butt at Lintang before pressing its palms in a tub of congealed fat, leaving telltale tiny handprints. Mother would definitely know a pixie had been in here now.

Lintang lunged. The fire whooshed. "Shoo!"

The pixie sped past her, out the open larder door. Lintang turned to chase it, only to find that the hanging panna leaves were alight. The wooden torch had caught them. Black smoke puffed to the ceiling and filled her nostrils.

"Uh-oh," she said.

The herbs caught fire too.

"Uh-oh," she said again.

She had been trying so hard to be responsible.

A piece of panna leaf fell to the floorboards and curled up, scorched. The thought of their timber house catching fire finally propelled Lintang into action. She ran out of the larder and returned the torch to its bracket. The wooden drum Mother used for scrubbing dishes in hung from the low rafters among the pots and pans, empty. If Lintang wanted water she'd have to go to the river, and that was too far, even if she sprinted as fast as a hurricane.

Ribbons of smoke unfurled from the larder, choking the midafternoon sunlight. Water, water . . . where else could she get water?

Of course—the household shrine. Their offerings to the Three Gods had been freshly laid on the stone altar that morning. She reached between a scattering of juicy burbleberries and thin, smoldering sticks of mollowood to take the earthen jug.

"Sorry, Niti, but this is an emergency."

Water sloshed over her sarong and onto her bare feet as she carried the jug into the larder. The smoke was now thick plumes that clung to the back of her throat and made her cough.

She tossed the entire contents of the jug over the blaze, but the parts she missed continued to grow. She set down the jug with a groan.

"Lintang!"

The front door burst open and Mother thundered into the house. She grabbed Lintang's arm to drag her out. Elder Wulan was waiting on the porch with a basket of washed clothes. Mother snatched a sopping pair of Father's pants and raced back inside.

Lintang tried to follow, but Elder Wulan snagged her sarong. "Not a chance."

They listened to the wet slaps as Mother tried to put out the fire. Smoke pulsed from the doorway.

Lintang gulped and turned to face Elder Wulan. Her teacher was the oldest person in Desa—she'd taught Lintang's grandfather when *he* was at school—but her age never stopped her from helping other villagers with their chores. She said as long as she kept moving, the Goddess of Death couldn't catch her.

"I didn't mean it."

Elder Wulan put the washing basket down. "Of course you didn't."

She didn't sound as if she believed Lintang, but it was true. Lintang never did these kinds of things on purpose. They just sort of . . . happened.

The slapping from inside stopped. Elder Wulan leaned toward the smoky doorway. "Shall I send Lintang to the village for help, Aanjay?"

"The fire's out," Mother said, her voice echoing from the larder. "But all my panna leaves are ruined."

Oh no. Mother was supposed to make fish wraps for the visitors tonight, but she couldn't without panna leaves. Mother prided herself on her fish wraps. The recipe had been passed down for generations. She refused to teach Lintang how to make them until Lintang proved herself a good housekeeper, which, by the way things were going, would be never.

Lintang sighed and turned to stare over the lush rainforest, down the hill to the lagoon. The visitors' ship bobbed beyond the reef. Its black sails were rolled up. A lone bird circled above as clouds clustered on the horizon. The heaviness of the air warned of an impending storm.

She closed her eyes as Mother's footsteps thumped toward her. "I'm going to get in trouble again, aren't I?"

"Yes, Lintang," said Elder Wulan with a long-suffering sigh. "I'm afraid you are."

The Worst Punishment

"**W**HAT AM I GOING to do with you? Father is going to return with his fish, and I have nothing to make with them!"

"I can explain."

Mother stopped pacing to throw her hands in the air, making her wooden bangles clack together. "She can always explain," she said to Elder Wulan. "What was it this time, Lintang? A piece of exploding meat? A dragon? Perhaps one of the Three Gods came down from the stars and set fire to my larder, hmm?"

Lintang picked up a sopping sarong. Elder Wulan always preached a truthful tongue, but every time Lintang admitted what really happened, Mother yelled at her. And if she told the truth now, she'd have to admit that she'd left the larder door open, which was another rule she'd broken.

How did she always end up in these messes?

She searched her mind for something believable. "Actually," she said, trying to sound indignant, "it was a pirate."

Mother snatched the sarong from her. "You're too much like your grandfather, may his gentle star shine forever." She strung the piece of cloth up on one of the thin ropes stretched across the porch. "Your uncle is the village storyteller now, not you."

Lintang flicked water from her fingers to hide the lurch of emotion. Her uncle told good tales, but no one could match her grandfather's ability to weave a legend before the bonfire in his coarse, vibrant voice.

"Perhaps it's not a story this time," Elder Wulan said under her breath, almost too quiet for Lintang to hear. "With the visitors due to arrive soon . . ."

"Yes, maybe the pirate came from the visitors' ship," Lintang said, pushing memories of her grandfather aside. "He was wearing a hat with a talross feather and had a sash and all these gold medals—"

"Stop." Mother picked up a wet shisea. The wraparound dress was so complicated and long it stretched across an entire line. Being allowed to wear a pretty shisea instead of a sarong was one of the only good things about becoming an adult.

"Why do you bring me such shame?" Mother said. "Why have the Gods tested me with such a daughter?"

"So that your star might shine as bright as any warrior," Elder Wulan said, digging into a small pouch tied around her waist and withdrawing a handful of plump dates.

Mother turned to glare at her, then said, "The ship on the bay is the *Winda*, Lintang. There's no man with a talross feather, and there are certainly no gold medals."

Lintang stopped in the middle of reaching for an offered date.

No. It couldn't be.

She'd thought the ship was just another group of Vierzans from across the sea. They always stalked through the village in their long coats and heavy boots, sweat across their brows as they talked to the villagers about boring things like trade and taxes.

Elder Wulan was from Vierz, but she'd been living in Desa so long she was practically one of the villagers. Her skin had darkened under the blazing sun, and she wore shiseas like the other women, as well as a blue kerchief around her thin, gray hair. She hardly counted as being like the Vierzans who visited.

Except it wasn't Vierzans visiting this time. It was so much better than that.

"The *Winda*?" Lintang asked, breathless. "Captain Shafira of Allay is here? In our lagoon?"

"Yes," Mother said irritably. "And stop speaking of her like that. She's a pirate, not a Goddess."

Lintang leaned on the porch railing to squint at the black-sailed ship. A group of colorful birds flapped up from the rainforest canopy. "Are we going to fight her? The Vierzans said we have to kill her on sight."

"There are rumors she's unkillable," said Elder Wulan, picking the pit from a date. "And with only eight people in the warriors' guild, the village hardly wants to fight pirates."

Lintang smiled, imagining her wooden sword in hand as she dueled some faceless attacker. She might've considered asking to join the warriors' guild, except nothing ever happened in Desa.

Until now.

"I heard Captain Shafira's innocent," she said. She liked the thought. If anyone understood what it was like to get in trouble when it wasn't their fault, it was Lintang. Really, they were the same, she and the pirate queen.

Mother snorted. "Where did you come up with that silly idea?"

"One of the merchants from the southern island said she came to their village. She only asked for food and to tell the story of how she was framed. She helped them get rid of a labak."

Recently, Lintang had gone to the inn to fetch more cups—one of the youngest children at school had knocked over the crockery shelf and broken their whole supply—when she'd overheard the merchant talking to the village elders. She'd lingered as the merchant explained how Captain Shafira had skillfully caught a predator mythie that was nothing more than a flying head with trailing organs. The tale had been gruesome, and Romi the innkeeper had made Lintang promise she'd never repeat it to her friends.

"What are you doing talking to merchants?" Mother said, snapping one of Father's wet shirts in the breeze. "No wonder you never get any chores done, if you're lazing about chatting to visitors."

Lazing about?

Lintang opened her mouth to defend herself, but before she could, Elder Wulan said, "That labak killed four people before Captain Shafira came along. It's why we're holding our usual welcome feast. Hopefully she'll leave us unharmed."

Lintang's gaze slid to the *Winda* again. "Will she need an Islander to get out?"

Elder Wulan chuckled dryly. "Pirate queens are not

exempt from the sea guardian's rules. If she wants to leave the Twin Islands, then yes, she'll need one of you."

Lintang rubbed the back of her neck, her fingers sliding over the small, shiny fish scale that had been in her skin since birth. Only Islanders had a scale like it. Merchants could come and go between the two islands without trouble, but Nyasamdra drowned ships that tried to leave her territory unless they carried someone who bore her mark.

"You're not thinking of asking to join a pirate ship, are you?" Mother said.

Lintang dropped her hand, wishing she hadn't been so obvious.

"You're not leaving Desa, even if all the governors in the United Regions begged for your service. You have work to do here in the village." Mother strung up a petticoat from one of her shiseas. "By the next harvest, when you finish school, your proper training will start."

"I don't want to be a housekeeper," Lintang said.

"We all have jobs to do." Mother's voice was brisk as she straightened the petticoat. "You will take over from me, and your brother will take over the fishing from your father."

Lintang gestured to the horizon. "I want to see the world and have adventures, like Captain Shafira."

"Don't be selfish," Mother said. "We do what's best for the village, not what's best for ourselves. Now, Elder Wulan, please take this child out of my sight."

Elder Wulan glanced at the incoming clouds and put the rest of her dates in her pouch. "Come, Lintang. It's time for afternoon class."

Lintang followed Elder Wulan down the steps, already plotting ways to convince Captain Shafira to take her, when Mother called out, "You won't be going to the feast tonight."

Lintang spun around. "What?"

"Did you think you were going to get away with burning down the larder?"

Niti's hat! The larder. She'd been so busy thinking of Captain Shafira she'd almost forgotten.

Mother picked up the empty washing basket. "You can stay home and scrub it until it's clean of soot."

"But I want to see Captain Shafira!"

Mother responded with her glare that could puncture a blowfish. Lintang's earlier excitement vanished.

She couldn't believe it. How would she ever get the chance to convince the pirate queen to take her away if she wasn't even allowed to meet her?

Bayani

T HE SCHOOL WAS IN the center of the village, surrounded by the blacksmith's shed, the warriors' guild, and a cluster of houses for villagers who didn't own farms. The smell of manure from the nearby stables was particularly strong, thanks to the muggy air. The younger kids were playing a skipping game in the dust outside, chanting an old rhyme about Nyasamdra.

Remember, remember, the guardian's rules.
Use them or you'll be a fool!
Don't you laugh or give her meat,
Pick your nails, or suck your teeth.
Don't let the palms of your hands be seen,
And most of all, don't wear green!

Lintang dodged a chicken and glanced around, hoping the visitors had already arrived. All she saw were the everyday people of Desa. There was a lot less conversation than normal, and there were a lot more worried faces.

"They say she's invincible," Camelia the woodcutter said to Romi the innkeeper as they scrubbed the long festival tables.

"I heard they've caught her before, but she escapes every time," Romi said. "Did you hear about her battle with Captain Moon?"

Lintang hung back, straining to hear Camelia's answer.

"The merchants tell me it was on a volcano in the sea, which is mad. But then, she's supposed to be not quite right in the head. She stabbed a man for trying to take her necklace."

Romi the innkeeper snorted. "Unsurprising. Wasn't there something about her in *The Mythie Guidebook*? I'm sure I remember seeing her under one of the entries, but it's been too long since I've read the Gods-forsaken thing . . ."

Elder Wulan called for Lintang to hurry up. She spoke in Vierse rather than Toli. At school they were always supposed to speak, read, and write Vierse, the language most spoken around the world. The Twin Islands hadn't officially joined the United Regions yet, but that was only because Nyasamdra was too dangerous for outsiders to travel through their waters.

Lintang reached Elder Wulan as the rest of the children went into the classroom to gather sacks so they could pick fruit for the feast. While morning classes were filled with reading and writing, afternoon classes were spent outdoors learning about different jobs in the village, whether it be angling on the lagoon with the fishermen, tending to farmyard animals, or harvesting seasonal crops.

Nimuel ran up to Lintang. Even strangers could tell they were brother and sister—their noses were petite but broad, their cheeks round, and their hair as dark as fertile soil. The only difference was that, unlike Lintang, Nimuel had inherited Mother's eyes, gray-green like the rainforest leaves at dusk. At the moment they were bright with excitement. "Did you see the ship?"

She brushed bread crumbs from his chin. He could be as messy as a blue-tailed howler sometimes. "Yes, but I'm not allowed to go to the welcome feast. I got into a bit of trouble at lunchtime."

He groaned. "What did you do now?" Some of the

kids stuck their heads out of the classroom, yelling for him. He waved. "All right, I'm coming!" To Lintang, he said, "Of all the days to get in trouble."

"You don't have to tell me," she said. He rolled his eyes and raced off to join the others.

He was only seven, but he'd made so many friends since starting school. Lintang could've made friends if she'd wanted to, of course, but the kids never did what she told them, even though she was the eldest. And they never accepted her challenges to duel. Who wanted to be friends with kids who didn't like dueling? A bunch of sea sponges, the lot of them.

Well, except one.

"Ah, Bayani, good." Elder Wulan headed to Bayani, who had been reading a book on the school steps. "Would you do me a favor?"

Bayani was twelve, like Lintang, but that was where their similarities ended. While Lintang and the other children came to class in sarongs or long, ragged shorts, he wore neat cotton shirts, clean pants, and boots. His black hair was carefully trimmed by his mother, and his skin was darker than Lintang's from working on the gaya farm. He was always polite, knew the correct answers in class, and loved learning. Normally Lintang would never have liked someone so responsible, but there was a good reason he was her best friend.

"As a reward for your excellent answers in history class this morning, you may stay behind and tidy the schoolhouse instead of picking fruit," Elder Wulan said to him.

He smiled. "Thank you, Elder Wulan."

She rounded on Lintang. "And," she said severely, "as punishment for giving your mother so much grief today, you must stay behind and tidy the schoolroom rather than come out to pick fruit."

Lintang scowled.

"Don't pull that face at me, Lintang of Desa."

Lintang forced her scowl to relax. She had to grit her teeth so she could answer without sounding resentful. "Yes, Elder Wulan."

It was so unfair. She'd been *trying* to do the right thing.

"Right." Elder Wulan turned to Bayani. "Don't let her leave the classroom, and don't let her get into any trouble."

Bayani grinned at Lintang. "I'll do my best."

Elder Wulan climbed the steps to check on the others, and Lintang peeked at the book Bayani had been reading. It was made of metal rather than papil, which meant it was an official textbook from Vierz. She caught sight of the cover.

The Mythie Guidebook
by
Leika of Zaiben

She should've known. He'd been obsessed with that book recently.

"So what did you do this time?" he asked while they waited.

"Nothing." When he looked at her, she added, "I singed the larder, that's all."

He shook his head, but he was smiling. "Of course you did. And who was to blame?"

"Pirates." Bayani laughed, and Lintang added glumly, "Yes, Mother didn't believe me either." She frowned at him. "Actually, it was that stupid pixie's fault."

"Which pixie?"

"Your favorite one. With the white glow."

"Pelita," Bayani said.

"Right."

The reason Bayani didn't have any friends besides Lintang was because he loved mythies. He gave them names and talked to them like people. He could usually be seen wandering through the village at dusk with two or three glowing fairies fluttering around his head. He even saved gnomes from wild-pig traps, and who would want to save an ugly old gnome?

She'd asked him about it before, but he'd just shrugged and said he felt sorry for them. Everyone thought he was strange, even the adults. But Lintang didn't mind if he was strange. It meant he wasn't boring.

The school group started down the wide, dusty road. Elder Wulan glanced back one last time and gave a warning glare before they headed out of the village. When they were gone, Lintang said, "I have a great idea."

Bayani sighed and went into the classroom.

She followed him. "Just listen."

It was darker than usual in the room. One side of a heavy world map drooped from its spot, blocking the windows. The room was cool, thanks to the concrete walls, though it smelled of chalk and the earthen floor. A fruit dove fluttered in the low rafters.

Bayani slid *The Mythie Guidebook* back on the shelf among all the other battered books. Lintang picked up a dry rag and started wiping each desk and slate clean.

"Mother's only mad because I burned her panna leaves."

Bayani beat two dusters together. Clouds of chalk exploded around him.

"If I get more panna leaves from the plantation, I could give them to her nice and early so she'll still be able to make her fish wraps. Then she can't be mad at me."

Bayani stopped beating the dusters. "Lintang . . ."

"This is important," Lintang said quickly. "It's to make Mother happy. I'm being responsible."

"Says the girl who set her mother's larder on fire and blamed pirates." Bayani stood on the little front stool to wipe down the blackboard. "Elder Wulan told you to stay here."

Lintang gave a dramatic sigh and threw her rag aside. "All right. You've forced me to do this. Bayani of Desa, as your elder, I order you to let me go."

Bayani snorted. "You're three days older than me. I hardly think—Hey!"

While his back was turned, Lintang had run to the storage cupboard. She hit the side of it in three special spots. The tired lock clicked; the door fell open. Two wooden swords, chipped and muddy and worn, sat on the top shelf. Mother had long ago regretted the day she'd had them made for Lintang. Elder Wulan was under the impression she'd managed to confiscate them for good, and Lintang was happy to let her keep thinking that.

She tossed one of the swords to Bayani. He caught it with a frown. His had a carving of a star on the hilt. Hers had a carving of a full moon, with two crescent moons on either side.

"Ordinary dueling rules apply," she said. "If I win, I can go to the panna plantation."

"I'm not dueling with you."

She smirked. "Yes, you are."

This was why Bayani made an excellent friend. Lintang could talk him into anything.

She edged forward and tapped her wooden blade against his. It made a delightful clack. "If you win," she said, "we both stay here, and I'll help you make this classroom spotless."

Bayani tapped his blade against hers, thoughtful. "We'd better not. We'll get in trouble."

"I saw you practicing last night in the paddock," she said. "You want to beat me, don't you? Come on. You never know. Today could be your lucky—"

He lunged. She yelped, blocking him just in time, then cackled as he attacked again. Usually she pretended to be Hantu, the legendary swordsman who battled a hundred soldiers on Malaki Mountain, but today she was Captain Shafira, fighting on a volcano in the sea.

"Take that!" she said, jabbing at Bayani and just missing as he spun away.

His attacks were fast, studied. She was right—he *had* improved. Maybe he had gotten tips from the warriors' guild.

Thwack! Clatter!

No one ever gave Lintang fighting tips. They were all scared that Mother would find out. Instead, Lintang had to use her reflexes, her strength, her knowledge of her sword.

Clack! Crack!

"You . . . you . . . wobbly jellyfish!" Bayani said.

Lintang laughed, climbing onto a desk. "We need to work on your insults." A slate fell to the floor. Chalk snapped beneath her bare heel. She jumped as he tried to swipe her legs. "You ebony-nosed loobatoon! You brown-tailed barbanees! You blood-eyed ruberrince!"

He snorted and stabbed at her legs again. "So while I was practicing sword-fighting, you were making up ridiculous words?"

She spun to dodge his attack and landed lithely on the floorboards near the front of the classroom. A toy landcraft clattered away on its wooden wheels. "And yet I'm still winning."

"You're not winning!"

Smack!

"I have to get those panna leaves. If I don't meet Captain Shafira, I'll die."

"Well, I'm glad you're not overreacting."

"I mean it. I have to be the Islander she chooses to get past Nyasamdra."

Bayani said nothing for a while. Lintang thought he was just concentrating—*Whack! Clack!*—but after a moment he said, "Do you think she'll consider taking me?"

Lintang lowered her sword. "You? On a pirate ship?" Rather than answer, Bayani swung, and she barely blocked his attack in time. "Why do you want to leave Desa?"

"Why do *you* want to leave Desa?"

"As if I want to be stuck here all my life. I'm sick of learning about these amazing places and not being allowed to see them." She hit her blade so hard against his, the wood shuddered in her hand.

"Same with me," he said.

"I don't believe you. You don't like traveling. It was only last season that you had to go to Sundriya, and you said you hated being away."

"I was in an infirmary the whole time, surrounded by other sick people. Of course I hated it."

"But why would you want to travel with pirates? They're criminals, you know."

Bayani used a three-move attack to back her up against a desk. "Forget it. It was just an idea."

She spun so the desk was between them. They stared at each other, panting. "What's going on, Bayani?"

He'd been acting strange ever since he'd come back from his seven-day trip to Sundriya, the capital city south of Desa. His fever had been too high for the village's traditional healers to save him. His mother had rushed him to a Vierzan medic instead, and when he'd come back, he wouldn't say a word about what had happened. Something there had changed him, though. He'd become secretive, often wandering around with a furrow in his brow. And he didn't always answer the first time his name was called anymore, as if he was constantly lost in thought. Whenever she asked him about it, he'd smile and say it was nothing.

"It's nothing," he said now, just as she'd expected. "Are you going to fight me or not?"

Fine. If he wasn't going to tell her, she wasn't going to play fair. The world map behind him was ready to fall. In one swooping movement, she picked up a duster and hurled it at the poster, which fell with a resounding crash. Bayani whipped around in alarm. While he was looking away, she lurched forward and thrust her blade at his throat.

"Surrender!"

Bayani's groan rumbled through the wood of her sword. He turned to face her. "You cheated."

She set her sword on the nearest desk. "I distracted you. That's not cheating."

He put his sword down too. "I can't believe you beat me. I've been training every day."

"This isn't some festival dance. There aren't special moves. You have to make it up as you go along."

"How? How do you do it so well?"

She shrugged. "I just . . . feel it."

He sighed noisily and started cleaning up the dropped chalk and slates. One of the slates was cracked. He examined it. "I don't know how we're going to explain this to Elder Wulan."

"Don't bother—she won't notice. Almost everything in this classroom is broken." She brightened. "And don't worry about cleaning now. Let's go to the plantation!"

"No." He picked up his sword and tried to reach for Lintang's, but she snatched it away. "The deal was that if you won, *you* could go to the plantation."

Her smile fell. "You're not coming with me?"

"I have to tidy this mess. Besides, the panna plantation is near the orchard. What if Elder Wulan catches us?"

"She won't. It'll be fine."

"No, Lintang." Bayani dropped a handful of broken chalk into the chalk bucket. "I am absolutely, positively not going with you."

The Mythie Guidebook Entry #87:
Propheseeds [common]

~~~~~~~~

Propheseeds are sky mythies that take the form of three glowing dandelion seeds. They appear harmless, giggling childishly, and do not physically attack.

Diet: Unknown.

Habitat: Worldwide.

Frequency: Moderately rare.

Behavior: The propheseeds will say your name three times, then, in the form of a riddle or rhyme, give you the time and details of your imminent death.

Eradication: There is no known way of banishing or killing the propheseeds, and no one has ever escaped their prophecies.

Did you know? In the ninety-fifth year of the Bauei period, the propheseeds predicted that General Lor would drown. He locked himself in an old fort in the Arobi Desert, which then flooded after a freak rainstorm, killing him and his five attendants.

Danger level: 1

Pero and the Propheseeds

◌৹

LINTANG STALKED TRIUMPHANTLY down the hill in front of Bayani, her wooden sword tucked into the sash around her sarong. She squinted at the bay over Farmer Johan's growing vegetables. The fishing boats were coming in for the day, but it was too hard to tell if the *Winda*'s rowboats were among them— thick gray clouds had cast dark shadows over the ocean.

She turned to ask Bayani if he could see them, only to find he'd stopped at the edge of his farm. Two gaya had wandered to the fence, vying for attention. He tousled the woolly blue head of one and patted a horn of the other.

"Oh, so we're friends again, are we?" Bayani said to the one with the torn ear. "You were certainly grumpy enough during dawn milking."

"By the gods," Lintang muttered. If it wasn't mythies he was busy chatting to, it was his beloved gaya herd. "Come on, Bayani!"

She turned on her heel and continued downhill without waiting. Pitter wrens darted around her, snapping at the tiny white rain moths that always swarmed before a storm. The grazing paddock soon petered out, replaced by tangled rainforest. It would be quicker cutting through than going around. She left the path and squelched through the warm leaf litter. The canopy twisted over her head, making it as dark as twilight. The buzzing insects were nearly deafening.

She took the path she knew, climbing onto a monstrous buttress root, then checking to make sure Bayani was still behind her. He was picking his way between two spiderwebs.

She cupped her hands around her mouth. "Stop being delicate! They'll build another one!"

He ignored her and continued in his careful manner. Leaves rustled above, probably blue-tailed howlers swinging from branch to branch in the canopy. A large flutterbee soared past her nose, its wings decorated in intricate patterns of black and orange.

"Over the mountains and across the sea," she said

dramatically as Bayani drew nearer, "there lived a warrior of legendary skill. His name was Pero."

"Oh good," he said, climbing up to join her. "I like the legends of Pero."

She jumped down from the buttress root. "But this is no ordinary tale, for Pero had seen the propheseeds."

Bayani groaned. "I don't want to hear about his death."

"Too bad, it's what you're getting."

They headed for the plantation.

"A good storyteller gives the audience what it wants."

"A good audience stays quiet. Now, Pero had returned to his village to take care of his sickly mother after his brave battle against the sea serpent. He enjoyed his time chopping firewood, fixing things around the house, and visiting the gaya girl, for they say those who take care of gaya make the best wives or husbands."

"You added that part in," Bayani said, reddening.

"True," she replied. "Actually, Pero visited the inn because he liked the barmaid. But on his way home one evening, beneath the shine of his ancestors' stars, he came across a trio of floating dandelion seeds. They swirled and giggled before him, and he knew his doom had come. 'Pero, Pero, Pero,' they said, and then they spoke in rhyme:

"Mother of monsters, ruler of all
She is the one to whom you will fall
Fifty days for you to fight
Mratzi will harvest you in the night."

Lintang stopped as she caught whiffs of sweet pannas mingling with the damp, earthy scent of leaf litter. And there was another smell—a delicious floral tang that reminded her of something. "We're almost there," she said, and broke into a run.

The first panna trees appeared suddenly, springing from the forest in knobbly, unkempt rows. Weeds grew taller than her, and fallen pannas squished pulpy and yellow beneath her bare feet. The rainforest canopy opened to reveal storm clouds rolling overhead. The air was so dense now, it felt as though she were swimming through it.

She slowed, and Bayani caught up to her, panting. "You can't stop a story halfway."

"I thought you didn't want to hear about Pero's death."

"Well, you've started it now, haven't you?"

"All right." She found a healthy tree nearby and thumbed one of its wide leaves. Perfect. Mother would love it. "Pero was not afraid of the Goddess of Death. He had faced the harvest many times during his battles. And the propheseeds had spoken of the mother of monsters —Lanme Vanyan herself—who was someone Pero had always wanted to fight. So he packed his bag, said goodbye to his mother, kissed the barmaid, and left."

Bayani narrowed his eyes. "He didn't kiss the barmaid."

"Who's telling the story here?"

As they talked, they pulled off panna leaves and stuck them in Lintang's sash so they sat like armor around her chest and back. The strange floral smell grew stronger.

"I would've run away," said Bayani, repositioning the fronds so they didn't tickle Lintang's chin. "If the propheseeds say Lanme Vanyan's going to kill you, why would you go after her?"

"You can't run from a prophecy."

"You can try."

"No, you can't. If Pero had stayed behind, Lanme Vanyan would've ruined his village. If he'd hidden in a cave, it would've been the exact cave she happened to be in at that moment. It's how prophecies work."

Rumbles of thunder echoed through the mountains. Under the thunder came a faint clicking.

Bayani paused in the middle of pulling down another leaf. "What's that noise?"

"The sound of you being a sapling about Pero the warrior. Of course he's not going to run away. He's the bravest person in history. He dared to go up against *Lanme Vanyan*. Sure, she killed him, but that doesn't mean—"

"Frangipani," Bayani said suddenly.

She blinked. "Huh?"

"Can't you smell it?"

So that was the floral scent. She knew she'd recognized it. Merchants from the southern island wore the flowers in their dark, curly hair.

"That's strange," she said, looking around. "I didn't know it grew here."

"It doesn't."

Something rustled behind them. Whatever it was whipped out of sight too quickly, though Lintang caught a flash of white. Had someone from school found them?

But no—it had looked more like a swishing dress than a sarong. Odd clothing for someone from the village.

Bayani stepped back as lightning flickered across the sky. The sun was long gone now, the afternoon dim.

"I think we should leave," he said. When Lintang frowned at him, he added, "I can hear clicking."

The faint sound persisted, barely audible beneath the insects. Her brain struggled to catch up with the drowsy sense of danger.

And then she remembered. The frangipani. The clicking. The panna trees.

She swore beneath her breath. "I thought they only appeared on the southern island."

"Not always." Bayani was starting to look sick.

This couldn't be happening. It was so ridiculous, so unlikely.

"It shouldn't be out," she said, as if logic could make everything safe again. "It's daytime!"

Even as she said it, she knew it didn't matter. With clouds overhead, there was no sunlight to protect them.

The sweet, floral smell turned rancid, like rotten meat. They stared at each other in panic.

A malam rasha was about to attack.

The Mythie Guidebook Entry #71:
Night Terror [Twin Islands]

∽ ∽ ∽ ∽ ∽ ∽ ∽ ∽

The night terror (malam rasha) is a humanoid forest mythie in the predator category. It appears as a woman with wooden skin, long dark hair, and a white dress. Instead of arms, it has tree roots, which are sharp enough to dig through flesh. It can be identified by the sound of its clicking wings and the smell of frangipani. When the night terror is about to attack, the sweet smell turns to one of rotten meat.

Diet: Human organs.

Habitat: Panna plantations on Thelkin Island, the southern half of the Twin Islands.

Frequency: Rare.

Behavior: When there is no sunlight, night terrors root their legs in a secret spot while their upper half searches for victims. They are impossible to outrun or to wound, as any injuries will heal. If you have your eyes open, it will suck them out of your head.

Eradication: The only way to kill these mythies is to smear ash or salt on the stump of their lower half, which keeps them from rejoining. If they are not whole when sunlight hits them, they will burn.

Did you know? Night terrors will not harm their home in any way.

Danger level: 4

Sword and Shield

S OMETHING MOVED BEHIND THEM. Lin-
tang twisted, drawing her wooden sword, but she
only saw a tendril of dark hair streaming behind a tree.
"What do we do?"

She didn't dare blink. Bayani stood perfectly still
beside her.

"Bayani," she said, throat tight. *"What do we do?"*

"I'm trying to remember what it says in the guidebook," he whispered. "But my brain is stuck . . ."

Lightning flashed again, blinding Lintang for a moment. When her eyes adjusted, she thought she saw another whip of white, but she couldn't be sure whether it
was just spots from the flash.

"Where did it go?" Bayani said. "Did you see it
move?"

Lintang glanced up and down the row of trees. The

stench of rotten meat was so strong she wanted to gag. "I don't know. I couldn't—"

She stopped. Out of the corner of her eye, right behind Bayani, she saw a dark shape.

Goose bumps erupted across her skin. She couldn't inhale. She couldn't turn to look at it properly.

Her lungs were bursting. She gasped and said, "I think it's behind you."

Bayani spun. His movement jolted Lintang from her panic. She turned too, lifting her sword as the mythie loomed before them. Its leathery wings clicked with each beat. Its long, black hair flowed around its wooden face. Its dress hung empty below its waist, where its legs should've been.

Before it could attack, a ball of white light zipped in front of its face. The malam rasha recoiled, snarling.

"Pelita!" Bayani cried.

Lintang used the malam rasha's distraction to grab Bayani's hand and drag him toward the rainforest.

Bayani glanced back, slowing their pace as he called for the pixie. Lintang checked over her shoulder too, but the panna leaves around her body constricted her movement.

The malam rasha batted Pelita away and flew down

the row after them. It was fast, much faster than they were. There was no outrunning a malam rasha, the guide-book said.

Well, then. If they couldn't run, they would have to fight.

Lintang whirled around and raised her sword. "Get back!"

The malam rasha reared up. It moved to strike with its arm of tree roots, but she stabbed and it retreated. *Stab. Dodge. Stab. Dodge.*

She let out a scream—not of fear, but of fury—as she continued to swing her sword, forcing the malam rasha back. She had to protect Bayani. She had to get this monster away somehow.

Pelita returned, buzzing around the malam rasha's face. Bayani yelled something. Why was the silly gnome not running to safety?

And then she heard what he was saying.

"Your sword—it's made of panna wood! *Panna wood!*"

Night terrors will not harm their home in any way.

She looked down at the leaves tucked into her sash and gasped. While Pelita was still distracting the malam rasha, Lintang ran to Bayani, shoved him to the ground, and threw herself over him. His cry was squashed from his lungs as she landed on his back. Her sword hit the grass beside them.

"Close your eyes!" she said, squeezing her own eyes shut.

Thunder crashed across the mountain and rumbled through the ground. There was a whoosh as the malam rasha descended upon them. Lintang cringed, praying to the Three Gods that her plan would work, and felt a spark of hope when nothing happened right away. The malam rasha hadn't attacked. Maybe they were safe . . .

Something raked the panna leaves in the back of her sash: tree roots, sharp enough to pierce flesh. They clattered against the veiny ridges of the leaves, the sound in harmony with the faint clicking noise of the creature's wings.

Lintang bit back a scream. It was trying to rip out her organs . . . but couldn't. The panna leaves protected them, just as she'd planned.

Bayani trembled beneath her. She dredged up a memory of a prayer from temple. "Hear me, Niti, Patiki, Mratzi—Gods of Ytzuam, givers of life, guardians of stars. Please protect us, please don't let the malam rasha eat us. Please protect us, please protect us, please protect us . . ."

Footsteps thumped on the grass. Were the malam rasha's legs coming to rejoin its body?

Lintang tucked her head down tight, expecting the final blow at any moment. But the reek of rotten meat vanished. Instead, she found herself inhaling the scent of squashed pannas and the clean smell of Bayani's hair. The clicking sound was gone too.

Bayani didn't move. Lintang turned her face to one side and cracked open an eye as a fat drop of rain landed on her nose. The plantation was empty. She turned the other way. Nothing.

Thunder rumbled again as she climbed to her feet. Bayani glanced up. "Is it gone?"

"I think so," she said, helping him stand.

"I thought we were going to die."

She picked up her sword. "Me too."

They headed toward the forest, keeping an eye out for movement between the panna trees. She strained her ears for any noise, but all she could hear was the insect commotion, which had swelled as the rain started.

"Did Pelita chase it away?" Bayani said when they reached the fringe of the forest.

"A malam rasha isn't afraid of a pixie." Lintang scanned the plantation one last time. "Didn't you hear the footsteps? I thought it was the malam rasha's legs at first, but now I think it was a person. Someone saved us."

"Who?"

"Lintang!" Elder Wulan hurried out of the rainforest with the rest of the class trailing behind. "What are you doing here? We heard you screaming from the orchard!"

Nimuel was behind her, biting into a mao. Watery orange juice trickled down his chin. "Hi, Lintang," he said through his mouthful.

"I can explain," Lintang said, but Elder Wulan shook her head.

"I don't want to hear your stories. What are those panna leaves doing in your sash? *And what are you doing with that sword? I confiscated it!*"

"There was a malam rasha! It was lucky I had the sword. We almost died—"

"Bayani, I'm disappointed in you." Elder Wulan grabbed Lintang's arm and marched her through the forest. Above them, howlers swung from branch to branch with their long, hairy arms, hooting and cackling as they sent showers of rain through the canopy. The other children followed Elder Wulan, chattering eagerly about their bulging sacks of fruit. They were used to Lintang getting in trouble.

Bayani rushed to keep up. "She's telling the truth."

"Oh, Bayani, not you too. Your parents will be furious if you start telling stories."

How could Elder Wulan think that Bayani, of all people, was lying? Did she really distrust Lintang that much?

"It's not a story!" Lintang said. "There was a malam rasha, but someone chased it away."

"Oh? Who?"

"I . . . I don't know."

The thrill of the attack started to ebb. Even to her, the explanation seemed far-fetched. Who would've been brave enough to chase away a malam rasha and not come back for the glory?

Elder Wulan gave Bayani an exasperated look.

"It sounds made-up," he said, "but she's telling the truth. You have to warn the warriors' guild there's a predator mythie nearby."

Lintang glanced at Nimuel, who was sharing extra fruit with his best friend. They were all in danger if she couldn't convince Elder Wulan she was telling the truth. There had to be a way to prove it. "I'll go to the feast tonight and ask the other villagers. Whoever saved us will come forward."

"Oh no." Elder Wulan pulled her up short. "I know what this is now. You made up a story so you could see the pirate queen. I'm sorry, Lintang, but your mother's word is final."

"What? No, that's not why I—"

"Stop arguing. You are to go straight home and stay inside. And, Bayani, if you don't want to be banned from the feast too, I suggest you stop playing along with her silly games."

Lintang and Bayani exchanged alarmed looks. How were the villagers supposed to defend themselves against one of the most vicious mythies on the Twin Islands if no one believed it existed?

Pirate Queen

WITH DARKNESS CAME rain that pounded on the thatched roof. Lintang sat on the little bench by the shrine, watching the knobbly sticks of mollowood burn low in their clay holders. Scented smoke coiled around her. Lightning flashed between the unevenly boarded walls, illuminating the room with its four straw mattresses, its shelf of bowls, and the two trunks where the family kept their clothes. Her stomach growled between rumbles of thunder.

The front door opened, bringing in a gust of wind that sent the hanging pots clattering.

Bayani entered. His best red shirt and pants were soaking wet and mud-splattered. Pelita fluttered around his head like a luminous flutterbee. He shut the door, dripping all over the floorboards. He looked wretched.

He must've gotten in lots of trouble for letting her sneak to the plantation.

"Are you all right?" she said.

"Come on." His voice was thick, as though he was coming down with a cold. He took her hand to pull her up. "Everyone's at the temple. We have to tell them about the malam rasha."

Lintang resisted. "Wait—"

"No," Bayani said. "The village is in danger. We have to do something."

Lintang studied him. His eyes were puffy in the flame light of the wooden torch. "What's wrong?"

He rubbed his nose with the back of his wrist. "Lintang, I . . . I saw . . ."

"You saw what?"

He looked away and swallowed hard. "Nothing."

Nothing, nothing, nothing. It was always nothing.

He smiled weakly, as if sensing her frustration and trying—poorly—to reassure her. "It's been a bad day, hasn't it?"

"You could say that." Lintang tugged her hand from his grip. "I'm not allowed to go to the feast, remember?"

He swiped at his wet face with his equally wet palms. "Since when has *not being allowed* stopped you from doing anything?"

Lintang returned her attention to the glowing mollowood. "Mother said if I go, she'll pull me out of school early and send me to one of the mining communities."

Mother would probably follow through with the threat too. Lintang had an uncle who lived on Malaki Mountain, spending all his days in dark tunnels digging out gemstones to be sent overseas. Mother had said it would do Lintang some good to learn what real hard work was.

Bayani hesitated. "Lintang—"

"No," she said. "I'll take any punishment, but not that. If the village doesn't want to know about the malam rasha, that's their problem."

Pelita fluttered down and patted her knee. Bayani was silent for a long time.

"What if someone dies?" he said at last.

"I don't care," Lintang said, and at once was hit with a surge of guilt. What if it was Nimuel who was attacked? Or Camelia the woodcutter, who'd crafted her wooden sword? Or Farmer Johan, who always gave her the biggest corn during the harvest? No—none of the villagers had done anything to deserve a horrible death.

Bayani must've seen where her thoughts were, because he held out his hand again.

She stared at it. "What if I get sent to a mining community? We'll never see each other again."

Pelita flew back to his shoulder. "Please," he said to Lintang. "Come with me."

She took his hand and stood. He led her to the door. "Where are your panna leaves?"

Lintang huffed, finding her energy again. "Mother used them for her fish wraps. You'd think she might've been nicer, considering I risked my life to get them."

They headed down the porch steps and into the rain. Her sarong was instantly soaked. Mud squelched beneath her bare feet. It was hard to see through the darkness, but with Pelita's glow they were able to make out their next few steps.

They hurried toward the temple. Lintang listened for any signs of the clicking noise through the storm.

"Thank you, by the way," Bayani said as they reached the center of the village. "You saved my life at the plantation today. I didn't really appreciate it until now."

"I was the one wearing the panna leaves. I had to cover you."

"You didn't *have* to."

"Sure I did." She frowned when she saw villagers in the market square hammering lids onto large barrels. "What are they doing?"

"The welcome feast was canceled. All food is being transported onto the ship. They've also taken a load of fresh water and cloth."

"So they were only here for supplies?" She slowed. "Wait, does this mean you've seen Captain Shafira?"

Bayani smiled. It was a slower response than usual, and it was only a small smile, but it was better than nothing. "I can't believe it took you so long to ask about her."

"I've had a busy day." She picked up the pace again. "What's she like? Is she amazing? I bet she is. I bet everyone stops when she walks into a room. What's her crew like?"

"She came in alone. I . . . I didn't like her."

"Of course you didn't like her—she's the pirate queen. Did she explain how she was framed?"

"She was talking about the ruler of her country being dead, and how there's a conspiracy to cover it up, but she was only just getting started when I left to find you . . ." He trailed off and said nothing more.

The temple came into view. They had to pass through a set of heavy gates to get inside. The temple was five stories high, each level a smaller block on top of the last. It was used by those who wanted to sit in peace and reflect on Ytzuam and the Gods. Lintang used to learn about the Gods from the priests there when she was younger, but the only time she visited now was during seasonal festivals.

They climbed the slippery stone steps. Pelita buzzed up to the second story of the temple and disappeared through a window, probably to wreak havoc in the priests' quarters.

Three hardwood statues guarded the doorless entry. Niti, the creator of stars, his hands cupped to hold new seeds. Patiki, the planter of stars, her basket tucked beneath her arm. Mratzi, the harvester of stars, wrapped in her ribbons, her lips and eyes sewn shut.

Bayani shivered as they passed the statues.

The stone floor was almost as muddy as the ground outside. Villagers sat on the long benches, their best clothes drenched. Rain and sweat dripped from their brows, making their faces glisten beneath the light of flaming torches lining the walls. They shifted in their spots, tense and wary, as if waiting for a sudden pirate attack.

Lintang walked beneath the ceiling of deep blue. It had swirls of painted stars representing Ytzuam and the shooting stars that had passed overhead when the mythies arrived. No one knew why the Three Gods had sent the mythies. The creatures had caused havoc throughout the world, but the priests always said in serene voices that the Gods had reasons for everything they did, even if humans couldn't understand them.

There was a woman on the stage at the front of the temple. She was speaking in Vierse, but her accent was heavy, the language new on her tongue. It was how most adults in the village spoke once they stopped going to school and using Vierse in daily conversation.

The woman was fearsome. Her deep purple top and pants hugged her body and blossomed out at the sleeves and ankles. From her belt hung a weapon with a spear on one end and a curved axe on the other, which was as scary as the chain of large fangs around her neck. Her thick lips were curled in a sneer, and her eyes, set wide apart, were narrowed in distrust. She didn't look like an Islander or a Vierzan.

"And so," she was saying, pacing the stage like a restless predator, "we need child to get past sea guardian."

A mutter rose from the adults, even as children's hands shot up to volunteer.

From the front row, Elder Wulan stood. "You want a *child* to get past the sea guardian?"

"Young girl not betray us," the captain said.

The muttering increased. Lintang drew in a hopeful breath. This was perfect. Forget the other kids. She was the one who had practiced dueling. She was the one who had fought a malam rasha and lived. If she could convince everyone the malam rasha existed, she'd be chosen to go aboard.

"We drop her in Zaiben after," the captain continued, ignoring the villagers' unease. "Vierzans send her back."

Bayani stiffened. "Zaiben?" he whispered, so softly Lintang knew she wasn't supposed to have heard.

Why did that interest him? Zaiben was the capital of Vierz. It was where Elder Wulan came from. It was supposed to be amazing, but Bayani had never shown an interest in actually visiting it before. Lintang was the one who dreamed of far-off places, not him. What had changed?

He nudged her before she could ask, keeping her moving down the aisle.

Oh, right. She had a job to do.

She took only a few steps before she realized he wasn't following. When she gestured for him to join her, he didn't move. His gaze darted around at the villagers. Some had already noticed them and were watching with frowns. Poor shy Bayani, always afraid to speak up, always afraid to get in trouble. What a dull life he would lead without her.

Lintang nodded to reassure him she could do it alone. She continued walking. More and more people turned to look. Sweat beaded on her palms. Her face felt hot. She couldn't see Mother yet, but it wouldn't be long before the yelling started.

She had to do this. She had to convince the villagers that they were in danger.

"We leave soon," the captain said. "We hunt sirens in Adina Sea. It is goodwill. You understand we are not criminals."

Lintang faltered again. She had almost forgotten that the pirate queen had helped get rid of a labak. This was good. This meant Captain Shafira could help find the malam rasha.

Elder Wulan frowned. "How do we know anything you've told us tonight is the truth?"

The captain started to reply, but at that moment she caught sight of Lintang in the aisle and her hand drifted to the weapon at her side. "What are you doing?"

Those in the front turned in their spots. Mother stood several benches away, the golden threads of her favorite shisea gleaming in the light. "Lintang!"

Lintang gulped. Water from her hair dripped down her back. She shivered despite the heat. "You have to listen to me."

Nimuel waved to her as Mother squeezed past people toward the aisle. Father stood too, shaking his head.

Once, Father had adored Lintang, taking her on his fishing boat where they would sit all morning with flagons of mao juice, talking and hauling in nets of fish when they were full. But ever since he'd started coming home to Mother's tales of Lintang's disobedience, he smiled at her less. Now it seemed he only had eyes for Nimuel, no longer interested in the daughter who caused so much trouble.

Lintang drew a breath and plowed on. "There's a malam rasha in the panna plantation. It tried to kill me and Bayani this afternoon."

"Lintang!" Mother whispered furiously. "I need to tether you to the house and never let you out!"

"No, it's true. I promise! I promise, in Niti's name!"

Other villagers whispered among themselves. Elder Wulan covered her eyes in shame.

Lintang's courage plummeted. She had sworn on a God, and still they didn't believe her. Couldn't they see that this time was different? Couldn't they tell she was serious?

She turned to the captain, the only person in the room who didn't know her as a storyteller. "I'm not making it up. We need your help."

"What is malam rasha?" the captain said.

"It's what we call a night terror. We only survived

because someone chased it away." Lintang searched the crowd of angry faces. "Who was it? Who saved us? Please come forward, we need to stop it—"

Mother reached the end of the bench and snatched Lintang's wrist. "Forget my daughter," she said in loud, hesitant Vierse. "She makes up stories to get out of trouble. She is a silly girl! She will be sent off to the mining community, mark my words."

She yanked Lintang's arm so hard it felt like Lintang's shoulder was being ripped from its socket. "Ow! Mother, I'm not making it up—"

Bayani tried to stand in the way as Mother stormed for the exit, but she shoved him aside. "Don't you dare bring shame to your family the way my daughter brings shame to hers."

Bayani stared helplessly after them. The other villagers had turned away, although the captain still watched with a thoughtful frown.

"Mother!" Lintang said again as she was dragged down the aisle. "I'm not lying, I'm not trying to embarrass you, *please*—"

"Stop."

The voice sliced through the temple, as sharp as the steel blade of a sword, but it didn't come from the stage behind them. It came from in front.

Mother halted so abruptly that Lintang bumped into her. Someone blocked the entrance, her figure momentarily silhouetted in a flash of lightning.

Silence blanketed the temple. The restlessness, the fidgeting, the movement—it all ceased.

Lintang peeked around Mother as the newcomer stepped inside, the clap of her boots echoing on the stone floor. She was dressed in leather armor across her chest and shoulders, and her brown pants were tucked into high, sturdy boots. Her undershirt had laces down the arms, and each of her wrists was capped with more leathery armor. Her black braids, tied together with a red kerchief, rippled like the veins of panna leaves. Her skin was as dark as timber burned through. Lintang had never seen anyone like her.

The woman advanced, her hand resting on the hilt of her sheathed sword. When she reached Mother, she simply swept her out of the way, exposing Lintang.

No one else in the temple moved.

"Your name," the woman said.

Lintang's tongue felt as though it were coated in sticky sap. She bade it to move as she parted her lips. She'd practiced her introduction a hundred times at school, which was lucky, because her brain had stopped working, and the words left her mouth from habit alone.

"Lintang of Desa, village on the island of Tolus, daughter of Aanjay and Arif, child of Nyasamdra."

The corner of the woman's lips twitched, but it was such a slight movement Lintang might've imagined it.

"Please." Mother's voice was breathless. "Please, she is trouble. She is a liar. Don't listen—"

"Are you a liar?" the woman said to Lintang.

Lintang couldn't look away. Power and strength and nobility pulsed from the woman's stance, from her voice, from her very presence. Lintang didn't dare lie to her. "Yes."

"There, you see?" Mother's voice was more confident now, although it trembled with what might have been relief.

"Would you lie to me?" the woman said.

"No," Lintang said.

"Would you ever disobey me?"

"No." Lintang's breath was stuck in her lungs. She felt caught in a spell, enchanted. This must be what it felt like to meet a Goddess.

"Disobeying me is a severe offense on my ship, Lintang of Desa," the woman said. "Do you understand?"

"Yes."

The woman pursed her lips, satisfied. "Show me the back of your neck."

Mother gave a small cry as Lintang lifted her hair to reveal the shiny scale embedded in her skin. When she turned back, Lintang said, "You're the real Captain Shafira, aren't you?"

The woman smiled, properly this time. Thunder cracked outside.

Mother heaved a shuddering breath. "No." She pulled Lintang into her arms. "I know what you are thinking. You cannot take my daughter."

Captain Shafira rested her hand on the hilt of her sword again. "I'll make you a deal. I'll rid your village of the night terror, and you give me this child so that we can pass through the sea guardian's waters safely."

Lintang gasped.

"No," Mother said.

Captain Shafira raised her eyebrows. "I'm making this deal out of kindness. If you don't accept, I'll still take her."

Spots appeared in front of Lintang's eyes. The Goddess wanted her. *Her.*

Mother's face warped into her terrible glare, but Captain Shafira didn't even flinch.

"If I may?" Elder Wulan stood again. "With respect, Captain, we have no proof this malam rasha even exists."

Mother opened her mouth to agree, but Captain Shafira cut her off.

"Of course it exists." She looked at Lintang, a gleam in her eye as if sharing some private joke. And it was wonderful, even if Lintang didn't know what the joke was yet, because the Goddess believed her, and everything, *everything*, would be all right.

"Are you sure?" Elder Wulan said, regarding Lintang suspiciously.

"Absolutely," Captain Shafira said. "I am the one who chased it away."

The Mythie Guidebook Entry #95:
Siren [common]

~ ~ ~ ~ ~ ~ ~ ~ ~

The siren is a sea mythie in the predator category. It is human-oid and made from a solid, shell-like stone. It nests with four to eight of its kind. It is most dangerous at midday, during calm seas.

Diet: Coral, rocks, seaweed, and occasionally, each other.

Habitat: Shallow reefs worldwide.

Frequency: Moderately common.

Behavior: Sirens put males under a spell with their enchanting song. The call causes men to either jump overboard or crash their ship into the reef. There is no cure. The best preparation is to have at least one female on board and a way to secure male crew until the nest is no longer in hearing range.

Eradication: As they have such tough exteriors, sirens can only be killed by dragon talons.

Did you know? Sirens are the cause of fifty-five percent of marine deaths.

Danger level: 4 for males. 1 for females.

The Black Blade

"I LOVE HER."

"Don't be a gnome."

Lintang stretched out and stared dreamily at the temple ceiling. "I do. I love her. I'm going to travel the seas with her for the rest of my life."

Bayani crossed his legs on the bench beside her. "Even if she does end up taking you, she'll dump you as soon as she's past Nyasamdra."

"Nuh-uh. I'm going to be so good that she'll want to keep me forever." Lintang smiled at the painted shooting stars. "I can be one of her crew and see the world and have adventures and never, ever be stuck doing chores again."

"So you want to be a killer?" Bayani said.

Lintang looked at him upside down. "What are you talking about?"

"She hunts mythies."

"Yes, but they're predator mythies. Like the malam rasha. Or the sirens."

Bayani winced and didn't reply.

"I think it's going to be amazing." Nimuel propped his chin on his knuckles on the back of the next bench. "You're so lucky. Do you think she'll take me, too?"

"Sorry," Lintang said. "No boy can resist the sirens' call. The siren hunters only want girls."

Some of the girls turned to her at that, looking envious and annoyed. Lintang resisted the pixie-ish urge to poke her tongue out at them. They probably regretted refusing to duel with her now.

Nimuel sighed and took a salted peanut from a platter that was going around. The village children had been left in the temple with Elder Wulan and Ramadel, head of the warriors' guild, guarding the entrance. The rest of the adults had left the temple to help Mother find the malam rasha before Captain Shafira could. Mother claimed that if they could kill it first, Captain Shafira wouldn't be able to take Lintang away.

Lintang had never imagined Mother could be so cruel. To go to such lengths, just to stop Lintang from being allowed to travel the world? And what would happen if she stayed in Desa? If Mother was serious, she'd be sent straight to the mining community. What good would she be there?

It didn't matter. Captain Shafira would win anyway. She had been in the panna plantation. She'd saved their lives. She was the greatest person to sail the five seas. If anyone was going to defeat the malam rasha, it would be her.

"Captain Shafira isn't going to find the malam rasha's legs first," Bayani said, his thoughts following the same path. "She isn't from here. She doesn't know the village like we do."

He had barely finished the sentence when a near-deafening clicking echoed through the temple. The children, who had been lounging around, talking or dozing, bolted upright. Lintang sat up too and stared at the entrance, where Ramadel and Elder Wulan had moved into defensive positions.

"Upstairs, into the priests' quarters," Elder Wulan said to the children. "Go quietly."

The children shrieked and screamed as they clambered toward the narrow staircase to the next level.

"I said quietly!" Elder Wulan bellowed after them.

Nimuel tugged at Lintang's hand. "Come on!"

She pulled from his grip. "You go. Stay with Bayani."

"What are you going to do?"

"I'll wait here in case Captain Shafira comes back." At Bayani's exasperated expression, she added, "You're the one who said she doesn't know the village. No one else will help her, so I'll have to do it."

"If you're staying, I'm staying," Bayani said.

Lintang was impressed. She hadn't expected that.

"I'll stay too!" Nimuel said.

Now, that, she'd expected. "No," she said, pushing her little brother toward the staircase. "This mythie is really dangerous. You need to go upstairs."

Nimuel folded his arms.

"He doesn't need to hide," Bayani said to Lintang, who gaped at him. To Nimuel, he said, "You're probably the bravest boy in the village. Go upstairs and find a cooking knife in the priests' quarters. Then you'll be able to protect the others. Can you do that?"

Nimuel touched his right fist to his temple, then over his heart, the way the soldiers of old used to salute. Then he sprinted across the stone floor and up the stairs, the last one to leave.

Lintang sagged as Nimuel's pattering footsteps faded. "You're brilliant."

"Thank you," Bayani said, frowning as the clicking persisted. "It wasn't this loud last time."

"I know. Strange, isn't it?" She led Bayani to the entrance.

The temple was a mess. Benches stood haphazardly from when the adults had rushed to follow Lintang's mother. Half-finished cups of water sat around, forgotten. The platter of salted peanuts lay smashed on the muddy floor. Rain continued to splatter the stone steps, and thunder rumbled beneath the clicking.

Ramadel eyed them as they drew nearer. "Elder Wulan told you to go upstairs."

Elder Wulan smiled tightly and said in Vierse, "Lintang is not one for following instructions."

"We're the only people in the village who've seen the malam rasha," Lintang said. "Maybe we can help."

"Your mother will gut me like a fish if I let you get hurt," Ramadel said.

He was a strong, broad-shouldered man, nearing the age when he would become an elder, and yet the thought of Mother was enough to make him nervous. Lintang didn't blame him, really.

Lightning flashed, illuminating their view of the village and the surrounding breezy forest. The market square was empty except for the barrels ready to be taken to the *Winda*.

"Mother's fish wraps will be somewhere in those barrels," Lintang said as the world went dark again. "Panna leaves protected us this afternoon. If we can find the fish wraps, we might be able to use them to keep the malam rasha away."

Elder Wulan gripped Lintang's arm. "I'm not letting you out of my sight. It's not safe. For either of you," she added when Bayani opened his mouth.

Lintang realized they didn't have to talk over the clicking anymore. It had grown quieter, as if the malam rasha was farther away. Rather than feeling relief, however, she felt her chest tighten, and she swapped glances with Bayani. Maybe the change in volume was part of the mythie's abilities. Maybe it was quieter the nearer it got, to put people off-guard.

As if proving her theory, Ramadel sheathed his sword. "Sounds like it's leaving."

Lintang didn't answer. She stared into the night, straining her eyes with the next flash of lightning, but she still couldn't see anything.

"We need those panna leaves," she said.

"No," Elder Wulan said. "Ramadel and I aren't leaving our post to get them."

"I'll take a shift."

Captain Shafira stepped out of the shadows. Ramadel drew his sword again.

"Put that away. I'm not here to hurt you." She nodded toward the temple. "I'll protect the children while you get the panna leaves."

Ramadel stood his ground. "No."

"It's best to go now. The night terror might come back." She raised her eyebrows at his sword. "Besides, you can't kill it with a blade, correct?"

He exhaled noisily and glowered at her.

She clapped her hands. "Chop-chop. And while you're down there, get some fishing nets. We'll need to keep it trapped until dawn."

"I'll go," Elder Wulan said. "Stay here, Ramadel."

Elder Wulan headed down the steps, and Lintang stole a glance at Captain Shafira. When she caught the captain's eye, she tilted her head in a subtle request to follow her inside. They left Ramadel standing guard at the entrance. Bayani followed in their wake.

Lintang waited until they were halfway across the temple before saying, "We'll help you find the legs—"

"I already have," Captain Shafira said, surveying their surroundings. "I fought a similar mythie that hid its legs beneath the tallest tree in the forest. The night terror did the same thing."

Lintang gave Bayani a gloating grin. Captain Shafira didn't need to know the village. She just had to know the mythie.

The captain walked along the side of the temple, checking the torches and feeling the stone wall. "Problem is, the salt I used to cover the stump dissolved in the rain. Ash would only wash off too. We have to come up with a different way to destroy it."

"What were you doing in the plantation earlier?" Bayani asked.

Captain Shafira started shifting the benches. There didn't seem to be any pattern to how she was placing them. "I was watching the children in the orchard to decide who to take with me when I heard the clicking. I recognized it and followed it." She threw Lintang a glance. "I saw you fight that monster with nothing but a wooden sword and a shield of panna leaves. It was . . . extraordinary."

The air left Lintang's lungs. The Goddess had *complimented* her.

"Thank you," she said, breathless.

"That was one of her prouder moments," Bayani said, shooting a wicked look at Lintang. "It's lucky you didn't see her jump off the school roof to check if she could fly."

Lintang elbowed him.

He elbowed her back playfully, then hesitated and said, "Captain Shafira, would it be possible for you to take me to Zaiben?"

Lintang stared at him. Zaiben again?

"Sorry," Captain Shafira said. "You can't be on board while I'm hunting sirens."

Bayani looked away, hiding his expression.

"What's in Zaiben?" Lintang said, but she already knew his answer.

"Nothing," he muttered.

Nothing, nothing, nothing.

Captain Shafira glanced up from moving benches. "The clicking's getting softer."

"Yes," Lintang said, tearing her gaze from her secretive best friend. "You know—"

"That the clicking is quieter the closer the malam rasha gets? It was the same with the other mythie."

"*The Mythie Guidebook* doesn't say anything about that."

"*The Mythie Guidebook* isn't exactly perfect." Captain Shafira unsheathed her sword. It shone not silver but glittering black beneath the torch light.

"Wow," Lintang said, peering at it. "Where did you get that from?"

"A volcano." Captain Shafira turned to the entrance. "I'm glad you're capable of defending yourself, Lintang, because these types of mythies don't like it when their prey gets away. If you escape, they'll keep coming back until they've killed you."

Lintang stared at her. "You mean it's hunting me?" She glanced at Bayani, whose eyes went wide. "Hunting *us*?"

"Of course," Captain Shafira said. "Why do you think I'm here?"

The Three Gods

L INTANG SAT ON THE STAGE, bouncing her
leg so her heel hit the wood with a rhythmic *thud
thud thud*. "We need to talk."

Bayani wandered restlessly along the side of the temple. He stopped at a torch that had nearly burned out.
Pelita flittered near his head. She'd come down from
upstairs, probably annoyed at the presence of so many
rowdy children in the priests' quarters.

"Just tell me what's wrong, Bayani," Lintang said,
watching him. "Let me help."

He didn't look at her. "You can't."

"You don't know that."

He said nothing as thunder rumbled in the distance.
The rain had eased, but the drizzle continued and probably would all night.

The clicking was still quiet, and the frangipani smell

drenched the air. Both of them pretended not to notice. It was too scary to think about.

Bayani climbed up to the stage and lay down, staring at the painted ceiling. "Why don't you tell Pelita the story of the Gods?"

"Don't change the subject. Pelita doesn't care about the Gods."

He tucked his hands behind his head. "She might. They created her, too, you know. Maybe she wants to hear about them. And"—he hesitated—"to be honest, a story about Ytzuam will make me feel better right now."

Lintang watched Pelita buzz around his head like an annoying blowfly. "Can she even understand us?"

"Sure. She knows Vierse and Toli."

"Really? How come she never does what anyone says?"

"She's a troublemaker." He looked at Lintang with a faint smile. "Kind of like someone else I know." When she didn't smile back, he said, "Will you tell the story? Please?"

Lintang opened her mouth to demand he tell her what was wrong so she could just fix it already. But his voice was small and his eyes were sad, so she let out her breath with a sigh and said instead, "High above, past the clouds, past the sun, there's a world in the stars."

Bayani's tense expression eased. Pelita flew down by the broken platter and licked salt from the spilled peanuts as Lintang continued.

"It's called Ytzuam." She gestured to the painted ceiling. "It's separated from our world by a single thin curtain. There are three Gods who live there: Niti, Patiki, and Mratzi." She waved her hand grandly toward the eastern wall, at the mural of a man in a field. His face was covered by a straw hat, and in his cupped hands was a tiny glowing star. "Niti's job is to create star seeds. He leaves them in the fallow fields of Ytzuam, waiting to be planted." On the western wall, a young woman holding a basket skipped through the same field. "Planting is Patiki's job. When she plants a star seed in a field of Ytzuam, it creates life here in our world. As we grow, the seed inside us blooms into a mature star." On the southern wall, Mratzi stood wrapped in her silver ribbons, holding a scythe. "Then, when we die, Mratzi harvests our star and puts it in the sky so that we may blaze for all time."

Pelita was still licking peanuts, but she might have been listening, because she'd looked at each of the walls as Lintang pointed them out.

"I like Niti the best," Lintang said. "He seems nice in the stories. Patiki's all right, I suppose, but she always looks so cheerful planting seeds in the pictures. No one should look *that* happy while they're working. And Mratzi . . ." She shuddered. "Mratzi scares me."

She glanced over at Bayani and started when she saw a tear trail down his cheek. Before she could ask, a gust of wind whooshed through the entrance, guttering torch flames and billowing the hem of her sarong. She scrambled to her feet.

The malam rasha swooped into the temple, its sharp roots reaching forward, bringing the stench of rotten meat.

Bayani jumped up and dived toward the side of the stage. Lintang leaped for the benches, but she was slow and the malam rasha was fast. The mythie barreled into her. She landed hard on the stone floor, winded. Pelita fluttered out of the way only just in time.

The malam rasha curled its lip and slashed at Lintang's stomach. Its roots ripped into her sarong . . . and stopped.

The malam rasha tried again, clawing and tearing, until the front of Lintang's sarong was in tatters. And yet not a single scratch made it onto her skin. Instead, the malam rasha kept coming across panna leaves, unraveled from their fish wraps and smeared onto Lintang's chest and stomach with sauce from the dish. A spicy scent drifted up between them.

The malam rasha stared at Lintang, its eyes bulging with fury.

Eyes.

Lintang slammed her eyes shut as the malam rasha lunged to suck them out. She had almost forgotten to keep them closed . . .

Except now she couldn't see.

Still fighting for breath, she scrabbled for something, anything, to protect herself with. Her fingers settled on the scattered peanuts. She tossed them at the malam rasha. Its weight lifted from her immediately.

Boots clapped across the stone floor, and the breeze from the malam rasha's wings disappeared.

"It's all right, Lintang. I'm here."

Lintang waited until the sound of boots was much farther away before daring to peek.

Captain Shafira aimed sword blows at the malam rasha so fiercely that it was forced to retreat. The red kerchief that had been in the captain's hair was now wrapped around her eyes, so her braids swung unrestrained. Being blind didn't seem to slow her down. She didn't even run into any of the wooden benches.

"Lintang!" Bayani crawled over to her with Pelita on his shoulder. "Are you hurt?"

"No," Lintang said, fingering the strips of her sarong.

"But Mother is going to sacrifice me to Nyasamdra for ruining this."

"Eire!" Captain Shafira yelled.

The woman in purple who had pretended to be the captain sprinted into the temple with a fishing net. She threw it over the malam rasha. Captain Shafira ripped the kerchief from around her eyes and grabbed the bottom of the net so she could yank the malam rasha to the stone floor. Eire stepped on one of its wings, pinning it. It squirmed and snarled. Its tree roots sliced through the net, but before it could escape, Captain Shafira brought her sword down and chopped off its arm. It released an earsplitting shriek.

Bayani spun away.

Lintang frowned. "What's the matter? Don't tell me you want that monster to live. It almost killed us!"

There was another shriek as Captain Shafira sliced the roots off its other arm. Bayani shuddered.

"Stop being silly," Lintang said. "It's just like when Camelia the woodcutter chops up a tree."

Bayani rubbed his eyes with his thumb and forefinger. "Please tell them not to hurt it anymore."

Lintang climbed to her feet and joined Captain Shafira.

"Are you injured?" Captain Shafira said, knotting the bottom of the net so the mythie couldn't escape.

"No," Lintang said.

"Good." Captain Shafira stepped on the creature's white dress to keep it on the ground. "How did you make it back off? I heard it recoil before I reached you."

Lintang held the pieces of her slashed sarong in place as she stared down at the malam rasha. "I threw peanuts at it."

"Peanuts?" Eire said, snorting.

"Salted. I thought if you're supposed to use salt to keep it from rejoining its legs, then it probably hates the stuff."

She caught Captain Shafira quirk an eyebrow at Eire, who pressed her lips together and looked away.

"That was imaginative," Captain Shafira said. She untied the kerchief that now hung loosely around her neck and wrapped it around her braids again. "But from what I hear, you're the most imaginative person on the island."

"How do you fight so well with your eyes closed?" Lintang said.

"Practice."

The malam rasha writhed, and Eire launched a kick at

it. Lintang flinched. "If you don't mind," she said, "Bayani asked that you not hurt it. Until sunrise, anyway."

He was still sitting on the floor where she'd left him, his face turned away.

Captain Shafira shrugged. "If it suits you." To Eire, she added, "This is where Xiang's darts would've come in handy." Then she directed a kick to the malam rasha's wooden head, and it slumped, unmoving.

Lintang gasped. "Did you kill it?"

"If it were that easy to kill a mythie, the world wouldn't be in such a mess." Captain Shafira nudged it with her boot. "It's just knocked out. Hopefully it'll stay that way through the night. Ah."

Her attention had moved to the staircase, where Ramadel and Elder Wulan stared uncertainly into the room.

"You've captured it?" Elder Wulan said. She eyed Lintang's tattered sarong. "Are the children harmed?"

"Both of them are fine," Captain Shafira said. She placed a hand on Lintang's shoulder. "And I'll be taking what I've earned, thank you."

Lintang's stomach swooped as violently as the malam rasha had.

Elder Wulan turned to Ramadel. "Oh my," she said in their native tongue. "I believe Aanjay's wrath will be equal to that of the Gods."

Her Most Precious Thing

"YOU ARE NOT TO TAKE HER. Not to take her!"
Mother clung to Lintang's arm with both hands.
Captain Shafira and Eire had tipped over their rowboat,
which had been upside down to protect it from the
storm, and were now dragging it down to the water.
The white sand of the beach was littered with branches
and debris, but the lapping waves of the lagoon reflected
bright blue sky.

Farther out on the reef, Captain Shafira's other rowboats headed smoothly to the *Winda*, carrying supplies.
Lintang hadn't had a chance to see the crew members
—they'd come before dawn to gather the barrels from
the market square.

Almost the entire village had been on the steps of the
temple at sunrise. Eire had dragged the malam rasha's
body into the light, and Lintang had stood with Captain

Shafira as it burst into flame, leaving only a silhouette of ash and the broken fishing net. Everyone had witnessed it, and now they were forced to honor their deal. Lintang was to go with the pirate queen.

Lintang squashed down the excitement that bubbled at the thought. There was still a chance Mother would tie her up and send her to the mining community.

Mother didn't release her grip. Lintang's hand was starting to tingle from lack of blood. Father stood at her other side. Nimuel waited a short way behind them. The rest of the villagers had gathered on the bay too but kept their distance, except for Elder Wulan, who stood by Mother.

"Please reconsider," Elder Wulan said to Captain Shafira. "She doesn't have the skills to handle the world out there."

"Yes, yes!" Mother said. "No skills! She cannot go!"

Lintang inhaled a breath of seaweedy air. Mother would find any excuse to stop her from escaping this boring old island.

"She will be a guest, not a crew member," Captain Shafira said, setting her rowboat at the water's edge. "She won't need skills." She held out a hand to Lintang.

Mother burst into tears. Lintang's face grew hot, and she ducked her head. Her wild stories were nothing compared with the embarrassing way her mother was behaving now. Why was Mother acting like this when she spent most of her time yelling? Why, if Lintang was such a terrible daughter, did she care if Lintang left at all?

She smoothed her best golden sarong and tried to pretend she couldn't hear her mother's sobs. She'd washed off the fish sauce and changed during the night. She wore her only pair of shoes too. They were made of thin, woven reed and rubbed at her big toes. The sack with the rest of her clothes — her wooden sword tucked carefully among them — was in her other hand. Mother had refused to let her take her sword, but Father, in an unexpected act of kindness, had secretly given it to her while she was packing.

"My aim is to have her home soon after Niti's festival," Captain Shafira said, gracious considering the circumstances. "You have my word."

"Word of the pirate queen?" Mother snapped through tears. "Forgive me, but I do not believe you."

Eire tapped a finger against the fangs strung around her neck and glanced impatiently at the *Winda*. It waited past the reef, its black sails still rolled up. Talrosses soared above it, so high their large bodies were nothing but white dots in the sky.

"You have terrible lives!" Mother said. "You will put

Lintang in danger. You are a bad influence. She thinks you are good. Pah!"

Lintang had had enough. She wrenched her arm from her mother's grip and spoke in their native tongue. "You made a deal with Captain Shafira. She needs to get past Nyasamdra, which means she needs me. Now stop wasting her time and let me go already."

Mother stepped back as though Lintang had spat at her. Lintang's stomach churned uncomfortably at her expression, but Mother got over it quickly enough. She scowled and snatched Lintang's arm once more. "You don't belong with these people," she said, speaking in Toli too. "This is your home. You'll grow up and run a household and contribute to the village like everyone else."

"I don't want to be like everyone else. I don't want to be stuck here my whole life. I want to see the rest of the world. I want to have adventures."

"You're not supposed to have adventures!"

Lintang was sick of arguing. Her bag was packed. The deal had been made. Mother wasn't going to win this time. Besides, she didn't want to be embarrassed in front of Captain Shafira any longer.

She pulled away from Mother and hugged Nimuel. "Goodbye, little brother. Look after the family for me."

"You're not going," Mother said.

Lintang ignored her. She scanned the thick green forest behind the watching villagers. Bayani's parents were on the shore, but he was nowhere in sight. He'd left long before the death of the malam rasha and hadn't returned. Why hadn't he come to see her off? Was he angry because she'd helped kill a mythie?

"If you see Bayani, say goodbye to him for me."

"I will," Nimuel said. "I think he's just jealous that you get to go and he doesn't." Then he stood on tiptoe and whispered in her ear, "I'm jealous too."

Lintang laughed and patted the top of his head. "I promise I'll tell you all about it when I get back."

She hugged Father and Elder Wulan, both of whom squeezed her harder than necessary. She hesitated at her mother.

"Goodbye."

Mother spun to Captain Shafira, her eyes still red. "You cannot take her," she said in Vierse. "She is my daughter."

"She's more capable than you think," Captain Shafira said. "She'll be fine."

Mother's chest shuddered with a sob. "*You* give up your most precious thing, and you will see it is not so easy."

Lintang gaped at her. "Most precious thing"? Had she gotten her Vierse mixed up?

Captain Shafira hesitated. For a heart-jolting moment, Lintang thought she was about to change her mind. But then Captain Shafira withdrew a chain from beneath her shirt. Unlike Eire's horrible fanged necklace, this one was beautiful. Red gems hung like teardrops from thick golden links. A large orange stone gleamed in the center.

There was a faint murmur from the villagers, and Elder Wulan gasped.

"Captain," Eire said in alarm, but Captain Shafira ignored her and unclasped the chain.

"Take care of this," she said, holding it out to Mother. "Keep it safe, and I will keep Lintang safe."

Mother stared fearfully at the necklace.

"Take it," Captain Shafira said again. "You can give it back to me once Lintang comes home."

"Mother," Lintang said.

Mother didn't move.

"Mother," Lintang said again. "I thought I brought you shame."

Mother swallowed, still gazing at the necklace. "You are my daughter." Tears wobbled in her eyes. In Toli, as if to prove there was no mistake, she said, "My most precious thing."

Words vanished from Lintang's tongue. Mother had hunted for the malam rasha last night, risking her life, not out of spite, but out of love. Why hadn't she said anything? Why had she waited until now?

"Captain," Eire said again, but Captain Shafira raised her free hand to silence her. She kept her attention on Mother.

Mother stepped tentatively across the sand and took the necklace. She held it up, examining the gems as if checking that they were real. Lintang didn't know what the necklace meant, but it seemed everyone else did. Elder Wulan had her hands clasped over her mouth. The villagers were silent and tense.

Mother clutched the chain to her chest. "You will drop Lintang in Zaiben?"

"Not if you take the necklace. If you take it, I'll accompany her all the way home."

"But then you will be stuck here again."

"I'll find another Islander. Time won't be important then. But it is now. Those sirens are out there, drowning ships. We have to leave."

Mother glanced at Father before shifting her teary gaze to Lintang.

"Very well," she said, her voice cracking as she turned away. "She may go."

The Mythie Guidebook Entry #69:
Lightning Bird [Allay]

~~~~~~~~~~~~

The lightning bird (impulu) is a sky mythie. It is avian, although there are no official descriptions available. It is supposed to be a symbol of dominance.

Diet: Unknown.

Habitat: Unknown.

Frequency: Extremely rare.

Behavior: Lightning birds follow ships. Unconfirmed reports say they are able to create lightning.

Eradication: Unknown.

Did you know? The only known lightning bird in existence flies with the *Winda*, the ship of the pirate queen.

Danger level: Unknown. Proceed with caution.

Across the Reef

AFTER HUGGING HER MOTHER, Lin-
tang climbed onto the middle seat of the rowboat. Captain Shafira and Eire pushed off. Both of them
took oars to row, while Lintang twisted around to wave
to the villagers. Only a few waved back. Father nodded
solemnly. Mother had turned away from Lintang. Her
shoulders shook. Nimuel jumped up and down, waving
with both arms.

A strange feeling surged through Lintang. It was a
powerful ache, like the time berry bugs had nested in
Jojo, her toy blue-tailed howler, and Father had had to
burn him. She'd stood by the fire, hardly six years old,
watching Jojo crumble to ash. She would never again be
able to cuddle him at night, or share him with Bayani,
or flop his long arms from side to side to make her baby
brother laugh. The loss had left a raw, empty space, and

she felt that same space now as the people on the bay grew farther and farther away.

There was still no sign of Bayani.

She breathed through the pain and turned away from the island to focus on where she was going rather than what she was leaving behind.

Past the reef lay ocean of deeper blue and bigger swell. The *Winda* looked much larger than it had from the shore.

She couldn't stop a grin from spreading at the sight of it. Her ache turned to flitters of excitement. The *Winda*, ship of the pirate queen. Unsinkable, uncatchable, unbeatable. It would take her across the Adina Sea, past Nyasamdra, toward adventure. It hardly seemed real.

Behind her, Eire grunted softly with effort. Captain Shafira sat in front, rowing backwards. Lintang could smell the leather of the captain's boots and the faint scent of sweat. She didn't dare look up at her face. If she looked too closely, she might discover it was only a dream, like the story of Tristin the priest. He had crossed the forbidden sea of stars into Ytzuam, only to be punished by Patiki and made to forget everything he had seen. Lintang wouldn't forget anything about this journey. Not a single precious heartbeat.

She trailed her hands in the clear, cool water of the lagoon. Iridescent fish darted between her fingers.

The rowboat passed over the reef, where colorful coral brimmed with creatures. She'd been here with Father to see how he caught all the delicious seafood he brought home, but she hadn't been as far as the *Winda* before. The excitement turned to panic, which turned to an urge to giggle nervously. How was it possible to feel so many emotions at once?

Lintang stuck her tongue out to taste the air, which was heavy with salt. Her heart swooped as they dipped down a wave, off the reef, into the true ocean.

She looked back one last time. The villagers were nothing but bright dots on the white beach. She searched for Mother and Father and Nimuel and Elder Wulan, but she could no longer see them in the crowd. The ache returned, so she faced front again and focused on the *Winda*.

The waves dropped lower and rose higher. Each time the boat descended, Lintang's stomach would stay up longer than the rest of her body. She clung to the side of the rowboat, her hands already starting to cramp.

Dark shadows flashed in the water below them. Mermaids? Sharks? Nyasamdra herself?

Talrosses circled above the *Winda* like flies around a carcass. From here she could hear the clack of masts, the creak of timber, the squeak of pulleys. Waves rumbled against the hull, which had a pretty gold pattern on the side.

And then came an unnatural screech. She looked up, trying to match the sound to the birds above.

"The lightning bird," Captain Shafira said as Lintang caught sight of a black dot soaring high above the talrosses.

"What does it do?" Lintang asked. "Is it safe?"

"Useless bird," Eire said between grunts. "It shrieks and makes skin bumpy from shivers."

"I thought it was supposed to have powers."

No answer.

"Does it at least make lightning?"

Eire shrugged.

Lintang pursed her lips, trying to hide her disappointment. She'd imagined the lightning bird to be as impressive as the pirate queen. Although, really, what could live up to a Goddess?

She dared a peek at the captain. From the stories she'd heard, she had expected the most wanted pirate in the world to have a harsh face, perhaps scarred from all her fights and wearing a constant scowl. Instead, Captain Shafira's face was smooth and unblemished, her brow and cheek round rather than angular, and often there would be a flash of amusement on her lips or in her eyes, as if she wanted to laugh, if only the world would give her a chance.

She heaved at the oars with the strength and rhythm of the ocean, her muscles defined even beneath her shirt. A few braids had escaped the red kerchief, curling like ribbons in the sea breeze. Lintang wished she had tied her own hair up. She kept getting hit in the eye with salty, dark strands.

Time moved on, the sun grew hotter, and they drew closer to the *Winda*.

Lintang had seen ships past the reef dozens of times, but she'd never realized how big they were. The *Winda* loomed so tall, she had to crane her neck to see the top.

When at last they reached the ship, ropes with hooks slithered down to attach to the rowboat, and they were winched up. She touched the *Winda*'s hull as they rose. The timber was damp beneath her hand, flecked with foamy sea spray. The wood had warped in places, lumpy but unchipped, and salt grains scratched at her palms.

"Beautiful, isn't she?" Captain Shafira said.

Lintang tore her attention away from the wood. "Where did you get her?"

Captain Shafira touched the side as Lintang had done. "She found me."

A woman of tremendous size reached down and dragged their rowboat up to the deck. Lintang stared. Her floral-pattern sarong was as big as a feast tablecloth.

"Lintang, this is Zazi, our helmswoman, among other things. Zazi, meet Lintang."

Zazi bared her few remaining teeth in a smile. Lintang managed a wobbly smile in return and accepted Zazi's help out of the rowboat, one hand clutching her sack of possessions. Eire and Captain Shafira climbed lithely after her. In contrast to the choppy rocking of the rowboat, the deck of the ship rolled beneath Lintang in gentle, sweeping arcs.

"Ah, good, most of you are here," Captain Shafira said.

Lintang turned away from Zazi to find a group of women crowded around them. Two looked to be in their twenties. Another was a young girl, maybe fourteen. There was also an elderly lady with springy, gray hair. She was the only one who wasn't staring at Lintang. Her shawl and dress were long despite the heat of the day. She stumped forward with a wide smile for Captain Shafira. At the thudding of every second step, Lintang realized she had a wooden pole for her left leg.

"Hello, Hewan," Captain Shafira said.

"Welcome home, Captain," Hewan said, beaming. "We missed you."

Captain Shafira patted her arm. To the others, she said, "This is Lintang. She'll be getting us past the sea guardian."

Lintang might have smiled or waved or said hello if they hadn't been eyeing her suspiciously. The teenage girl actually scowled. She had short, shaggy hair, hem-torn pants held up by rope, and a filthy shirt that would've revolted Bayani's mother. Considering she was closest to Lintang's age, she could've been a friend, but from her expression it didn't look as if it was going to work out that way.

Lintang resisted the urge to edge closer to Captain Shafira as the group continued to stare.

"Have you unloaded barrels?" Eire said, pushing past Lintang, at last breaking the silence. "I am hungry."

The other women broke into chatter, leading Eire away as they discussed the supplies they had taken from Desa. No one gave Lintang a second glance.

Zazi secured the rowboat as Captain Shafira said to Lintang, "They'll grow on you like barnacles, I promise."

"Captain." Someone else wandered over. "We're ready to set sail when you are."

Lintang's eyes widened. This woman had an adult face and body, but she was shorter than Nimuel. She wore a knitted hat with thick ropes dangling over her hair, which gave the impression of a woolly octopus sitting on her head.

"Lintang, this is Quahah, our navigator," Captain

Shafira said. "Best person to have in charge when you're sailing. I don't know how I ever survived without her."

Quahah waved Captain Shafira's words away. "Aw, stop it. You make me feel a hundred masts tall."

"But . . . you're tiny," Lintang said.

Quahah glanced down at her body and gave a dramatic gasp. "So I am! Fish on a stick, thanks for letting me know. That might've been really awkward." She grinned at Lintang, whose face scorched when she realized she'd been rude. Barely a heartbeat on the ship, and already she'd made a mistake.

"Sorry," she mumbled.

"Quahah, please show Lintang to a cabin," Captain Shafira said. "Lintang, stay off the top deck so you don't get in the way as we set sail."

Quahah gave a casual salute and gestured for Lintang to follow her down a large hatch.

"There are a lot of people in the world, kipper," Quahah said as they headed down the wooden steps. "Most will be different from what you know, but treat them with the respect they deserve and you'll do fine."

"I'm sorry," Lintang said again.

Quahah smirked. "I'm only giving you fair warning," she said, "because you'll need it for when you meet our cook."

Unexpected Crew

~

T HE STAIRCASE LED DOWN to a wide corridor lit by candles in frosted glass balls that were blackened from long exposure to smoke. Even so, patches of golden light shimmered on the wooden walls and ceiling like sunlight reflecting off a hidden body of water. The corridor rocked with the sea as they walked. It was an odd feeling.

Half-open doors revealed comfortable cabins with different types of beds. Most were variations of hammocks, although nothing like the simple woven ones at home. These were colorful or cushioned or hanging from the ceiling in the shape of an egg or strung up like a swaying basket. One room had a sideways giant barrel carved open with a little ladder to get to the bedding inside. Another was simply a net that looked fun to bounce on.

Each room had a wooden chest to hold possessions, though few seemed to be used for that. Most cabins had clothes strewn over the lid of the chest, or boots in the corner, or weapons like swords and arrows and other unusual artifacts hanging in brackets on the wall. In the room with the bouncy net, countless trinkets overflowed the chest and spilled across the floor in puddles of mess.

"What's that smell?" Lintang said, inhaling deeply. "It's like trees and rain, but it's also . . . spicy?"

"Euco oil rubbed onto the timber," Quahah said, patting the wall. "Does wonders for keeping away insects and rodents. It'll stop you from being sick too, considering you haven't had the Curall."

"Curall?"

"A medicine. Protects you against diseases. Ah— here's a good room for you."

Quahah stopped outside a cabin with a circular hammock, which had thick strings lifting the frame and joining at a single point in the ceiling so it looked like an upside-down cone. A brass lantern hung from the wall, swaying with the rocking of the ship.

Lintang stared inside. "This? This whole thing? It's mine?"

"You're not going to ask to share with me, are you? Because I'm a kicker."

"No, no," Lintang said quickly. "It's just . . ." She smiled, thinking of her tiny house. "I've never had a place to myself before."

She took her wooden sword out of her sack. It was too short to fit in the brackets, but she was able to balance the hilt on one of the iron pegs.

"You can dim the flame here," Quahah said, twisting a knob on the lantern.

"You can control fire?" Lintang tossed her sack in the wooden chest so she could try turning the knob herself. "Wow."

Quahah laughed. "You have so much to learn, kipper. Now, are you all right by yourself? I need to go back to the top deck."

"I'll be fine," Lintang said, kicking off her shoes and climbing into the hammock. It was big enough to stretch out in. Her muscles enjoyed unfolding after spending so long in the rowboat.

She gazed around the room as Quahah left. It was all hers. No little brother to argue with, no mother telling her to clean up after herself, no father snoring the night away. Why had she felt sad to leave?

The hammock continued to sway as the ship bobbed —they must've started moving by now. Wood creaked around her, and the euco oil was a soothing smell. She might've fallen asleep if her mind weren't buzzing. She was really here, traveling with the pirate queen, leaving Desa to see the world. She was going to meet Nyasamdra. Mother and Father hadn't met Nyasamdra. Ramadel, head of the warriors' guild, hadn't met Nyasamdra. Even Elder Wulan hadn't met Nyasamdra, since she had only traveled to Tolus and hadn't left the island again.

The thought of all the adventures she was going to have kept Lintang fidgeting. When she couldn't stay still any longer, she hopped out of the hammock and padded barefoot down the corridor to explore more of the *Winda*.

She peeked at the other cabins, the cargo hold, the large dining room, and a stinky space that held slop buckets and green goop.

And then she found the kitchen. She heard it first. There was a lot of clamor and sizzling, with smoke drifting out to the corridor.

She poked her head in. The place was larger than she expected. A fire roared in an iron box, pots bubbled on the stove above it, and knives and ladles swung from the ceiling around a bright lantern.

A big woman stood at the counter. She had a shaved head and golden hoops dangling from her earlobes. She was hacking carrots with a cleaver.

"Hello," Lintang said over the crackles and sputters of the fire.

The woman jumped so violently that the cleaver went flying out of her hand and lodged in the wall behind her.

"Mother of monsters, you scared the petticoats off me!" Which was strange, because she was wearing tight pants, a wide belt, and a food-spattered tunic, without a petticoat to be seen. "Look, Ma, we have a visitor!"

Lintang peered behind the woman, but she couldn't see anyone else.

"You must be our Islander," said the woman. She picked up a large clamshell from the counter. "I'm Dee, and this is my mother, Farah."

Lintang wasn't sure where Dee's mother was hiding until Dee snapped the clamshell open and closed and said in a squawky voice, "Pleased to meet you."

Lintang blinked at the shell. Then at Dee. Then at the shell again. On the top of the shell were two eyes drawn crudely with ink.

"Look at her face," Dee said in the squawky voice, snapping the shell's mouth again. "You'd think she's never seen a mother-daughter cooking team before."

"Er . . ." said Lintang.

"Let's take a look at you." Dee spun Lintang around with her free hand and lifted Lintang's hair to expose the back of her neck. "And there it is. That shiny scale's worth a bundle on the black market."

Lintang shivered.

"Don't scare the poor girl," said the squawky voice.

Dee dropped Lintang's hair. "Don't worry; I'm not going to sell you on the black market. To be honest, I'm worth more, since I'm a crew member of the *Winda*."

"No one would pay a quartz for you once they realize you're more trouble than you're worth," said the shell to Dee.

Lintang turned to face her again. "So . . ." she said slowly. "You're Dee. And that's your mother, Farah."

"She's a bit slow, this one," said Farah the clamshell.

"Hush, Ma, don't be rude," Dee said, and to Lintang, "What's your name, starflower?"

Lintang drew a breath. "Lintang of Desa, village on the island of Tolus, daughter of Aanjay and Arif, child of Nyasamdra."

Dee burst into screams of laughter. "Hear that, Ma? What a mouthful."

"I remember when you used to be able to introduce yourself so eloquently," Farah the clamshell said.

"Those days are long gone, old woman."

Farah the clamshell addressed Lintang again. "Best

not reveal so much about yourself out in the world. The less people know about you, the better."

Lintang was going to ask why, but a pot behind them started bubbling over.

"Give us a grain—the stove's turning dragon," Dee said, which was something Lintang didn't understand, but Dee didn't need an answer. She tucked the shell into her wide belt and hurried to shut the iron box with her foot while scooping up the chopped carrots and tossing them into a pot large enough to hold a small child.

"I suppose you've never seen anything like this before, have you?" Dee said, yanking the cleaver from the wall. "This room's called the galley. This is the stove. These big spoons hanging from the ceiling are ladles— although maybe you've got those at home?"

She explained all the things in the room, and when Lintang's stomach growled, she dug into a crate for a loaf of crusty bread. Lintang ate a slice thick with butter while they talked. Dee showed her how the smoke went up a pipe from the iron stove and ex- plained how it was released over the ship and how the bellows worked.

"Are you happy to be here?" Dee said, unwrapping a cloth filled with lobsters from Desa and dumping them into the pot.

"Definitely," Lintang said through her last mouthful of bread. "I've always wanted to travel the world. And you should've heard what I went through to get aboard. Captain Shafira had to give Mother her necklace as a promise to bring me home."

Dee stopped stirring the soup. "Her necklace?"

Lintang swallowed her mouthful. "Yes, the gold one with the gems."

Dee set down the ladle. She looked worried.

"What is it?" Lintang said.

"Sorry." Dee ushered Lintang toward the door. "We're busy in here right now. Why don't you get yourself a copper basin from the cargo hold? You can keep it in your room with a pitcher of water. Always nice to wash your face first thing in the morning."

"But—"

Dee shoved her into the passage. "That's a good girl," she said, and closed the door.

Lintang stared at it for a heartbeat before wiping crumbs from her mouth and walking away. She'd made another mistake, said the wrong thing again, but this time, she didn't know what it was.

What was so important about the necklace? Eire had looked upset when Captain Shafira had offered it up, and the villagers of Desa had been horrified. Was it valuable?

Was it a family heirloom? Would all the crew shut doors in Lintang's face when they discovered the necklace was now in her village? How would she ever make friends this way?

The thoughts plagued her as she headed down the steps to the cargo hold. A pile of copper basins sat in a crate among silver pitchers and extra plates, and she was just reaching to pick one up when she heard a *thunk* farther along. She paused, listening. Maybe something had fallen with the movement of the ship.

Or maybe not.

She straightened and crept toward a collection of barrels. The floor was cold under her feet. It was a forest of shadows in here, with only a single lantern near the stairs.

She held her breath, listening, but there was no other sound. Then, through the scent of the euco oil came a cloud of spices and—

"ACHOO!"

Lintang jumped back, knocking the top layer off a pile of firewood. "Who's there?" she said through the clatter.

There was a familiar buzzing sound, and a ball of bright light zipped up from behind the barrels. Lintang placed a hand over her heart to make sure it was still beating. How embarrassing—she'd been frightened by a pixie!

Although . . . how could a tiny mythie sneeze so loudly?

Before she could investigate further, a sigh echoed through the silence, and in the same place the pixie had been hiding, Bayani stood up.

The Mythie Guidebook Entry #73:
Mermaid [Caletrom]

∘ ∘ ∘ ∘ ∘ ∘ ∘ ∘ ∘

The Caletromian mermaid (syrena) is a sea mythie in the predator category. It is the most dangerous of the mermaid species. It is a combination of humanoid and serpentine and can be distinguished from the common mermaid by its snakelike tail.

Diet: Caletromian mermaids will eat any meat available, whether it be turtle, shark, or human.

Habitat: Throughout the five seas.

Frequency: Moderately rare.

Behavior: Caletromian mermaids release a calming drug called lunjin that puts their victims in a state of suggestibility. As soon as they catch their prey, they reveal their true face and drag the unsuspecting creature to the bottom of the sea.

Eradication: Staying on guard against the effects of the lunjin is the hardest part of killing these mythies, as their humanoid halves are easily pierced with a sharp blade.

Did you know? Lunjin is now used during surgical procedures.

Danger level: 3

Choices

"**W**HAT ARE YOU DOING HERE?"

Bayani flinched at Lintang's shout and gestured for her to keep quiet. The pixie zipped around the room delightedly. Now that Lintang's eyes had adjusted to the bright glow, she could tell it was Pelita. She should've known.

"We hid in one of the barrels," Bayani said.

Lintang exhaled through her teeth. Her fear had eased, and her frustration billowed like storm clouds. "You gnome. Now we're going to have to turn around!"

"No!" Bayani clamped his mouth shut and tried again in a softer voice. "Please don't tell anyone I'm here. I need to go to Zaiben."

"*Why?*" She couldn't believe that Bayani—smart, mature, obedient Bayani—had stowed away. On a pirate ship, no less.

Pelita settled on his shoulder. Her white glow illuminated his face, and for the first time Lintang saw the cuts and bruises that must've come from being transported in the barrel. He was in the previous night's clothes, looking quite rumpled now, with his red shirt torn in one place and his pants still muddy.

"What were you thinking?" Lintang said, fighting a peculiar motherly urge to brush him down and wash his face. "What about your parents?"

"I left a note in the schoolroom explaining where I am. No one was there this morning because they were seeing you off. I needed enough time to sneak on board without anyone realizing I was missing."

Lintang frowned. "At least this explains why you didn't come to say goodbye."

His posture relaxed, and he dared a smile.

"Don't think I'm not angry with you," Lintang said. "Now, come on. Let's go see Captain Shafira."

His smile vanished. "We can't. Not yet. We're still too close to Desa. She'll make me go back."

"Maybe she'll give you a fair hearing. If you tell her why you want to go to Zaiben—"

"No. It's not . . . She won't . . ." He blew his bangs from his eyes as if he had an excuse for being annoyed, when Lintang was the one who would get in trouble.

What if Captain Shafira thought she'd helped him stow away?

"You can't tell anyone we're here," Bayani said.

Pelita buzzed her wings in agreement.

"You can't do that to me!" Lintang said. "I promised not to lie to Captain Shafira."

"Please."

Lintang huffed like an angry gaya. "We're not even going to Zaiben anymore. Captain Shafira's dropping me back home when this is over."

Bayani chewed his lip, staring thoughtfully at a spot over her shoulder. "After we've passed Nyasamdra's territory, I'll come out of hiding and ask the captain to take me to Zaiben. We'll be closer to Vierz than the Twin Islands by that stage—hopefully I can talk her into making the extra trip."

Lintang dragged her hands down her face. Bayani was her best friend, but she was supposed to be impressing the captain, not keeping secrets from her. "Why are you doing this?"

"I can't tell you."

"Bayani!"

"I'm so sorry," he said.

Lintang turned on her heel and stalked toward the

steps. Bayani rushed to stand in front of her. "Please don't tell on me. Please."

Pelita took off from his shoulder and fluttered away to investigate the toppled firewood.

"Why shouldn't I?" Lintang said. "This is my one chance to get away from Desa. I'm going to have adventures, and meet Nyasamdra, and slay sirens. You will ruin everything."

Pelita started stripping bark from the wood, making a mess like the destructive little thing she was.

"I know, but . . ." Bayani grasped Lintang's hands. His skin was cold. "Getting to Zaiben is the most important thing in the world. I need you to trust me."

She frowned. The most important thing in the world? That sounded too dramatic for Bayani. It was more like something she would say.

Because she exaggerated and lied and never did what she was told.

And he always, *always,* went along with it, or got her out of trouble.

He accepted her challenges to a duel when no one else would. He'd gone with her to pick panna leaves, even though they'd ended up being attacked by a malam rasha. And he'd convinced her to go to the temple the night before, which was probably the only reason she'd ended up meeting Captain Shafira in the first place.

But if Captain Shafira found out Lintang had kept his presence a secret, it would ruin everything.

Before Lintang could decide what to do, footsteps thumped on the stairs. Bayani threw himself behind the pile of firewood. Pelita burrowed between logs so her light wouldn't show.

Lintang turned as Eire appeared. "Here you are," Eire said, scowling. "I look all over ship for you."

Lintang hurried forward and snatched up a copper basin and silver pitcher. "Sorry. I was just getting—"

"I am not caring," Eire said. "Captain wants you. Come."

It took all Lintang's willpower not to glance back as she followed Eire up the stairs. She dropped the basin and pitcher in her room on her way to the top deck. When she stepped outside, she had to squint against the brightness. It had been so gloomy below in comparison. The sun was halfway down the sky now. It gave hiccups of warmth between gusts of fresh breezes. The sails snapped as the ship soared over the waves.

Eire scanned the deck. "Captain may be in cabin. Stay." Rather than return below, Eire headed to the front of the ship, where there was a door. Lintang thought

Captain Shafira must have a big room on the top deck all to herself.

Eire wasn't gone long before the younger, unpleasant girl shoved past Lintang, and growled, "Out of the way."

Lintang edged to the side of the ship. It was better here anyway—she could hold on to the railing as they rose and sank with the swell.

She stared back the way they'd come. The island of Tolus already looked so far behind them.

She didn't have room to feel that ache again—she was too busy thinking of Bayani and what reason he could have for stowing away.

And why had Captain Shafira summoned her? Was she somehow already aware that Bayani was below deck? Would she yell at Lintang? Would she bother to listen as Lintang professed her innocence, or would she believe Lintang a liar, just like everyone said?

While Lintang imagined the crew cheering as she was thrown overboard, movement caught her eye below. She glanced down to find two girls grinning at her from the waves. They dived and splashed, revealing their scaly tails as they followed the ship.

Mermaids.

Lintang had only seen a mermaid once before. She'd been on the reef with Father, helping haul in his nets, when he'd pointed at the mythie sunbathing on dry rocks by the cliffs. Father saw lots of mermaids while he worked. They usually brought the fishermen shiny objects or helped untangle bigger animals like dolphins when they got caught in the nets.

But the mermaid Lintang had seen that day with Father had had a tail like a fish. These two mermaids had tails like serpents.

They continued to leap over waves as they chased the ship. They laughed with each breach of the water. They looked as though they were having fun. More fun than Lintang was having . . . although at the moment, she couldn't remember why she was upset. Watching them was as soothing as the euco oil had been to her lungs. She found herself laughing along with them. How lovely it must be to play in the sea all day, carefree, with no household chores and no adults to scold them.

Her insides felt buoyed with bubbles. When the mermaids beckoned her, she couldn't refuse. She already felt as though she were one of them. She hefted herself onto the railing. A sound snagged in the wind—someone calling her name?—but she was already soaring over the side. The water rushed toward her, the wind tearing at her clothes. The ship rose on a wave behind her, and she hit the ocean hard. Stinging spread across her body, from both the impact and the chill. It didn't matter. Nothing mattered anymore. She was with the mermaids now.

Bubbles rushed against her face as the mermaids' hands found her, welcoming her . . .

No. They were pulling her. Dragging her down.

She kicked out, the air in her lungs fast disappearing, but she weakened as the hands continued to keep her from the surface.

Her senses returned, and she felt the pain and the cold . . . and the panic.

She struggled to free herself. One mermaid shoved its face against Lintang's, and it was grotesque, more monstrous than the malam rasha.

Splinters sliced at Lintang's lungs. Her head felt light. An odd floating feeling overcame her. She barely noticed the flash of steel, or the clouds of blood in the water, or the fact that the mermaids had released their deadly grip. She drifted, dazed, as arms wrapped around her and tugged her toward the surface.

Captain's Cabin

LINTANG WOKE IN A BED that rocked like a cradle. She tried to sit up, but the blankets tucked around her body constricted her movement.

The bed had four pillars, with plush red curtains and a springy mattress, not at all like Lintang's straw mat at home. She realized it wasn't the bed itself that was rocking—it was the whole cabin.

A single candle burned in its frosted glass container, illuminating the room. Several steps led up to a tall, paned window. Beyond the glass, the sky was creamy indigo and bursting with stars.

Her saturated clothes hung from a wooden chair. There was a finely carved desk covered with papil scrolls and sticks of charcoal and bottles of ink. Glass jars held precious stones that sparkled rainbow colors when they caught the candlelight. An hourglass hung from the back of the door, filled with running sand that made a steady *shhhhh* sound. A beautiful map stretched across an entire wall, blocked by—

Eire.

Lintang started. Eire seemed even fiercer in the shadows, her head slightly lowered so her wide-set eyes made her look like a predator watching its prey. She waited a beat before saying, "Stupid girl."

Lintang didn't know how to answer.

Eire moved from the shadows. "Captain should not have rescued you, but she gave up necklace, and now she risk everything to keep you safe." Her hand moved to her hip, where she usually kept her weapon. The axe-spear thing was not on her at the moment, Lintang noticed with relief.

"I'm sorry," Lintang said. She hadn't wanted to annoy anyone on the ship, especially not the captain's second-in-command. "I didn't mean—"

"Save your sorries." Eire flicked her hand. "We are turned around. You will be off this ship by tomorrow."

Lintang choked, but before she could reply, the door swung open and Captain Shafira stalked in. She had a steaming bowl in her hands and one of Lintang's spare sarongs draped over her arm.

"That will do, Eire."

Eire sneered at Lintang before slinking out and shutting the door behind her.

Captain Shafira cleared a space between scrolls to set the bowl on the desk. She'd changed her outfit, but her braids were still wet.

"Thank you for saving me." Lintang's voice cracked. She inhaled a lungful of euco oil to steady her breathing. She had never felt so horrible for doing the wrong thing, not ever.

Captain Shafira perched on the corner of the desk, the sarong still hanging from her folded arms. "What was the instruction Eire gave you when you reached the top deck?"

Lintang wriggled in her blankets. "One of the crew told me to get out of the way, so I—"

"You're not answering my question."

Lintang's face burned. Any story that entered her head disappeared like smoke on her tongue. She'd promised not to lie to the captain. She swallowed hard and said, "She told me to stay where I was."

Captain Shafira tossed the sarong onto Lintang's lap. "There are good reasons for the instructions we give. If you don't follow orders, you may get yourself or someone else killed. Do you understand?"

Lintang nodded. She freed her arms from the blankets

and pretended to examine her sarong so she wouldn't have to look Captain Shafira in the eye. It was pale blue, one of her old ones. She'd probably still be wearing it when she arrived back in Desa tomorrow, disgraced. Father would shake his head in shame. Elder Wulan would say she'd tried to warn Captain Shafira: *That Lintang, she just doesn't know how to follow instructions.* And Mother . . .

Well, Mother would be happy to have Lintang back, at least. Maybe happy enough not to send her away to the mining community.

But Lintang would still be sentenced to domestic duties for the rest of her life, stuck doing nothing but chores while the *Winda* sailed around the world, with other, luckier people on board.

She pulled on the sarong and climbed out of bed. Her stomach rumbled at the aroma of pepper and lobster soup.

"Eat," Captain Shafira said, gesturing to it. "Dee fought hard to save it for you. The crew are vicious at mealtimes."

She grinned, but Lintang couldn't smile back. Instead, she sat on the chair, careful to avoid her wet golden sarong, and slurped at the soup. Dee had infused the broth with mao juice. And as well as being peppery, it was . . . sweet?

"Her cooking is interesting," Captain Shafira said,

"and it's certainly better than her sailing." She was still perched on the desk, so close that Lintang could detect an unfamiliar floral scent from her skin.

Lintang's throat tightened and she put the bowl down. She didn't want to go home. How could she, now that she knew there were better options? She had almost, *almost* gone on an adventure, and the fact she had been so close only to ruin it left her feeling ill.

Captain Shafira unfolded her arms, staring at the unfinished soup. "I didn't think it was that bad."

"I'm sorry about the mermaids," Lintang said. "I promise I'll never do it again."

"The mermaids were why I'd sent for you in the first place. I wanted you to learn an important lesson . . . I suppose you won't forget it now." At Lintang's puzzled frown, Captain Shafira added, "Just because the mermaids you know from home are safe doesn't make them all safe. Different countries have different versions of mythies. In some places, fey are human-size and cast spells. In others, gnomes are cunning and try to kill people. The waters are dangerous because aquatic mythies roam out of their territory. You don't know whether you're facing a gentle common mermaid or a killer mermaid from Caletrom."

Lintang had read about different mythie species in the guidebook, but it was one thing to learn about them and another to come across them. She'd lived her whole life knowing only safe mermaids—how could she have expected this?

Captain Shafira pushed the bowl forward. "Keep eating."

Lintang picked it up and took another sip, even though she'd lost her appetite. "I really am sorry."

"We all make mistakes, Lintang."

How could she be so understanding, even after Lintang had disobeyed her? How was she the same ferocious pirate queen everyone spoke about?

Lintang licked broth from her lips and lowered the bowl again. "You know, you're nothing like the stories."

Captain Shafira laughed. "What stories have you heard?"

"You and Captain Moon battled on a volcano."

"Oh, that one's true."

"Really? What about the one where you stabbed a man for touching your necklace?"

"Lie."

"What's so special about your necklace, anyway?"

"You know, I don't think even the governors asked this many questions last time they caught me."

Lintang clicked her tongue. "Everyone makes a big deal about it. It must be important."

"It has a sunstone. It's a gem found only in Allay, so it's worth a great deal to the rest of the world."

"Is that all? A single gem?"

"Well, it's also the crown of Allay."

Lintang, who had slurped again at her soup, nearly choked. "The what?"

"The leader of my country isn't a king or a queen, but a Zulttania. The title's passed down from mother to daughter, along with that necklace. I took it when I discovered the Zulttania was dead. I was going to use it as proof, but I was labeled a thief by her council instead, and now there's a huge reward for its return. There, are you satisfied? Now finish your soup." Captain Shafira waited until Lintang's mouth was full before adding, "Listen, my point about the Caletromian mermaids—"

This time Lintang really did choke. She had almost forgotten they were on their way back to Desa.

She let the bowl clatter to the desk and scraped her chair away as the peppery broth burned her throat.

Captain Shafira thumped on her back. "Are you all right?"

"Please," Lintang gasped, "please don't make me go home. I promise I'll follow all your instructions; I promise I'll do whatever the other crew members say. Give me another chance, please, please—"

"Make you go home? Why would I do that? You know perfectly well I need you to get past the sea guardian, and we already wasted enough time in Desa."

Lintang sat up, her coughs subsiding. She stared at the captain through watery eyes. "You're not taking me home? But . . . but Eire said—"

"Oh, Eire." Captain Shafira let out a breath through her teeth. "She likes to stir up trouble."

"Isn't she your first mate?"

"More or less," Captain Shafira said, then corrected herself. "Yes, she is."

"So why does she stir up trouble?"

"It doesn't matter. The important thing is, I'm not sending you home. I need you."

Lintang couldn't help it. Laughter fell from her lips between a few extra coughs. She was still going to meet Nyasamdra; she was still going to hunt sirens; she was still going to stand on the deck every day, and sleep in her hammock at night, and feel the wind in her hair as they ventured over the horizon.

But then the laughter faded. A cold dread settled over her like a blanket. After everything that had happened, she'd almost forgotten her other monstrous problem.

What was she going to do about Bayani?

The Weapons Master

LINTANG KNEW EXACTLY WHERE she was when she woke the next morning. She didn't need to open her eyes to feel the rocking of the ship, or hear the creak of timber, or smell the euco oil. She breathed in, long and deep, and smiled.

After changing into her sarong, she headed toward the aromas of breakfast. She'd gone straight to bed the night before, even though there had been raucous sounds of games and laughter from the dining room. She hadn't been ready to face everyone after her embarrassment with the mermaids. She still wasn't sure she was ready.

But Quahah was the only one in the dining room when Lintang arrived. She was reading an enormous book with a bronze cover. The tentacles of her woolly octopus hat hung over the pages, which were made of thick, rubbery material.

"It's about time," Quahah said as Lintang sat beside her. "We usually get up with the dawn bell, you know."

"I . . . had a busy day yesterday," Lintang said, ducking her head to hide her face.

"Yes, I heard about that." Quahah gave a sly smile. "We had a good laugh about it last night."

"I'm sure Eire wasn't laughing," Lintang muttered.

"Oh no, Eire doesn't laugh. It wastes precious scowling muscles."

Lintang peeked at the open book, but it was written in another language. It had sketches of islands between the scrawl.

"This was my father's," Quahah said, shifting it so Lintang could see better. "He was an explorer. Taught me everything I know."

"What language is that?"

"Phaizen. I come from the island of Phaize. Eire's from there too."

"Did you know each other before you came on the ship?"

"Thankfully, no. Captain Shafira needed to travel through Phaize, and she enlisted me as a guide and translator. We found Eire deep in the forest with her tribe."

Lintang crinkled her nose. "Why did Captain Shafira choose her to be first mate?"

"I thought I heard your voice." Dee wandered into the dining room, her arms laden with plates of food. She set the plates down and took Farah the clamshell out of her belt.

"She looks a little peaky," Farah the clamshell said in her squawking voice. "That dip in the ocean did her no good."

"Swimming's supposed to be refreshing," Dee said.

"Not if you almost drown, you gnome!" said Farah the clamshell.

Lintang stared at the spread. Scrambled eggs with cheese and herbs, fat sausages, bacon, yogurt, ripe burble-berries, crabmeat, a whole roasted fish, wild mushrooms, a bowl of rice, half a loaf of bread, and seven hard-boiled eggs.

"Is that enough?" Dee sounded concerned. "Do I need to bring out more?"

Lintang picked up a hard-boiled egg. "Who else is coming?"

"This is just for you," Quahah said, helping herself to a sliver of crabmeat. "The captain said you'd need a hearty meal."

"Swimming makes you hungry," Dee agreed.

"I don't think I need any more," Lintang said. "Er . . . thank you."

Dee beamed. "I can brew you a cup of tea later, if you're still peckish."

She wandered out of the dining room, and Lintang started on her meal. "What were we talking about?" she said, her cheeks bulging.

"Why the captain chose Eire as first mate," Quahah said, closing her book and sliding it well away from the food. "See, Eire's a skilled warrior. Very useful when traveling the world. She can defeat any creature, large or small. The captain saw her potential and offered her a place on board, but Eire would only accept if she was given a position as second-in-command." Quahah cut into the roasted fish. "That was before we came across most of the other crew. I don't think the captain realized she'd find more suitable people for the job and regret her decision."

"Then why doesn't she just kick Eire off?"

Quahah tossed a stray woolly tentacle over her shoulder. "Her word is law, even for herself. She made a promise to Eire, and now she has to keep it."

Lintang's mouth was too full by this stage to answer, so she made a face to show her disapproval instead. She shouldn't have felt so bad about annoying Eire, after all.

She'd been hoping to sneak to the cargo hold and give Bayani something to eat, but Quahah stuck with her through breakfast and helped her carry the leftovers into the galley. Dee tried to talk them into a cup of tea. Lintang said that if she had anything else, her stomach would explode.

Poor Bayani, meanwhile, would be picking at cold rations from barrels.

Unfortunately, Quahah didn't seem to have anything important to do. She followed Lintang out of the galley, and when she suggested they go to the top deck, Lintang couldn't think of a reason to say no.

It was a beautiful, clear day with a warm breeze that kept the sails full. Most of the others were up here. Captain Shafira was at the wheel with Zazi. Eire prowled by the railing. Something overhead caught Lintang's eye, and she looked up to find one of the crew flipping across the rigging as naturally as a howler in the rainforest.

"Mei used to be an acrobat," Quahah said. "Ah, here's Xiang."

A tall Vierzan woman approached them. There was something graceful about her, so even her loose, casual clothes appeared as if they belonged to royalty. Her glossy hair was pinned in a bun with a thin stick that looked like a spindle.

"Xiang's the weapons master," Quahah said.

Xiang dipped her head in acknowledgment.

"Weapons master?" Lintang said, perking up. "Can you fight?"

Xiang arched a thin eyebrow. "Is that supposed to be a joke?"

"Great! I challenge you to a duel!" At last—a real opponent. Lintang was bored with beating Bayani all the time.

Xiang inspected Lintang's outfit, and asked, "Where's your sword?"

"I'll get it."

Lintang raced downstairs and snagged her wooden sword. She regretted moving so fast as she climbed the stairs again—her bloated stomach protested noisily. When she returned, Xiang was still in the same spot, but now she held a long silver blade.

"Where did you get that?" Lintang said, slowing.

"Am I not the weapons master?"

Lintang lifted her sword. "True. Are you ready?"

There was a blur of movement, and before she'd even blinked, her sword was knocked from her hand, clattering onto the deck.

"Wait," she said, scrambling to pick it up. "I didn't say go."

Captain Shafira started toward them, leaving Zazi at the wheel. Lintang was determined to impress her captain, so she lifted her sword and faced Xiang again. "Right. Go."

Another blur of movement. Another clatter as her sword hit the ground.

"What? Stop it! Go slower!"

"Very well," Xiang said. She lifted her sword in a sweeping arc, exaggerating slowness.

Lintang lifted her own blade to block it, only for Xiang to change direction suddenly and, with a twirl of her wrist, disarm Lintang a third time.

Lintang said a bad word in her own language and picked up her sword, heat rising in her cheeks. Quahah chuckled.

"I'm still full from breakfast!" Lintang said.

Without warning this time, Lintang lunged. Xiang blocked her first attack, then her second. And her next.

"How are you doing that?" Lintang said, her voice a pitch too high.

Captain Shafira laughed softly behind her.

"She's got fire," Xiang said as she continued to block Lintang's attacks. She didn't even seem to be trying.

"I know," Captain Shafira said. "Stop teasing her, will you?"

"As you wish."

Lintang released a final flurry of attacks, knowing what was coming, but despite her best efforts, her sword still fell uselessly to the deck. Before she could pick it up, Captain Shafira grabbed it.

"Not bad," Captain Shafira said, examining it. At first Lintang thought she was talking about the craftship, but instead, she grinned at Xiang. "You didn't even leave a notch."

"Of course I didn't," Xiang said, sounding offended.

Captain Shafira handed the sword back to Lintang. "Xiang's blade can cut through wood like this in a single blow."

Lintang whirled to Xiang. "Teach me how to fight. Properly fight."

"Oh no," Xiang said, sheathing her sword. "Don't you understand the rules of a duel at sea? You challenged me and lost. You must throw yourself overboard."

Lintang lowered her blade. "What?" The roar of the waves dulled to a whisper.

How was she going to talk her way out of this one? Why was she *always* getting into trouble?

But then Xiang's solemn expression broke, and she burst into giggles.

"What?" Lintang asked again as Quahah started

laughing too, and Mei above them, and Zazi at the wheel. Even Captain Shafira's lips twitched. Eire at the bow was the only one who didn't look amused.

Xiang no longer had an air of grace or formality. She clutched her sides, her cheeks turning red from her fit of laughter. "You should've seen your face," she said through tears. "How could you have believed me?"

"That was mean," Lintang said weakly.

"Well, we are supposed to be pirates," Quahah said, which brought about another string of giggles from Xiang.

Lintang managed a smile. Whoever was trying to convince the world that this crazy crew was criminals obviously hadn't met a single one of them.

Mythie Guidebook Information Page:
Reproduction

~~~~~~~~

Despite falling under different classifications, all mythies reproduce by laying an egg in a host body. Eyewitness accounts describe various species of mythies "bursting" from humans without warning. No information has been collected as to how mythies lay their eggs, or why the host has no knowledge of the egg's existence until it's too late.

Mythies are born fully grown. There have been no sightings of mythical creatures at any stage of life except maturity. Studies show that mythies do not age and do not possess reproductive organs.

Scientists theorize that mythies send out invisible spores that can be absorbed by humans. Some go as far as to say that these spores are sent out during the death of a mythie, as it has been found that many hunters, both amateurs and professionals, become hosts to various species of mythies. Other experts disagree, as these hunters are rarely the host of the same mythical creature as the ones they kill.

No plausible explanation has yet been given for this phenomenon.

Life on the *Winda*

⟲

THAT EVENING, DEE and Farah the clamshell taught Lintang some creative cooking tips with rations from Desa and freshly caught seafood. They made hot soup, burbleberry tarts, smoked salmon with cream cheese, and olive-stuffed pastries. It was messy work, and Lintang's sarong ended up dusted with flour and splattered with broth, but it was worth it. If cooking at home had been as fun as cooking with Dee and her clamshell mother, Lintang might've enjoyed it more.

When it was time to serve up, Dee hollered, *"Yamini!"* and the ragged teenager walked in. She was bony and angular—her clothes seemed to hang on her. Her hair formed a curtain over her face to hide her high cheekbones and pointed chin. She took the plate for the captain without a word.

"Can I help?" Lintang said. She really wanted to make friends.

But Yamini curled her lip and looked at Lintang as if she were a slop bucket. "I don't need help from anyone, especially *you*."

She stalked out with the plate. Lintang frowned after her.

"Yamini's the cabin girl," Dee said. "She serves the food by herself."

"She doesn't have to be rude about it."

Dee loaded a new round of plates. "Ah, but see, it's punishment."

"The crew used to share the chores," Farah the clamshell said. "Scrubbing floors, cleaning slop buckets, washing dishes. Now she has to do it all herself."

"Why?"

"She let the captain down."

"Really?" Lintang ladled soup into bowls. "What did she do?"

"It's not for me to say."

"Nor me," Farah the clamshell said.

Lintang had been planning on taking a plate down to Bayani while everyone was eating, but now she stared at the spread of food and imagined what would happen if someone caught her. What if she was sentenced to be cabin girl too? What if she had to empty slop buckets all day, and scrub floors, and clean up after dinner? If she'd wanted to do chores, she would've stayed at home.

She put the extra plate away while Dee's back was turned. There were plenty of rations in the cargo hold. Bayani would be fine on his own for just a little longer, until she figured out the best way to visit him without making anyone suspicious.

Dinner was a noisy affair. The dining room was called the mess, which was a good name for it. The crew had loosened up since Lintang's duel against Xiang. They regaled Lintang with tales of the famous creatures they had fought—a kraken, a giant jellyfish, a carnivorous eel. In return, she told the story of Pero's last battle against Lanme Vanyan. When she was finished, Xiang said Lintang was the best storyteller she'd ever heard. Lintang hoped her grandfather's star, blazing high in the sky, agreed. Unlike Mother, he had never been ashamed of her stories.

When the plates were licked clean, they sang songs beneath the light of the swaying lanterns. Zazi the helmsperson played a funny instrument that was like the bellows from the galley, only it made all kinds of sounds when she squeezed it. Mei the rigger played a stringed instrument with a bow, and Quahah blew into a wooden pipe.

Afterward, Eire called for Yamini to set up rouls. Flat wooden boards were assembled as an upright track, with cranks to make it move. While Yamini turned the cranks, the players threw darts or daggers at pictures painted on the moving boards. The smaller the picture the player hit, the more points she got.

It was a fun game that caused a lot of fights, especially when Eire lost to Xiang. Lintang tried once with a dagger, but on her first throw she almost hit Eire, who immediately banned her from playing again. Lintang resolved to practice when no one else was around.

She went to bed buzzing and hardly expected to sleep, but in the blink of an eye the dawn bell was ringing and Captain Shafira was knocking at her door to give her a proper tour of the ship.

The captain taught her nautical language as they walked—port and starboard and rigging and helm— then showed her the big map across her cabin wall, pointing out where they were and where they were going, and where she expected Nyasamdra would appear.

Lintang had seen world maps before, but they hadn't

been detailed and colorful like this one. The parchment was strong and the ink was vibrant. Bayani would've loved it.

"Why are the countries drawn in different colors?" she said, tracing her finger over the green outline of the Twin Islands. Almost every other country was red except two—a small island and a big southern country—which were blue.

"How closely did you listen to lessons at school?" Captain Shafira said.

Lintang chewed the inside of her cheek. "I may have been daydreaming every now and then."

"Good. That means you haven't been brainwashed yet." Captain Shafira smiled wryly and pointed at the red countries. "These are the ones under the control of the Vierzans. All these countries together are called the United Regions."

"Yes, I know about the United Regions," Lintang said, staring at the many red markings.

"Here's Vierz," Captain Shafira said, pointing to a big country west of the Twin Islands. "The governors who run the United Regions want the whole world under their rule."

One of the coastal cities was highlighted in deeper

red. Zaiben—the capital. The place Bayani had been desperate to go.

"I thought being part of the United Regions was a good thing."

"And who told you that?"

"Elder Wulan."

"Is Elder Wulan an Islander?"

"No, she's . . ." Lintang trailed off.

"She's from Vierz," Captain Shafira said. "Whenever Vierzans visit the Twin Islands, they bring building materials, supplies to help with mythies, medics, and *teachers*. They tell you everything you want to hear, so that your village ends up wanting to join the UR. And then when every other village on the Twin Islands agrees too, before you know it, this green outline turns red, just like everywhere else." She tapped the ocean next to the Twin Islands. "The only thing keeping you safe at the moment is the sea guardian. Vierzans can't come in and out easily with her protecting your waters."

Lintang stared at her. "Are you saying Elder Wulan is bad?"

She couldn't imagine Elder Wulan, dear old Elder Wulan, who helped Mother with the chores and taught Lintang how to write, as some kind of enemy.

"No," Captain Shafira said. "She just believes you should live like Vierzans, which is ridiculous. There's nothing wrong with how you live now." She tapped the two blue-outlined countries. "Caletrom and Allay are the only truly independent places left in the world. They don't have anything to do with the United Regions."

"Allay," Lintang said. "Where you're from."

She hadn't heard much about it. Elder Wulan barely touched on it in her geography lessons. Some merchants even called it the forbidden island, because it had been closed to trade ever since the Kaneko Brown war. No one had been allowed to go in or out of Allay for almost twenty years.

Captain Shafira looked at the blue island for a long time. "Yes," she said at last. "My home." Then she turned away to talk of other things. Their conversation about Allay was over, and neither of them brought it up again.

Avalon

OVER THE NEXT FEW days, Mei the rigger took Lintang climbing across the ropes, which turned out to be scarier than it looked.

Despite her fearlessness, Mei was the gentlest person on board. There was kindness in her eyes, and her round cheeks gave her a youthful, innocent appearance. She was quiet, too, and let Lintang work out things on her own. Once, Lintang heard her singing in a different language, but when Lintang asked about her home country, Mei simply smiled, the wind whipping her dark hair across her face, and climbed higher.

On the third day of exploring the rigging, Mei showed Lintang the upper basket—an enclosed platform near the top of the mainmast—and Lintang used a collapsible brass telescope to scan the ever-blue horizon. It was exhilarating being so far up as the ship rose and fell with the swell. Lintang stayed long after Mei had climbed down. She looked back with the telescope, her breath catching when all she saw was water. She was truly far from home now.

Maybe Captain Shafira would let her visit another country. Vierz was straight ahead, and when Bayani gave himself up, they'd have to drop him off in Zaiben.

She strained to remember what Elder Wulan had said about the capital city. Half of it had been destroyed by a dragon during the first years of the mythie infestation. Hundreds of people had been killed. The Vierzans had found a way to create clouds that constantly hung over the city, hiding them from other attacks. A deep ravine surrounded the place, so people could only enter and exit via three bridges. Gate guardians checked everyone who came in or out. They had landcrafts on the streets, buildings rising high almost into the clouds, and water running through pipes without a river.

Lintang's entire body tingled at the thought of being able to see it for herself. She imagined taking that first step onto the soil of another country. It would be the best feeling in the world.

She was so wrapped up in the idea that at first she didn't notice the bird land on the basket railing. It warbled at her, breaking her daydream.

"Hello," she said. "You're a friendly one, aren't you?"

It wasn't a talross. It had black feathers, a long neck, and a yellow crest. It cocked its head this way and that, examining her.

She glanced around, but there was no sign of its friends.

"Are you alone?"

It hopped closer.

She laughed. "I don't have any food, sorry."

Lintang reached out tentatively, wondering whether it would let her stroke it, and smiled when her fingers brushed its silky feathers. It warbled again, this time drowsily.

"Bayani would love you," she said. "He likes animals. He names them and everything."

Guilt washed through her. She'd been meaning to check on him. Really. It was just that she'd been so busy with lessons and games and climbing, and besides, the crew seemed to be everywhere—she could never find a time when it was safe to sneak downstairs.

She swallowed hard and studied the bird's yellow crest. "Well. Since he's not here, I'll call you Keelee."

Smoke belched from the pipe at the bow of the ship. Dee must've started dinner. Lintang lifted her face to sniff the air. "We're so lucky, Keelee," she said, pushing thoughts of Bayani aside. "This is the best place in the world."

The bird cocked its head again, chirruped, then stretched its wings and flapped away. Lintang watched it disappear into the blue before returning her gaze to the snapping sails of the ship.

A flash of movement caught her attention. Someone with pale skin and dark clothing was on the deck.

It was a man.

He walked to the bridge and opened a hatch behind the helm. Lintang stiffened. How had he gotten on board?

She scrambled down the rigging, heart thumping. She hadn't been to the bridge before, since she wasn't allowed near the helm, but this was an emergency.

Her foot had barely touched the first step when a voice rang out.

"What do you think you're doing?"

Lintang whirled around as Yamini the cabin girl stalked across the deck.

"There's a stranger on board," Lintang said urgently. "A man. You have to get the captain."

Yamini's expression changed from alarm to amusement. She gave Lintang the once-over and said, "There aren't any ships around for a hundred measures. No way can there be a stranger on board."

"I saw him!"

"You must've been imagining things." Yamini eyed Lintang's foot, which was still on the first step to the bridge. "Or maybe you're coming up with an excuse for being somewhere you're not supposed to be."

Lintang groaned and kept climbing. "Just fetch the captain."

"You'll get in trouble."

Lintang ignored her. When she reached the bridge, she ducked behind the helm, which had been fastened securely to keep the ship on course, and lifted the hatch. A staircase led to the next level. A single lantern lit a room with an extra tiller. The man was nowhere to be seen.

Why was he here? Had he snuck aboard to kill the pirate queen? Was it possible there were *two* stowaways on this ship?

A quick search led to the discovery of another hatch behind the tiller. With a fierce tug she swung it open to reveal a second set of steps. Light glowed warmly on her face. The sound of coarse scraping echoed up to her. What was he doing?

The angle wasn't right for her to see anything. If she wanted to catch him, she was going to have to go down.

She had to do it. She had to protect her captain.

After a breath to steady her nerves, she descended the staircase, leaving the hatch open above her. The scraping continued. A wonderful foresty smell lingered over the euco oil. She reached the bottom and peeked inside.

The stranger was at a carpentry work station, sanding a piece of timber with rough bark. She stopped with a gasp.

He must've been a mythie. His skin was as white as the sand on Desa's bay. His dark hair made his complexion look sickly. A furry silver animal like a squirrel with long ears sat on his shoulder, reminding her of Pelita watching over Bayani.

The man stopped sanding, and she realized too late that her gasp had been heard. He dropped the rough bark. The silver animal chittered angrily, darting from one of his shoulders to the other.

He wasn't as old as she'd first thought. In fact, he looked Yamini's age, maybe fourteen or fifteen. And if he was working, he probably wasn't a stowaway.

"Who are you?" she said.

He stared at her, unmoving. The silver animal continued to scold her in its own twittery language.

Lintang gazed around the room. A variety of carpentry tools hung from the walls, but there were also weapons in brackets—all sorts of weapons. They gleamed in the light of the lanterns.

More frightening was the giant cage against the wall.

"Are you a crew member?" Lintang said, daring a step closer. "How come I've never seen you before?"

The boy picked up the rough bark but didn't continue sanding.

Lintang edged forward. "I'm Lintang of Desa, village on . . . Oh, never mind. I'm Lintang."

Still no answer.

She caught sight of a hammock in the corner, with an empty plate from lunch and a wooden chest like in all the other cabins.

"Is this your room?"

At last, he muttered, "It's Xiang's storage room."

Lintang looked at the weapons on the wall again. "But you sleep here?"

"Yes."

"And you work here?"

"Yes."

"And you spend all your time here?"

A shrug.

"Then it's kind of your room too, isn't it?"

The silver animal finally stopped chittering and started grooming itself. The boy resumed his sanding.

She watched him for some time before saying, "Why are you in here all alone?"

"I don't like people" was the gruff reply.

"What people?"

"Everyone."

"Even your parents?" No answer. "Even your brothers and sisters? Even your friends?" Lintang frowned at his silence and said, "Even Captain Shafira?"

At that he looked up.

Lintang nodded, satisfied. "So," she said, continuing toward him, "how come you're allowed on board if you're a boy?"

He hesitated, but before he could answer, another voice said, "Avalon dresses like boy, but she is girl."

Lintang turned to find Eire at the foot of the stairs. Yamini stood behind her.

"See?" Yamini said. "I told you she was snooping."

"Leave, cabin girl," Eire said.

Yamini raised her eyebrows at Lintang before swaggering back upstairs.

"I was trying to help," Lintang said, glaring after her. "I thought someone had snuck on board. The rules don't technically say anything about the hatch on the bridge, and I thought—"

"Thought what?" Eire crinkled her nose. "You take on trespasser alone?"

Lintang faltered. She hadn't thought that far ahead. She didn't even have her wooden sword.

Eire bared her teeth in a cruel smile. "I tell captain this."

"But I didn't do anything wrong!"

"Leave her alone, Eire," Avalon said, setting down his rough bark.

Eire's eyebrows shot up. "You are not to order first mate, cupaal."

The muscle in Avalon's jaw twitched. His pale face had turned a strange reddish color. "Don't call me that."

"You are ordering me again, cupaal?"

"What?" Lintang said. "What are you saying?"

"I am saying truth," Eire said. "Avalon pretends she is boy. I remind her she is not."

Avalon held out his hands for the silver squirrel to scamper down from his shoulder. "I *am* a boy."

Eire raised her eyebrows. "We will find out when you meet sirens, yes?"

"What's going on?"

They turned as Captain Shafira came down the stairs. She took in the three of them and said, "Eire, Lintang —there's no need for you to be down here."

Eire gave Lintang a dirty look. "Girl was snooping."

"I thought someone had snuck on board," Lintang said quickly.

Eire started to argue, but Captain Shafira held up her hand for silence. "Go, Eire. Lintang, we need to talk."

Eire stalked away in Yamini's wake.

"I didn't—" Lintang started, but Captain Shafira wandered over to Avalon and said, "So now you've met the best carpenter to sail the five seas. He did Hewan's peg leg, you know. Expert piece of craftsmanship." She clapped his shoulder. He ducked his head, embarrassed.

"But . . ." Lintang said, looking from him to Captain Shafira. "You . . . I mean . . . He . . . and . . . the sirens . . ."

"It's a risk, but we need him," Captain Shafira said. "Why do you think we have the cage?"

"But Eire . . ."

Captain Shafira raised her eyebrows. "I already told you she likes to stir up trouble."

Lintang put her arm against Avalon's so that her brown skin stood out against his sea-foam white. He was definitely warm, and definitely real, and definitely not a mythie.

"Avalon comes from a country where skin like his is normal," Captain Shafira said.

The silver creature on Avalon's shoulder chirruped.

"Who's your friend?" Lintang said.

"This is Twip." Avalon used his index finger to stroke Twip's nose. "He's from my home."

"Where's that?"

"A long way away."

Captain Shafira opened the wooden chest. "While we're here, Avalon, can Lintang try on some of your old clothes? She'll need something warmer than sarongs as we head north."

"I guess," Avalon said hesitantly.

"Thank you. Lintang, come here. See if there's anything you like."

Lintang hurried over. The chest was filled with clothes that seemed almost small enough to fit her.

"These are from when Avalon was younger," Captain Shafira said. "He's too sentimental to throw them away, and they're going to waste sitting here."

"They might be useful as rags later," Avalon said.

"Sure, sure," said Captain Shafira. "In the meantime, at least let them go to good use."

Lintang pawed through the clothes. There were pants and shirts, well worn but clean, and . . . dresses? She looked at Avalon again.

"What?" he said, sounding defensive.

She shook her head. "Nothing."

"You think I'm strange."

Lintang dug deeper in the chest. "Not really. Dee's mother is a clamshell."

"Hmm. Fair point."

Her fingers touched leather, and with a gasp she pulled out a pair of boots. They were lined with creases like an old woman's face, but they were sturdy, and the fur lining was soft.

"Try them on," Captain Shafira said.

Lintang wriggled into them. They were a touch too big, but they were better than her woven shoes, and she could clomp around in them like a pirate. She rummaged through the rest of the things. When she couldn't find any other clothes that looked like the captain's, she picked out a dress of rainforest green.

"It's made of velvet," Avalon said as Lintang trailed her fingers along the fabric. She'd never heard of velvet.

"Here's a skivvy to go beneath it." Captain Shafira held up a gray top with a high neck. Lintang also found stretchy black pants like the ones Dee wore. Tights, Captain Shafira called them.

Lintang changed into the clothes and held her arms out for a proper inspection.

"Much better," Captain Shafira said. "Thank you, Avalon."

Avalon grunted, but the corner of his lips twitched as Lintang twirled around the room in her new clothes. She'd never owned anything so lovely.

The Mythie Guidebook Entry #81:
Sea Guardian [Twin Islands]

~~~~~~~~~

The sea guardian (Nyasamdra) is a sea mythie and the largest humanoid, appearing as a giantess in a green dress. She's considered the guardian of the Twin Islands. Humans born in her territory have a fish scale on the back of their neck to mark them as hers.

Diet: Unknown.

Habitat: The seas around the Twin Islands.

Frequency: Single entity.

Behavior: The sea guardian allows anyone to enter her waters but only lets them leave if they have her mark. If they try to escape without giving her the proper tribute,* she will drown the ship.

Eradication: Unknown.

Did you know? There are three hundred and forty-five rules when dealing with the sea guardian. Please refer to *The Sea Guardian's Guidebook* for a comprehensive list.

Danger level: 4 for non-Islanders. 2 for Islanders.

* *The sea guardian's tribute:* "I am _____ (insert name) of _____ (insert birthplace), son/daughter of _____ (insert mother's name) and _____ (insert father's name), child of Nyasamdra. Please allow us to pass." (Head must be bowed low.)

Nyasamdra

A FEW AFTERNOONS LATER the waves calmed to ripples, the wind died, and the sky became gray and drizzly. The talrosses that had been following the ship flew away.

The entire crew—even Avalon—stood on the deck looking out to sea in a hush. Lintang edged behind Zazi's massive form. It was as if all of their voices had vanished with the waves.

From the upper basket Mei cried out, shattering the silence. As soon as she did, the wind picked up, catching the black sails. Captain Shafira raced to the bridge to take control of the helm.

Lintang hurried to help with the ropes, but Mei was still yelling, and the crew looked to where she was pointing. Lintang shielded her eyes against the drizzle. Water churned in the distance in a glowing green whirlpool.

Her breath choked. She had to grip the railing at a sudden rush of shivers.

It was Nyasamdra.

"I didn't reckon her to appear this soon," Quahah said, taking off her woolly octopus hat and squinting at the whirlpool.

The swell grew. Lintang wrapped her whole arm around the railing so she wouldn't get jolted overboard. "She doesn't always show up in the same place. No one knows when they're going to come across her." Her voice was breathy. Her stomach churned as violently as the sea. If she threw up in front of Nyasamdra, she'd never forgive herself.

A dark bulge rose from the swirling green, growing larger and larger, until a smooth part appeared, glistening; then eyebrows, eyes, a nose—

"It's just her face," Avalon said, gaping. "How big is this thing?"

Nyasamdra's head was as high as the mast of the ship. She stood taller and taller, looming like a mountain before them. Water cascaded down her hair and sparkling dress —a dress that was green like Lintang's new velvet one . . .

"Oh no," Lintang whispered.

She couldn't move, couldn't hide, not with the giant woman peering down at them.

The ocean sloshed around Nyasamdra's thighs as though she were merely wading through a stream. She examined the crew one by one, her smile expectant. Even without looking, Lintang could sense the stillness of those around her. Only Captain Shafira moved, struggling to keep the ship on course.

"Leaving?" said Nyasamdra pleasantly. Her voice boomed around them, as powerful as the waves. But she didn't speak Vierse—she spoke in Lintang's native tongue, which meant no one else knew what she was saying.

Nyasamdra tilted her head. "Have you one of mine?"

Lintang couldn't answer. As on the night she had met Captain Shafira, her tongue felt sticky.

"Lintang," Eire said sharply.

Lintang didn't speak. When the silence stretched on, Nyasamdra frowned. "Have you one of mine or haven't you?"

"Lintang!" Eire said again. When Lintang didn't answer, Eire spoke to Nyasamdra herself, using Vierse. "We have Islander. Let us pass."

Lintang sucked in a breath so fast it was painful. Who would dare speak to Nyasamdra that way? If she understood, she would take offense and drown them all.

But Nyasamdra blinked slowly and didn't answer.

Eire gestured to Lintang. "This is Islan—"

"No!" Lintang lunged to shove her arm down. The rest of the crew spun to them. "I'm sorry," she said. She spoke loud enough for Captain Shafira to hear but used Vierse so Nyasamdra didn't understand. "I'm sorry, I made a mistake, a *stupid* mistake."

"What do you mean?" Xiang said.

Lintang pointed to her velvet dress, which was now soaked through. "I'm not supposed to wear green. I can't believe I forgot. Nyasamdra has very particular rules, and that is one of them."

The crew glanced at Nyasamdra's sparkling outfit. Eire muttered something in her own language, then staggered with everyone else as the ship lurched.

Nyasamdra had grown bored with them and was swirling the water as if their ship were a toy.

The ship lurched again and began to spin in a circle. Captain Shafira strained with the wheel, but it was useless.

"Tell her anyway," Eire said, stumbling to the foremast to keep herself steady.

"Nothing makes her angrier than one of her children wearing her color. Trust me." Lintang grabbed the same mast. She considered pulling her dress off and tossing it overboard, but the deck was rocking too hard, and she didn't want to risk drawing Nyasamdra's attention.

"Last generation, a Vierzan ship took an Islander wearing green and Nyasamdra drowned them all."

"Then you are useless!" Eire roared.

Lintang squeezed her eyes shut as the ship spun faster. She hadn't thought about Nyasamdra's rules since putting on the dress. She'd been taken in by the softness, by the pretty color. She'd felt special. She shouldn't have felt special—she should have remembered the most obvious reason she'd never worn green.

Eire raised her hand. "You stupid—"

A shriek pierced the sky, and a flash of black swooped between them. Eire staggered back.

Keelee the bird soared up between the sails and into the clouds. Eire watched it, hissing, but they had a new problem now. Nyasamdra had cupped her hands over the ship. A film of water appeared from her palms, surrounding them. All the rushing noise from the ocean disappeared. The wind stopped. The black sails drooped.

They were in a bubble.

Nyasamdra picked them up and let them float in the air. She watched them swirl inside the bubble, her face childlike with curiosity.

Lintang leaned over the side. Some of the ocean water whooshed in the bubble with them, but below that the sea was getting farther away.

Dee clung to the railing. Raindrops spattered on her shaved head. "This is not good," she said with a moan.

Xiang snagged a knife from her boot and threw it at the bubble. The knife simply bounced off.

"This is *not* good," Farah the clamshell said from Dee's belt.

Keelee soared over Nyasamdra, who batted at the bird.

"Keelee!" Lintang cried.

But the bird darted past Nyasamdra's fingers and pecked the bubble. There was a *pop*, and everyone had to hold on as the ship plummeted back into the waves. Lintang felt as though her stomach had left her body. They hit the water with a painful jolt.

Keelee disappeared into the clouds again, which flashed with brilliant white light. Lintang straightened, her legs trembling so hard they threatened to give out beneath her. She slotted the pieces together.

Keelee was the lightning bird.

"Did you just call our protector *Keelee*?" Xiang said.

"I thought it was an ordinary bird!" Lintang said. She spun to Captain Shafira on the bridge. "I didn't know —I'm sorry!"

"You mean you've met it before?" Quahah asked. "You actually saw it up close?"

Captain Shafira laughed. "You doubt me now, Eire?"

Nyasamdra scowled down at the *Winda*. She seemed angry that she'd lost her toy. She raised her hand to squash them.

Lintang covered her head uselessly. Nyasamdra's palm was as big as the ship—they would be smashed to pieces.

"What's that?" Avalon cried.

Lintang jerked up. A familiar ball of light sped out from below deck: Pelita, the pixie. Which meant—

Bayani sprinted after her, past the staggering crew and an open-mouthed Eire. He dived to his knees at the bow of the ship.

"I am Bayani of Desa, village on the island of Tolus, son of Devina and Saam, child of Nyasamdra." He spoke in their native tongue, with his head bowed so low the shiny scale on the back of his neck was visible. "Please," he said, "allow us to pass."

Nyasamdra paused. Bayani kept his head down. He struggled to stay steady as the ship rocked and swirled with the unsettled waters.

Lintang stared at him, heart pounding. Now she really felt as if she was going to be sick. It was over. He was out in the open for everyone to see.

The crew was silent. Above them, lightning illuminated the clouds once more.

At last, Nyasamdra lowered her hand and returned Bayani's bow. "Safe passage is granted."

Then she sank into the water, vanishing with the same slow, smooth movement with which she had arrived. Only when her mass of dark hair had disappeared did Lintang dare to breathe properly.

But several heartbeats later, Mei yelled from the upper basket again. Lintang whirled to find the giant face behind the ship. Instead of attacking them, though, Nyasamdra puffed her cheeks and blew, so that their ship turned to point west once more. Her breath filled their sails and sent them speeding away, out of the waters of the Twin Islands.

It didn't take long for the crew to return to their senses. Some raced to secure the ropes. Quahah snagged her woolly octopus cap, which had gotten tangled in the rigging.

Xiang and Eire lunged to grab Bayani. Pelita zipped angrily around them, but when Eire almost squashed her, she fluttered to hide in a pile of toppled barrels by the mainmast.

Lintang's legs were too shaky to move. She watched, helpless, as Eire and Xiang hauled Bayani to his feet.

"I know this boy," Eire said crisply. "He—"

"Requested to come with us." Captain Shafira came

toward them. Zazi had taken the wheel, but there wasn't much steering required, since Nyasamdra had them directly on course. Captain Shafira stood before Bayani. "What are you doing here?"

"I have to go to Zaiben," Bayani said.

"The sirens' song will drive you mad," Xiang said, keeping a firm grip on his arm. "You'll do anything to go to them, including putting us in danger."

Bayani's gaze fell to Avalon. "But you already have a boy here."

"Avalon and I have an agreement," Captain Shafira said. "I won't make the same deal with you."

Eire jolted Bayani. "We throw him overboard."

"No!" Lintang hadn't been able to stop her cry, and it drew the attention of everyone around her, including Captain Shafira.

"Did you help him stow away?" Captain Shafira said.

"No," Lintang said. "No, I swear to the Gods, I had no idea he'd sneaked aboard, and when I found him I was so mad—"

Bayani shook his head frantically, and it was only then Lintang realized her mistake.

"You knew he was aboard the ship?" Captain Shafira's voice turned cold. "How long?"

Lintang's heart hammered in her throat, blocking her

ability to answer. Behind Captain Shafira, Yamini raised her eyebrows.

"How long, Lintang?" The captain's voice was loud now. Fierce.

Heat flushed through Lintang's cheeks. "Since the first day." She couldn't look at anyone.

"We toss them both overboard." Eire sounded triumphant.

"No one's going overboard," Captain Shafira said. "The boy saved our lives—the least we can do is spare his. He'll be dealt with," she continued over the cries of outrage. "But he will come with me first. I'd like a word in private."

"And the girl?" Xiang said, speaking as though Lintang hadn't been traveling with them all this time, as though they hadn't eaten together, or practiced fighting, or even met one another before. "Remember your necklace, Captain."

Captain Shafira stalked toward her cabin. Eire and Xiang followed with Bayani between them. "I'll speak with her after I speak to the boy. Don't worry. You can be sure she too will be punished."

Cabin Girl

LINTANG WAS ENRAGED. She was enraged by the unfairness of it all, by the fact she had been stuck between loyalty to her best friend and loyalty to Captain Shafira, with no possible way to win. She was enraged with Bayani, who still wouldn't tell her why he'd stowed away, even after she'd been demoted to cabin girl, even after she'd lost the friendship of the crew—and worse, the respect of Captain Shafira. She was especially enraged at Yamini, who was now her new boss.

Yamini was the worst boss in the world. She loved making Lintang do all the horrible chores, like cleaning the dirty rags and slop buckets. Lintang had no choice but to follow her orders, because Captain Shafira had made a promise to the rest of the crew that if Lintang disobeyed her superiors one more time, she'd be off the *Winda* for good.

It was just like the legend of Princess Gree, who had been captured and forced into slavery. Lintang had to move out of her big cabin and into the smallest one at the end of the ship. It was bare except for one small gray blanket covering the simple woven hammock. There weren't even brackets on the wall—Lintang had to set her wooden sword in the corner. Yamini watched Lintang carry all her things without helping, hissing nasty names like "useless swill" and "spineless jellyfish."

When the dawn bell rang, Yamini pounded on the wall between their rooms to wake Lintang. They worked all day and well into the night while everyone else played rouls and sang songs. None of the crew spoke to them. They cleaned the mess after the rest of the crew went to bed. They had to scrub and mop the entire room, and Yamini always assigned Lintang the bigger, grubbier side. Then, when Yamini had finished, she'd stand over Lintang and point out the places Lintang had missed. Sometimes Yamini made Lintang mop the floor all over again just because she found a single streak of dirt.

Lintang learned to be thorough with her cleaning, or she wouldn't get to bed until almost dawn.

There you go, Mother, Lintang thought wryly as she scrubbed a glob of spit from the deck. *I finally know how to be a good housekeeper.*

She found herself craving Mother's sweet fish wraps. Who would've thought she'd miss that?

The ache for home had returned with a vengeance —that same hollow feeling she'd had when her toy Jojo had burned to ash.

She wanted to sit on her porch at home in the sun, listening to the droning insects and watching the colorful birds in the rainforest canopy. She wanted to wander down to the beach with Father, collecting interesting shells, to share sweetsap-roasted nuts with Nimuel after supper. She even missed those sticky nights when it was too hot to sleep, when Mother would fan her with a panna leaf and hum absently to herself.

She missed her mother.

The temperature dropped. Gone were the warm breezes of the tropics, replaced by gusts that bit her skin and made her teeth chatter. Her breath came out as steam, which made her look like a dragon. She was allowed to keep her velvet dress, but neither it nor the skivvy nor the tights kept her warm enough. Even the sea spray was painful. She had thought the ocean was cold before—but it was nothing compared to now. The mornings were filled with a thick white cloud called fog. It made for dangerous sailing.

They had changed course since Nyasamdra. Instead

of going directly west, they moved northwest, toward Vierz. They had to drop Bayani off in Zaiben before they could chase the sirens. He was finally headed for the place he was so desperate to get to. He wouldn't tell Lintang what he and Captain Shafira had talked about in private. She gave up asking. She gave up talking to him altogether. Why should she be friends with someone who had ruined her dream life and wouldn't even tell her why?

Captain Shafira had put Bayani in the cage in the weapons room. Avalon gave him fresh clothes.

It was Lintang's job to feed him and clean up after him, as well as take him for walks around the deck in the cold sunshine when Eire decided it was safe. He was quiet during the walks, staring out to sea, lost in thought as Pelita fluttered around his head.

Lintang stomped into his room one evening with a pitcher of fresh water and a tray of scraps from the galley. She was already in a bad mood—she'd spent a good portion of the day scrubbing the slop room, but then Yamini had "accidentally" tipped dirty mop water all over the floor. Lintang had flown at her in a rage, but while Yamini was bony, she was much stronger than Lintang and simply pushed her into the puddle and told her to start again. The last thing Lintang felt like doing was dealing with her traitorous ex–best friend and swatting Pelita away while she tried to work.

When she got to the carpentry room, she found Bayani on his back, one arm flopped across his stomach, the other draped over his eyes. Pelita sat on his chest, which rose and fell with his breaths.

Lintang slowed at the foot of the staircase. "Are you sick?"

The last time he'd been ill, he'd had to go to Sundriya and she hadn't been sure she'd ever see him again.

It took a long time for him to answer. At last, a groan dragged past his lips and he said, "It's nothing."

Nothing, nothing, nothing.

She huffed. "Fine."

He sat up. Pelita almost tumbled off him. She rose into the air, buzzing angrily. For once, Bayani ignored her. He watched as Lintang slid up the small door in his cage to pass through his food. She refused to look at him, but she could feel his stare.

He scooted over and took the plate. Pelita buzzed down to poke at the mashed potatoes. She glared at Lintang in disgust.

"Don't look at me; it's not my fault," Lintang said to her.

"No," said Bayani miserably, scooping up the potato with his fingers, "it's mine. It's all mine. I'm so sorry."

"You've said that already. About a hundred times."

"Why is she so angry?"

Both of them turned to find Avalon sitting on the steps, Twip on his shoulder. He kept his gaze on Bayani. "I've never seen anyone hold on to anger for that long. Usually people sentenced to cabin duties break down and cry after the first day. And yet she's still raging." He tickled Twip's chin.

"Why don't you ask me yourself?" Lintang snapped.

"You see, Bayani," Avalon said, "the crew's been given instructions not to speak to Lintang unless they're giving her direct orders, and I won't disobey the captain. But there were no rules about not talking to you."

Lintang scowled and dragged out Bayani's pitcher to refill it. So that was why everyone on the ship was ignoring her—Captain Shafira had *ordered* them to. She dumped the fresh water into Bayani's pitcher, sloshing some onto the deck.

"Lintang's not angry," Bayani said.

"Are you sure about that?" Lintang said through her teeth.

"She's not," Bayani said. "She's sad."

Lintang banged her empty pitcher on the ground. "I'm not sad!"

"Captain Shafira is her hero," Bayani continued, as if he had been ordered to ignore her too. "And she's always wanted to travel the world. Being chosen for the *Winda* meant everything to her."

"Now she's cabin girl, set to go home as soon as this is over," Avalon said.

Pelita bobbed over to Twip and pulled one of his long ears. He chittered at her.

Lintang glared at the ground. "I wouldn't be surprised if Captain Shafira dumped me in Zaiben with Bayani."

"She wouldn't do that," Bayani said.

"No." Lintang climbed to her feet, taking the empty pitcher and tray. "I suppose she needs her necklace back."

"Does Lintang think Captain Shafira doesn't care about her?" Avalon said to Bayani.

"I hope not," Bayani said. "Because Captain Shafira didn't want to punish Lintang."

Lintang spun to him. "What?"

Pelita darted past her, picked up some leftover mashed potatoes, and flicked them at Twip. Twip screeched. Most of the mess ended up on the floor, leaving spots of grayish-white that Lintang would have to scrub later.

"Of course she didn't want to punish Lintang," Avalon said over the noise. "She has to put on a show, though."

"So the rest of the crew will see that she doesn't tolerate disobedience," Bayani said. "Otherwise *they* might start disobeying her."

Avalon nodded, stroking Twip to calm him down. When Twip finally stopped shrieking and started grooming the flecks of potato from his fur instead, Avalon said, "Captain Shafira wants to let Lintang off the hook. She just needs a reason."

Lintang stared around at the various weapons on the walls. Three harpoons stood out. They weren't like the ones from Desa. These had curled tips, like claws, that gleamed in the lantern light. If she had to fight another mythie to impress the captain, those were the ones she'd use.

"I think," Avalon continued, still looking carefully at Bayani, "if Lintang works hard, if she follows all orders, she has a chance to win back the captain's favor."

Hope bubbled inside her. "Really?"

"I don't see why not."

Lintang's grip tightened on the tray and pitcher. "Why are you helping me?"

Avalon smiled at Bayani. "Not everyone accepts who I am. I thought our Islander visitor would be the same.

Instead, she found a loophole in the captain's rules, came barging down, and chattered away to me as if I were just like everyone else. She showed me kindness, Bayani, when the rest of the world is rarely so friendly." He shrugged and got to his feet. "I'm simply returning the favor."

Avalon walked up the steps, the sound of his boots disappearing to the upper deck, and Lintang whirled to Bayani. "Do you honestly think Captain Shafira will forgive me?"

"Of course. If anyone can impress her, it's you."

Lintang's heart was as warm as sunshine. There was still a chance for her after all.

But her smile died as she met Bayani's dark gaze. She looked away and cleared her throat.

"Bayani," she said, the words clogging her throat, even though they'd been in the back of her mind all these days. "Um . . . When you were in the cargo hold . . . I meant to visit you . . ."

"It's all right, Lintang."

"No. It's not." She stared at the floor, face burning. "I kept finding reasons not to go down. People were watching, or I had a lesson on the rigging, or Dee needed me in the kitchen."

"You were worried about being caught."

She hugged the tray to her chest. "I should have

checked on you. You could've died down there, and no one would've known."

"I wouldn't have died. I had food, fresh water, and extra blankets to keep me warm. Hey." He stepped up to the bars so she would look at him. "I promise I would've gone above deck if it had gotten too much. And Pelita would've fetched you if I'd hurt myself. You have no reason to feel guilty. I'm the one who decided to stow away."

She studied him between the metal bars of the cage. His dark hair was greasy, he looked sickly, and there were lines beneath his eyes from sleepless nights. He could be at home right now. He could be well fed and comfortable. *Why* had he stowed away?

"Why are you going to Zaiben?" she said.

His brow creased, but he didn't answer.

"Are you in trouble?"

He hesitated. Then at last, at long last, he said, "Yes."

She released a breath. It was the first proper answer he'd given her. "Is it bad?"

He lowered his gaze. "Yes."

She couldn't imagine how Bayani could've gotten into trouble so terrible that he had to go all the way to Zaiben. "What can I do to help?"

Bayani smiled a sad smile, and said—*of course*—"Nothing."

The Mythie Guidebook Entry #92:
Sea Serpent (common)

∽∽∽∽∽∽∽∽

The sea serpent is a sea mythie in the predator category. It is serpentine and has been found at lengths of over one hundred measures.

Diet: Meat, mostly humans.

Habitat: Deep seawaters.

Frequency: Moderately rare.

Behavior: Sea serpents bring down ships by wrapping their bodies either longways around the hull or over the deck and squeezing until the ship splinters. They then devour all crew aboard.

Eradication: The scales of these mythies are impenetrable, but with enough force and a powerful weapon, the serpents can be beheaded.

Did you know? Sea serpents have three rows of teeth.

Danger level: 4

Hero

T HE *WINDA* CONTINUED NORTHWEST, and the weather grew impossibly colder. Occasionally they passed land on either side, but no one showed any interest except Mei, who stood in the upper basket and stared south, singing in her own language.

Lintang worked hard through her shivers. In fact, she worked so hard, she was now doing twice as much as Yamini. She whistled the same tune Father did while he cleaned his fishing tools. When her lips were too cold to whistle, she hummed. She greeted every crew member, even if they weren't allowed to talk back. They found ways to show they appreciated her attitude, though. Dee slipped her extra rations. Xiang demonstrated how to load a crossbow to a dozing talross while Lintang was nearby. A fur blanket that used to be in Quahah's room mysteriously appeared in Lintang's cabin one evening.

Captain Shafira did not specifically acknowledge Lintang's change, but Lintang often caught the captain watching her with a careful expression on her face. That had to mean something. Lintang was making progress, slowly.

One clear day when the ocean sparkled as blue as the sky, Mei cried out and Keelee shrieked from above.

Captain Shafira stepped down from the bridge. The rest of the crew followed her to the bow. Lintang, who had been gutting freshly caught fish, set down her knife and washed her hands in a little bucket of water. The fish lay stinking on the deck as she climbed to her feet.

"Is it the sirens?" Xiang said. "Has anyone checked on Bayani or Avalon recently?"

"We're too far north of the reef," Quahah said, shielding her face from the sun.

Captain Shafira studied the horizon. Lintang peeked between people to see what they were looking at.

Water swirled and churned in the distance. It wasn't glowing green, so at least it wasn't Nyasamdra again.

"Xiang," Captain Shafira said.

"On it." Xiang almost barreled into Lintang as she sprinted to the hatch on the bridge. She was fetching weapons.

Yamini shoved past Lintang to get to the railing.

Lintang was too busy watching the turbulent water to care.

It was different telling stories at dinner of flesh-eating eels, or turtles as big as islands, or the ferocious Lanme Vanyan. Now that they were facing the cold, frothing truth, Lintang couldn't laugh.

"Mei!" Captain Shafira called to the upper basket. "Any chance of getting around it?"

"I don't think so, Captain," Mei said, peering through the collapsible brass telescope. "It's heading toward us."

She was right. The swirling water disappeared and reappeared closer. Every now and then Lintang thought she saw a lump of scales.

Only when the sun glistened on scales did Captain Shafira roar, "Sea serpent!"

The crew immediately scrambled across the deck. Lintang had to throw herself out of the way to avoid being knocked over.

At first, the crew's movements looked chaotic, but there seemed to be a method to their frenzy. Maybe they'd done this before. Or maybe they'd had drills, the way Desa practiced preparations for all the dragons that never came.

The sails went up and loose objects were thrown below. Captain Shafira ushered Lintang toward the main hatch. "Stay in your cabin until I come for you." She lifted her voice and added, "Yamini, you too."

Then she was off, helping Mei with the ropes. Lintang gathered her tools and tossed the fish guts overboard. Xiang burst from the hatch on the bridge with three harpoons that had tops curved like claws — the ones Lintang had seen earlier. A white ball of light zipped up after Xiang, but Lintang didn't stop to take a proper look. She was going to follow Captain Shafira's orders this time, just as Avalon said. No mistakes.

She carried her things below deck, leaping out of the way as Dee thundered up the stairs. Hewan the medic stumped to her room, her shawl wrapped tightly around her shoulders, muttering under her breath about how she'd just wanted to enjoy a nice cup of tea.

Lintang made it into the galley right as the ship lurched. She tumbled against the wall, barely missing the hot stove. The iron door had been fastened shut, which was lucky because the ship lurched again and she fell the other way. One of the doors to the storage shelves burst open. She covered her head as chopping boards and plates tumbled down. The knives and cleavers swung from their places on the ceiling, but nothing sharp landed on her.

It wouldn't be the same for Bayani.

She clambered to her feet. He was in the weapons room, surrounded by blades and carpentry tools. Had anyone thought about that?

And what if the ship sank? He'd be stuck in the cage, unable to swim for safety. He'd *drown*.

She was supposed to go to her cabin. The captain had ordered it. But how could she leave Bayani locked in that cage when they were under attack?

She staggered out of the galley. Something thunked against the outer walls. It was followed by a sickening crack.

How much damage could a sea serpent do?

Yamini snagged Lintang's dress before she could get to the stairs. "What do you think you're doing?" She yanked Lintang back. "No, I know what you're doing —you want to impress the captain."

Lintang wrenched at Yamini's fingers. "Let go!"

"The captain gave us orders to stay down here."

Lintang stomped on Yamini's foot. Yamini shrieked and released her, and Lintang raced to the top deck. She didn't get far. Everyone was leaning over the edge, staring and shouting and hitting downward, no matter what part of the ship they were on. Lintang hurried to peer over the side.

No wonder the timber was cracking and groaning:

the sea serpent had wrapped its body around the entire ship longways and was squeezing the way a python suffocates its prey. Its thick bulk was just above the waterline and its scales flashed silver in the sunlight. It stank of old fish.

The crew tried to hack at it with their weapons, but it was too low and no one could reach. Xiang's special harpoons lay at her boots as she hurled slim daggers at the serpent's body. The daggers simply bounced off the scales and spun into the water, lost forever. After the third throw, she pulled out the spindle holding her bun in place. Her glossy hair tumbled down her back. She put one end of the spindle in her mouth and blew. Something sped from the tip. It glanced uselessly off the scales like the daggers. She opened a pouch hanging from her waist and reloaded the stick with dart after dart, sending each of them at the serpent. These weren't like the darts she played with during rouls. They were tiny pins. Some pierced between the serpent's scales, but nothing else happened.

She shoved the spindle into her pouch. "Serpent's too big to react to the poison."

Lintang picked up one of the special harpoons and examined the curved tip. It was lighter than she'd expected. "Why don't you throw these?"

"They're dragon talon harpoons," Xiang replied. "Worth a fortune, and the only thing that will kill the sirens."

"Who cares about the sirens when we're going to die?"

Xiang pointed to Mei and Eire, who were tying ropes around their waists. "They'll lower themselves down and hack at the serpent from there. Hopefully that will do the job, or at least make it let go. If only we could find the head. Then we could—" She broke off and groaned.

Lintang turned to see what she was looking at and found Captain Shafira tying a rope around her waist with the other two.

"She's always got to be a hero," Xiang muttered, then stalked over to them.

Lintang tightened her grip on the harpoon. If only *she* could be the hero this time.

Yamini burst out of the hatch and ran across the deck. "Let me help, Captain."

The cheater! She'd probably tried to stop Lintang to get the glory for herself.

But Captain Shafira whirled to Yamini with a face like thunder. "What are you doing here? I told you to stay below deck!"

Before Yamini could respond, the ship rocked steeply,

throwing everyone off their feet. Lintang was still scrambling to stand when the serpent's head lifted behind Captain Shafira, snapping its jaws. It took a heartbeat for Lintang to realize there was a little ball of white light speeding around its face.

"The harpoons!" Captain Shafira said. Xiang turned to fetch them, but the serpent dived at Captain Shafira's voice, fangs bared.

Lintang acted without thinking. She raced forward and shoved a harpoon into the serpent's mouth to wedge it open. The serpent started to snap but stopped as the dragon's claw dug into the roof of its mouth and sprayed blood across the deck.

A thread of pain sliced down Lintang's arm. She staggered and fell back.

Pelita buzzed around the serpent, again making it lift its head. Keelee gave a piercing screech, and lightning split the blue sky. The serpent thrashed in pain as Lintang blinked away spots.

"Now, while it's blinded!" Captain Shafira said.

Eire jumped onto the rigging. Xiang hurled one of the remaining harpoons through the air. Eire swung out on a rope, caught the harpoon with one hand, and used the dragon talon to slash the serpent through the neck.

The serpent fell back, slopping into the ocean, its

body unfurling from the hull like a rope let loose. Lintang hadn't realized how its grip had affected the ship until they bobbed higher onto the waves. The crew leaned over all sides to watch the mythie's torso sink into the depths.

Eire landed back on the deck, the harpoon still in her hand. Some of the crew cheered, but the rest were already starting to assess the damage done to the ship.

Lintang didn't get up. She checked her stinging arm. Her shirtsleeve had torn, and there was a ribbon of blood from her shoulder to her elbow.

Captain Shafira jogged over. "Are you hurt?"

Lintang wanted to say no, it was only a scratch, but the stinging had grown worse.

Quahah leaned her hands on her knees to inspect it. "Fish on a stick, is that a wound from the serpent's fang?"

"You need to get that fixed up." Captain Shafira took Lintang's good arm and helped her to her feet. "Come on, we'll get you to Hewan."

"She was very brave," said Xiang as they passed her.

"Yes, I suppose she was," Captain Shafira said. Lintang's heart lifted in hope — *The captain thinks I was brave* — until Captain Shafira added, "Except that she disobeyed my orders. Again."

Banished

CAPTAIN SHAFIRA SAT LINTANG on one of the mess's tables and rolled up her skivvy sleeve.

"Oh, the poor thing," Farah the clamshell said.

"Maybe they'll have to cut her arm off," Dee said in a hushed tone.

Lintang sucked in a sharp breath.

Captain Shafira gave Dee a warning glare before yelling, "Hewan!"

The rest of the crew gathered around. Eire took one look at Lintang's arm and huffed. "She is fine. Why is there fuss?"

"Yamini, fetch me some salve." Captain Shafira took a bundle of clean cloth from Avalon and pressed it against Lintang's wound, which sent sparks of pain up and down her arm.

"I'm sorry I didn't stay below deck," Lintang said. "I

just wanted to make sure Bayani was safe. He's in a room filled with weapons, and—"

"Don't you think I know that?" Captain Shafira said. "Don't you think we're prepared? Avalon would be in dire trouble down there if we hit turbulent waters, otherwise. The weapons are always secured against the wall."

Lintang untangled her tongue. "But if the ship sank—"

"The ship will not sink." Captain Shafira couldn't know that for certain, but she sounded incredibly sure of herself.

Lintang hesitated. "Keelee . . . the lightning bird . . . it *does* have powers, doesn't it?"

"It protects me, and the ship," Captain Shafira said. "So there was no need for you to act. Your constant disobedience is giving others the idea that they too can ignore my orders." She shot an annoyed glance in the direction Yamini had gone. "Not to mention you lost me a valuable harpoon."

Lintang sagged, then winced as the action tugged at her wound.

"She was only trying to save you," Avalon said.

Captain Shafira didn't answer.

Avalon persisted. "She won't have to leave the *Winda*. Right?"

Lintang's breath caught.

"You made promise," Eire said. "If girl disobeyed, she would be off ship."

Captain Shafira looked at Lintang. There was regret in her eyes.

"No," Lintang said. Hurt crept into her voice.

"Vierzans will take you home," Eire said, maybe to appear reassuring, but she looked pleased, and Lintang knew she didn't really care what happened as long as Lintang was gone.

Xiang stepped forward. "What about your necklace, Captain?"

"We will go to Twin Islands later," Eire said.

"I didn't ask you," Xiang said, frowning.

"I'm here." Hewan stumped in with a wooden box. "Who's hurt?"

Captain Shafira withdrew the cloth, and Hewan peered at Lintang's arm. "Oh dear," she said. "Looks like it needs stitches."

Lintang barely heard her. "Captain, please—"

"Don't speak," Captain Shafira said.

"But—"

"For once in your life, Lintang, just do what I say!"

Lintang recoiled. Captain Shafira sounded angry. Truly angry.

Mother had yelled at her. Elder Wulan had yelled at her. That was nothing compared to this. The Goddess had had enough. Lintang had broken the rules one too many times, had opened her mouth when she shouldn't have, had been as disobedient and troublesome as Mother had warned.

Heat flooded Lintang's face as the rest of the crew shifted uncomfortably. Eire nodded to herself, satisfied the captain could finally see the truth. Lintang was not fit to be a crew member of the *Winda*.

Yamini returned with a cloth filled with the green goop from the slop bucket room. She was smirking—she must've heard Lintang being told off.

Hewan scooped up the goop. Lintang had learned that it killed germs and kept the body clean. She used it every night instead of having a bath. But when Hewan smeared it on the wound, it felt as hot as a hornet's sting. Lintang cried out, surprised.

"We haven't even started yet," Hewan said.

Captain Shafira held out a hand. "Here." Her voice was tight.

Lintang didn't move. She felt raw and exposed. Any movement, even to reach out to the captain, seemed like it would somehow make her humiliation worse.

But then Hewan pulled out a thread and a needle,

and they were very alarming, so Lintang clutched at Captain Shafira's fingers as though her grip alone would keep the pain away.

"Don't watch, starflower," Dee said gently, as Hewan threaded the needle.

Lintang shut her eyes. She wished everyone would leave.

When Hewan pinched the top of her cut together she let out a small gasp and squeezed Captain Shafira's hand tighter. Captain Shafira squeezed back.

The noise dimmed as the needle pierced Lintang's skin. She could *feel* the thread being pulled through. She whispered a string of swearwords in her own language.

"Avalon, get Bayani," Captain Shafira said. "He can keep Lintang company while Hewan works."

Eire snorted. "Why?" she asked as Avalon left the room. "They will be company in Zaiben, yes?"

"Yes," said Captain Shafira quietly. "I suppose they will."

The Defiant Boy

⌒⌒

BAYANI ENTERED THE MESS alone. Lintang didn't look up. The tears had come uninvited, and she hated when people saw her cry, even him.

Captain Shafira stood so he could take her spot. He sat down and squeezed Lintang's fingers.

"Avalon said you fought a sea serpent," he said. "Just like Pero the warrior."

She stifled a sob and didn't answer. She was overly aware of the rest of the crew standing around, murmuring to each other. Hewan continued her agonizing work.

Bayani added lightly, "You've had worse than this. Remember when you swam through the rapids and broke your arm?"

Lintang finally looked at him. "I have to leave the *Winda*."

His halfhearted smile faded. "I heard." He cupped

her hand in both of his. "We'll go home together. It'll be all right."

No. It would never be all right again.

She said nothing, and he said nothing, and the silence stretched on. Twip and Pelita passed by in the corridor outside the mess, Twip chasing Pelita with high-pitched screeches while Pelita dodged and zipped about in glee.

"I'm so sorry, Lintang," Bayani said at last. "I heard you broke the rules to try to save me. I've ruined everything, haven't I?" He loosened his grip on her hand. "I can go back to the cage if you want."

She clutched at his fingers, keeping him in his spot. Yes, she was embarrassed. No, she didn't want him to leave.

So even though neither of them spoke, he waited by her side while Hewan worked. Captain Shafira and Xiang spoke in the corner, their voices too low to hear. Everyone else had given up their conversations.

Pelita finally joined Bayani, settling on his shoulder.

"Are you done tormenting poor Twip now?" he said.

She buzzed her wings in satisfaction.

"Finished," Hewan said at last, and cut the leftover thread from the wound. "It will leave a scar, I'm afraid." She examined her work. "I suppose you haven't had the Curall."

Lintang released Bayani's hand and flexed her fingers. "No."

Hewan nodded, unsurprised.

"What's Curall?" Bayani said.

Hewan rummaged in her medical box. "A new medicine developed by Vierzans. It kills dangerous things in your body. Stops illnesses, diseases; you name it, the Curall fixes it."

"We could use that in Desa," Bayani said.

"I'm sure you could," Hewan said. "But only people who are part of the United Regions are entitled to it."

Lintang thought of her grandfather, his body shuddering with blood-filled coughs, the healer's broths doing nothing to save him. She thought of the plagues that swept through the village, taking so many lives on their way. She thought of how sick Bayani had been last season; how helpless she'd felt when he'd been rushed to Sundriya, so delirious with fever he spoke only nonsense, while his father quietly made preparations for his funeral. They'd desperately needed medicine then.

"That's not fair," she whispered.

"No," Captain Shafira said, looking up from her conversation with Xiang, "it isn't. It's just another reason Vierzans are able to talk countries into joining the UR. I can't believe—"

She broke off abruptly as Bayani straightened up, gasping.

"What?" Captain Shafira said at the same time Hewan said, "Here it is," and pulled out a small glass vial with a pump on the top. "I have one left. It's a spray. Just aim for the back of your throat."

She held the vial out for Lintang, but Bayani snatched it from her hand. "Let me see that."

Lintang pulled away in surprise. Since when did Bayani snatch?

He whirled to Pelita too fast for anyone to stop him and sprayed her directly in the face.

Hewan cried out, Captain Shafira stepped forward, and the crew tensed for a fight. Eire even drew her weapon.

"Have you lost your mind?" Lintang said.

"Bayani," said Captain Shafira slowly, "that was Lintang's best chance of avoiding infection."

Pelita hovered beside him, spluttering.

"I'm sorry," Bayani said. "But I have two days left. I had to try."

"Try what?" Lintang said, but Captain Shafira spoke over her.

"You think this is going to prove it?"

"I hope so."

"Prove what?" Lintang said. "What do you mean, you have two days left?"

Xiang looked from Captain Shafira to Bayani, puzzled. "What's going on?"

"The boy is defiant," Eire said, pointing the spear side of her weapon at him.

"He used up the last Curall!" Hewan cried.

"Everybody stop talking, and Eire, for the love of Mratzi, put your khwando away."

Eire scowled and reluctantly returned her weapon to her belt.

Captain Shafira peered at Pelita. "How long do you think it will take to work?"

"I have no idea." Bayani held his hand out for Pelita to sit on. She did so begrudgingly, giving him her worst glare. "Sorry," he said again. "But hopefully it will be worth it."

"What will be worth it?" Lintang said.

Captain Shafira and Bayani were working together. They had a secret, something neither of them had shared with Lintang. She frowned at them as they watched Pelita.

"Wait," Bayani said. "Just wait."

The Little Girl

～⚬～

PELITA BUZZED ABOUT FOR A BIT, then sat down on the table, yawned, and curled up to sleep. The crew grew bored and wandered away. Though no one said it, their looks toward Bayani were clear. They didn't know what he was up to, and they didn't like it. Lintang didn't like it either.

Captain Shafira placed a hand on his shoulder. "It was only a theory."

"Can you please tell me what's going on now?" Lintang said.

Before Bayani could answer, Pelita woke with a squeak and squirmed in her spot.

Bayani jerked forward. "Look."

Pelita's white glow was getting brighter.

"Yes." The word rushed out of Bayani as a breath.

"Mratzi's scythe," Captain Shafira said, stepping toward the table. She stared at Pelita, mouth open.

The glow grew so bright they couldn't look directly at it.

Lintang pushed her chair away and stood. "What's happening?"

"Dee!" Captain Shafira said.

Dee stuck her head into the room. "What's wrong, Captain?"

"Fetch Hewan. And get a fur cloak from the cargo, now."

Dee's eyes widened at Pelita's glow, but she nodded and hurried off.

Pelita's squeaks turned to tiny shrieks. She sounded like she was in pain.

From beside Lintang, Bayani was whispering, "Please work, please work, please be worth it, please work—"

And then, as swiftly as a sneeze, a human body burst out of the pixie. A girl lay in Pelita's place, an Islander barely ten years old. She opened her eyes and screamed.

Lintang staggered backwards.

Captain Shafira lunged to hold the girl still. "It's all right, little one, it's all right—" She glanced at Bayani over her shoulder and said breathlessly, "You were right. By the Gods, Bayani, you were right all along."

Lintang looked at him. He was staring at the girl as if he couldn't believe it either.

Dee returned with a fur coat, and Captain Shafira wrapped it around the girl's body, both to cover her and to pin her arms in place. "Get some food and fresh water prepared."

"Wh—what's happening?" Lintang said as Dee left again. "Who is that?"

Hewan returned with her medical box. "What —*Oh.*" She put the box down. Other crew members crowded in. The girl continued to scream.

"A little help, Bayani," Captain Shafira said.

Bayani hesitated, then leaned over the girl. "I'm here," he said softly. "You're safe now."

She cut off midscream and stared at him, mouth agape, chest heaving.

"Wa . . . ter . . ." She had to speak through wheezes, and she used Vierse.

"Dee, hurry with that water!" Captain Shafira said.

The girl continued to stare at Bayani. "You . . ."

"Bayani," he said. "My name's Bayani."

Her brow creased. *"Bayani, Bayani, Bayani."* She said

it like a chant, and something about it sparked in the back of Lintang's memory.

Bayani's face paled.

The little girl drew another shuddering breath. "Water."

"Dee!" Captain Shafira said.

"Water," the girl said again, still staring at Bayani. "The water will call for you."

"Shh." He stroked her hair. "It's all right."

She sobbed. "The water will call for you. The harvester will come."

"What's she talking about?" Lintang said.

"Nothing," Bayani said, avoiding her gaze.

Nothing, nothing, nothing.

The girl closed her eyes again.

Hewan picked up her medical box and joined them. "What do you need, Captain?"

"Make sure she's all right," Captain Shafira said. "I'll have her taken to your room."

Dee hurried in with a jar of pickled fish and a flagon of water. She pushed through the crowd, the gold hoops in her ears swinging frantically. "Where do you want this?"

"In Hewan's room."

"She's a little girl," Mei said, staring. "She's just a little girl."

Bayani touched the girl's shoulder. "Who are you?"

The girl didn't open her eyes. "P–Pelita."

"No, who were you before Pelita? Before you became a pixie?"

She frowned. "There was fire. In the sky."

"A dragon?"

"Dra . . . gon?"

"Was the fire from a dragon?"

"Stars. Stars falling."

Lintang had lost track of the conversation. So much was happening. Where was Pelita? Who was this girl? Why did she talk about the harvester, the Goddess of Death?

Bayani exchanged a glance with Captain Shafira. "Is there a mythie that makes stars fall?"

Pelita finally opened her eyes again. "What's a mythie?"

"You can ask her questions later," Hewan said. "I have to make sure she's not in need of urgent medical attention. Xiang, if you please."

"Bayani, Bayani, Bayani," Pelita said as Xiang scooped her up. A tear rolled down her cheek. "Bayani, Bayani, Bayani."

Bayani lifted the back of her hair, checking her neck, before Xiang took her away.

"Why is she saying your name like that?" Lintang said. Her mind was trying to bring the sparked memory to the surface, but the chaos had confused her. She was frightened—she just didn't know why.

Bayani said nothing.

"What's a mythie." Captain Shafira frowned at him. "That's what she said."

Bayani nodded slowly. "And she spoke about the shooting stars."

"The shooting stars? As in, the ones that were said to go overhead before the mythie infestation? Bayani, that was over a century ago. You're telling me that girl is a hundred and thirty years old?"

"How else do you explain that she doesn't know what mythies are? Besides, she's an Islander, but she doesn't have Nyasamdra's mark. She was born before the sea guardian."

Lintang was sick of this. They had secrets, the captain and Bayani, and neither of them had bothered to say a word to her. "Tell me what's going on!"

The rest of the crew waited, silent. Xiang returned and stood by Captain Shafira's side.

"The mythies are humans," Captain Shafira said.

"Just sick humans. It looks like Curall can turn them back."

"*What?*" Yamini said.

Lintang's breath whooshed past her lips. It couldn't be true. It was a mistake, an awful mistake.

Xiang looked at Bayani, puzzled. "How did you know?"

"Mratzi came to me when I was ill last season and explained everything."

There was a silence. The ship lurched as the swell grew heavier. Candles flickered in their frosted glass, and the lanterns swung above them.

"Mratzi," Quahah said. "The harvester of stars."

Bayani stared at the ground and nodded.

Quahah scrutinized him. "She just . . . dropped in for a chat? Do you often have the Goddess of Death over for a visit? Do I need to start brushing my teeth again?"

"I . . ." Bayani said, hesitating and glancing at Lintang. "I died in Sundriya."

Lintang sat down. It was a violent movement, accompanied by a painful thud when she hit the chair.

She'd feared for him while he was away, of course she had, but he'd come back fit and healthy, and she'd assumed her worry had been for nothing.

It hadn't been for nothing. He'd *died*.

"So Mratzi came to you to harvest your star," Xiang said, understanding. "But instead of taking you to Ytzuam, she told you that mythies are humans and let you live so you could . . . what? Spread the word?"

Bayani hung his head. "No one believed me. The medic blamed the fever. Mother was going to leave me behind for more tests, but I didn't want to stay in Sundriya. I just wanted to go home. I told them I'd dreamed the whole thing. I didn't know what to do. My last hope was stowing away and seeing Leika of Zaiben—"

"Who?"

"The author of *The Mythie Guidebook*. I thought she could help, considering she wrote a whole book on mythies, except . . ."

"Except I told him she wasn't real," Captain Shafira said. "Leika is just a code name for a group of Vierzans who traveled the world collecting stories to compile into a single volume."

Xiang frowned at her. "You knew about all this?"

"Bayani told me after we faced the sea guardian. I thought he'd probably imagined it because of the fever, but . . ." She looked at him. "I was wrong. I'm so sorry I doubted you."

He gave a wan smile. "At least you let me explain. I can't say the same for anyone else."

"You didn't even try to explain to me." The words were poison in Lintang's mouth. She felt sick. All this time . . . He had kept these secrets from her *all this time*.

He'd died, and met the harvester, and discovered the world's biggest lie, and he hadn't told her any of it.

"I thought you'd laugh," he said weakly. "Imagine if I'd walked up to you out of nowhere and said I'd met Mratzi. You'd think I was mad."

"It sounds crazy without proof, believe me," Captain Shafira said.

Bayani stared at the ground. "You're the storyteller, Lintang. How could you possibly have believed me?"

"You didn't give me a chance! I offered to help you. I *wanted* to help you. I . . ." She trailed off, the words lodged in her throat.

"What was Mratzi like?" Mei said.

Bayani looked at Lintang. Their argument wasn't over, they both knew that, but they couldn't continue with everyone else listening.

"I couldn't see her," he said, turning away from Lintang. "I could only sense her presence."

Mei nodded thoughtfully. "Did she speak Vierse or your native language?"

"She didn't speak at all. She kind of . . . pushed her thoughts into my head. It wasn't words. It was ideas. She showed me images of humans and mythies being the same."

"What were the shooting stars, if they weren't the Gods sending mythies to our world?" Xiang said.

"How did sickness begin?" Eire said.

"Is it contagious?" Yamini said.

Bayani dropped his head into his hands. "I don't know. I don't know anything else. I'm sorry."

"There are stories," Quahah said slowly, "of people becoming hosts to mythie eggs after slaying a mythie."

"But not everyone," Xiang said. "We haven't."

"We've had the Curall," Captain Shafira said.

Bayani glanced at Lintang. "How close were you to the malam rasha when it died? Or the sea serpent?"

"Or the Caletromian mermaids?" Quahah said.

They all turned to Lintang.

"I don't know," she said. Who cared? What mattered was why Bayani hadn't told her the truth in the first place.

She turned away. It hurt to look at him. "I need some air."

"Lintang—" Bayani said, but she ignored him, pushing through the crew to get to the door.

"Lintang, wait."

Lintang stopped, but only because it was Captain

Shafira who spoke this time. Lintang half turned to face her.

"You need to know—" Captain Shafira started, but Bayani spoke over her.

"Don't. Please."

Captain Shafira frowned. "Bayani, you have to tell her."

Lintang brushed at angry tears. "Tell me what? No, let me guess," she said as Bayani opened his mouth. "*Nothing.* Nothing, nothing, nothing!"

"I'm just trying to make it easier." Pleading crept into Bayani's voice. "There are some things you don't want to know."

"If you don't want to tell me, fine. You don't have to. Who needs a best friend, anyway?" And before Captain Shafira could order her to stay and listen, she walked out.

The Mythie Guidebook Entry #70:
Lidao [Vierz]

∽∽∽∽∽∽∽∽

The lidao is a river mythie with an insatiable appetite for shiny rocks. It's amphibian and is commonly mistaken for a toad. The only difference is its long tongue, which is blue instead of pink. In sunny weather, the sound of a bell will drive it away. In rainy weather, the sound of a bell will lure it closer.

Diet: Gems, crystals, and precious stones.

Habitat: Riverbanks in Vierz, mostly near populated areas where gems are abundant.

Frequency: Common.

Behavior: While they are usually slow, stupid creatures, these mythies can hop with erratic speed if chased. They live in burrows and spend every waking moment searching for food.

Eradication: Lidao can be captured by placing a strip of wood on their back, which causes them to become immobile. Once caught they can be squashed or pierced.

Did you know? One recorded instance in the thirty-fifth year of the Bauei period claimed that a single lidao ate an entire warehouse of carnelian gemstones overnight.

Danger level: 1

Gems and Bridges

LINTANG SAT ON HER LITTLE HAMMOCK with her sack from home in her lap. She breathed in the euco oil, trying to commit to memory the soothing way it swirled in her nose and lungs. Even after everything, she was still being banished from the ship. As if Bayani's betrayal hadn't been enough.

His extraordinary secret hadn't made a difference. The captain's word remained law. He and Lintang would be dropped in Zaiben, where they would have to find their own way home. Lintang hadn't imagined it was possible to feel so miserable.

She'd decided to wear her usual outfit to cover her scar, which was still searing with pain. Someone had sewn up her skivvy and washed her dress and tights while she slept. It wasn't ideal, washing with seawater

—everything was stiff and crusted with salt—but it was better than being dirty.

There was a knock at her door. She tensed.

"Lintang?"

Lintang opened it up to find Avalon. He ducked his head so his dark hair fell over his eyes. "I'm supposed to take you to the captain."

Twip *twip*ped from the crook of his neck.

Lintang wanted to speak, wanted to tell him that she would miss him terribly, but her throat was dry and the words wouldn't come.

He gazed past her. "Don't forget your sword."

She glanced carelessly at the corner of her room. "Don't need it."

"Oh."

After an awkward silence, he held out the fur coat that was bundled in his arms. "From Xiang. Just in case."

Lintang moved to take it, but he held it at a funny angle and said, "Careful." There was a small bundle beneath the fur. A pouch. And from what she could feel, it had Xiang's darts inside.

Avalon turned and headed down the passage without a word. Lintang withdrew the pouch as she followed. It had a rope for slipping around her neck so she could hide it neatly beneath her dress. She wanted to hug both Avalon and Xiang, but they probably wouldn't be allowed to hug her back. She tucked the pouch out of sight and slipped on the coat, instantly engulfed in warmth.

They reached the mess to find Captain Shafira wearing a hooded cloak of deep sea-green. She stood with her back to the door while Xiang pinned colorful jewels in her braids.

"Why couldn't I keep my big mouth shut?" Captain Shafira was saying quietly.

"It'll be fine," Xiang said. "Once we get back to—"

Avalon cleared his throat. Xiang and Captain Shafira turned. Captain Shafira's gaze fell on Lintang, who found herself unable to speak. Very soon, she would leave, never to see the Goddess again.

Xiang finished pinning the last of the jewels in Captain Shafira's braids. "Done."

"Thank you, Xiang. Remember our arrangement."

"Of course." For a heartbeat it looked as though Xiang might smile, but when she turned to Lintang there was only sadness in her eyes. "Safe traveling."

"Are you hungry?" asked Captain Shafira.

As if Lintang could eat. She shook her head. There was a lump in her throat that was threatening to turn into tears.

"What's going to happen?" she said.

Captain Shafira tied her red kerchief around her neck. "I'll take you as far as the bridge into Zaiben. Once you're in the city you can ask a vigil—that's anyone in a gray uniform—for directions to Parliament House. Bayani and I discussed it, and we think he should try to convince the governors that mythies are human. Leika of Zaiben might not be real, but the governors certainly are, and they have the power to help. And whether they believe him or not, they'll still arrange to have a merchant ship take you back to Desa."

Lintang swallowed hard, her mind stuck on the first thing Captain Shafira had said. "You're not coming into Zaiben with us?"

Captain Shafira smiled grimly. "Considering I have a bounty on my head worth the cost of a small island, no, I think it's better I keep away. Now come on. The others are waiting." She swept out of the mess. Avalon gave Lintang's hand one last squeeze before they followed the captain up the stairs to the sunny deck. It was a fine morning, with no fog, though still cool.

They headed for the rowboats, where the rest of the crew was waiting for them. Everyone looked solemn.

Lintang felt like Cass, the legendary village girl from one of her grandfather's stories, who had to be sacrificed to a river monster. Every step seemed to be taking her toward her doom.

Zazi waited to lower one of the rowboats. Her large body cast a shadow on Bayani, who was already inside, holding a helping of fishcakes that steamed in the cold air. He smiled weakly at Lintang. She didn't smile back.

She put her sack of belongings in the rowboat. "Where's Pelita?"

"Sleeping," Captain Shafira said. "Hewan's watching her. I'm sorry, but she can't go with you. We have to work out what's happened to her and what needs to be done now. Obviously we can't hunt the sirens anymore —maybe we can cure them instead."

"Here," Dee said, passing Lintang more fishcakes. "For the trip." Her voice cracked on the last word. She sniffled and wiped her eyes.

"Be safe," said Farah the clamshell from Dee's belt.

Lintang climbed in next to Bayani.

Quahah took off her woolly octopus hat and held it to her chest. "Take care, kippers."

Yamini stood by Zazi, hugging herself against the chill. She didn't look sad that Lintang was going, but she didn't gloat, either. Lintang had never thought she would be envious of a cabin girl. It didn't matter how horrible the chores were—at least Yamini got to stay.

Captain Shafira hopped into the rowboat, and Eire handed her an empty sack. "I am not to come, Captain?"

"No," Captain Shafira said. "I'll be back soon."

Lintang took one last look at the crew. It really was like being sent to a river monster.

Zazi winched them down, and before Lintang could properly grasp that she'd never see her or Dee or Quahah or Mei or Avalon again, they hit the sea with a jarring thud. Then they were off, heading toward the shore, Captain Shafira rowing backwards with swift, powerful strokes.

Lintang bit into one of the fishcakes. It was probably delicious, but she was so upset that it crumbled tasteless in her mouth. She stared dully at the misty coastline. The land rose and fell in folds like a blanket strewn over a bed, covered with clumpy grass of various greens. To the northeast were steep cliffs with a collection of gray clouds at the top, despite the blue sky all around.

Zaiben.

Bayani twisted to see behind them. "Where are they going?"

Lintang turned too and found the other three rowboats heading south.

"To get timber for repairs and stock up on food," Captain Shafira said.

They'd have a feast tonight. They'd play rouls and sing songs and tell stories, and Lintang wouldn't be there.

Captain Shafira looked over Lintang as she heaved at the oars, her attention fixed on her ship.

Everything was different from their first journey together. Lintang stared at the captain's boots, remembering the smell of leather and the feeling of utter awe at being chosen by the pirate queen. She'd been so desperate to make a good impression.

And Captain Shafira had *wanted* her to do well. Hadn't she said to Xiang that she wished she'd kept her mouth shut? Hadn't she looked at Lintang with regret when she realized she was going to have to banish her from the ship?

"I'm sorry." Lintang's voice almost disappeared in the breeze. "I'm sorry I disobeyed you. I'm sorry I let you down. I'm so sorry, Captain."

Captain Shafira paused for barely a heartbeat as her gaze slid to Lintang. There was emotion in her eyes — dismay? Hope? Then she continued rowing as if Lintang hadn't spoken.

They drew closer to the rocks. Talrosses much bigger

and darker than the ones in Desa plunged into the green water and surfaced with plump fish.

The waves grew choppier. Droplets splashed onto Lintang's bare hands, so cold they were like teeth against her skin. She was even too cold to pull Xiang's coat tighter around her body. She clung to the edge of the rowboat as they rose and fell violently. Each dip had her losing her stomach, and her spine kept getting jarred as they hit the bottom. The wound on her arm stung with each jolt.

Captain Shafira swung the boat around so they narrowly missed a jagged outcrop that had been hidden by a swell moments before.

Lintang wanted to ask the captain if she was sure this was the best way into Zaiben, but the heaving sea took her breath and fear took her voice, so she placed her trust in the pirate queen and prayed to Niti she wasn't wrong.

They were so close to the rocks now that she could see tiny perforations in them, like the pores in a sea sponge. Crabs watched them from small outcrops.

Captain Shafira navigated around a curve of rocks, headed toward a sheltered beach. She jumped out to push the rowboat ashore. Lintang and Bayani helped her drag it up, away from the later tides. Lintang's legs were so wobbly she felt like a jellyfish trying to walk on its tentacles. The ground seemed to be rocking. She'd been on the *Winda* too long—she'd forgotten what steady land felt like.

Captain Shafira grabbed the empty sack and headed up the beach.

Lintang took her own sack and followed. What she'd first thought was clumpy grass was actually squat, sturdy trees with hard leaves.

"Hey," Bayani whispered. Lintang glanced at him. He gave her a small smile. "We're in Vierz."

She stared at the earth beneath her feet. She was standing in another country. The dirt was beige rather than brown, and soft like flour. The faint sour smell of foreign plants mingled with the briny air. Her breath would have to cross an ocean before it touched her island home.

If only all these wondrous things didn't mean she was banished from the *Winda*.

"I wish we didn't have to leave Pelita behind," Bayani said, checking over his shoulder.

Lintang continued in Captain Shafira's wake. "She'll be all right. She's in the safest place in the world."

"What makes you say that?"

"Keelee—the lightning bird—protects the ship. Pelita will be fine."

Bayani flashed another smile, but this time it was a sly, knowing one.

"What?" Lintang said.

"You named the lightning bird?"

She pursed her lips. "Its yellow crest reminded me of the warrior—"

"Who wore a strip of yellow cloth around his head. Yes, I remember the legend of Keelee."

And despite how upset she was with her friend, Lintang was suddenly grateful that she would not be alone in this far-off country.

Captain Shafira slowed at a narrow river that rushed down the slope toward the ocean. She untied a clinking pouch from her waist and withdrew a clear gem that gleamed in the sun.

"What's that?" Lintang said.

"Just a quartz." Captain Shafira threw it toward the bushes growing near the river, picked up a flat piece of bark, and sat on a rock with the empty sack on her lap. "Now we wait."

Lintang sat beside her. "What for?"

"Shhh."

Bayani settled down on Captain Shafira's other side, and the three of them lazed in the sun, listening to the burble of the river and the unfamiliar calls of the birds around them.

Lintang didn't know what they were doing, but if they stayed here all day, it was fine by her. Anything to postpone Captain Shafira's departure. Besides, it was warm in the sun when the breeze wasn't blowing.

They waited.

And waited.

She wriggled, the rock hard and jagged beneath her. Captain Shafira placed a hand on her knee and mouthed to her to keep still. They waited some more.

She was almost happy, despite everything. She was with her two favorite people in the world. She thought about that as she sat there. Then she thought about how she had let Captain Shafira down. And how Bayani had let *her* down. There were so many secrets between them all. Stowaways and death and mythies and Zaiben. Why couldn't they just be honest with one another? For Bayani to have kept that important, world-changing secret . . .

The image of Pelita bursting apart replayed in her mind. There were so many questions left unanswered. What had happened to the pixie body? Where had the pixie come from in the first place? Would the girl survive?

Lintang would never find out. She would go home and never see the girl or any of the *Winda*'s crew again. Everyone in Desa would know that she'd failed. She hadn't managed to complete even a single journey without being kicked off. Worse, none of them would be surprised. They'd shrug and say, *That's Lintang for you. Troublemaker. Storyteller. What did she expect?*

And she wouldn't be able to answer them.

She pulled Xiang's coat tighter around her, any trace of happiness gone. The sun rose higher. The waves at the shoreline crept inland with the tide. A large bird circled overhead, as if it were waiting for them to die.

They might as well have been dying. Who sat still for this long anyway? What was the point of—

Captain Shafira stiffened. Lintang glanced at the quartz by the bushes and smothered a gasp.

A fat, ugly toad hopped toward the gem.

Captain Shafira moved soundlessly to her feet. Lintang and Bayani watched as she slunk forward with the prowess of a predator.

The creature's blue tongue darted out and gulped down the gem, and at the same time Captain Shafira tossed her flat piece of bark onto its back.

The creature became still as stone. Captain Shafira crunched over and slipped it into the sack.

"What is that?" Lintang said.

"A lidao," Bayani said. "It's in *The Mythie Guidebook*."

"What does it do?"

"Eats gems."

"And . . . ?"

Bayani shrugged. "That's it."

"But that's a person," Lintang said as it finally sank in. "That's . . . that's a real person."

"Scary, isn't it?" Bayani said.

She'd been overwhelmed by everything that had happened yesterday—the lies, the betrayal, Pelita's violent transformation. She hadn't really thought about what it meant until now.

Nyasamdra. The malam rasha. The sea serpent. The Caletromian mermaids.

They had been *people*.

"By the Gods," she whispered. "How could you have known all this time and not said anything?"

"I should have," Bayani muttered. "I should've told everyone in the village. I should've screamed it from the temple rooftop. I should've been brave, and I definitely should've told you."

"Yes, you should've."

"Will you forgive me?"

"That depends. Are you going to tell me what your other secret is?"

He didn't answer.

She pursed her lips. When was he going to trust her to share his burdens? Even if she couldn't help, she could at least listen.

"Come on, you two." Captain Shafira slung the sack over her shoulder and started for the slope. "We have a hard climb ahead of us."

Lintang followed her through the shrubs. "Why do we need a lidao?"

"So you can repeat what happened on the ship. Show the governors your wound and explain that you're an Islander. They should supply you with Curall. When they hand you a vial, Bayani can spray the lidao and wait to prove his story."

"Oh," said Lintang, but she couldn't say anything else because the hill was steep and she was already feeling out of breath. The whoosh of the waves became a distant sound.

Her feet slid in her too-big boots. Unseen animals rustled in the bushes.

Briefly, she wondered what mythie she would become if she really were infected. A mermaid, maybe?

Not a Caletromian one; one from Desa, playful and carefree. Could people choose the mythie they became? How did the illness decide who turned into what?

After several turns of the timepiece, they came across a well-worn path that led up the cliffs. The huge stone walls of Zaiben loomed before them, their tops hidden by cloud. The shrubs disappeared, and the three climbers scrambled over small stones instead.

"Is this the only way to Zaiben?" Bayani said, puffing.

"No, but it's the worst way." Captain Shafira pulled a flask from her belt and offered them each a drink of water. "Which is good for us. The other entrances are usually bustling. The fewer people we see on this trip, the better."

When they reached the top of the windy cliff, Captain Shafira pulled her hood up to hide her face and jeweled braids. The path dropped away to crashing waves on one side and a ravine on the other. The entire strip of ground they walked along was only as wide as ten adults lying side by side.

A scattering of people sat on the rocky ground, catching their breath from the climb. All of them were Vierzan. Lintang wanted to flop down and join them, but Captain Shafira kept walking.

There was a tunnel attaching their side to Zaiben.

People gathered around the entrance in a line. A man and a woman in aqua coats checked each person before they were allowed to go through. They must've been the Gate Guardians Elder Wulan had spoken about.

The woman had a stack of metal sheets taller than her waist and was using a crystal stick to carve into one as if it were as soft as warm tree gum. Five armed guards in gray uniforms blocked the entrance, stepping aside only when the aqua-coated people approved each visitor.

When Lintang got a proper look at the entrance, she pulled up short. It wasn't just made of stone.

It was the gaping, skeletal jaw of a dragon.

Into Zaiben

"**T**HAT'S HORRIBLE!"

"Shh," Captain Shafira said.

"But—"

"I know. The interior of the tunnel is an entire dragon skeleton. All three bridges to Zaiben look like this."

That was right—Elder Wulan had told them about the bridges being made out of dragon skeletons. At the time Lintang had loved the idea. Now, just like everything else, it made her ill.

They drew level with the crowd, and for the first time she noticed people passing flat crystals to the Gate Guardians.

"What are those?"

"Identity tags. Every citizen of the United Regions has a special crystal with their name and birthplace engraved on it. You can't get into Zaiben without one."

Lintang stared at her pointedly.

Captain Shafira's lips twitched. "You think I'm not prepared?" She pulled out her clinking pouch and held it open for Lintang and Bayani to see. Between a handful of gemstones were dozens of identity tags of all different colors—green and purple and brown and black and everything in between.

Lintang reached for a brilliant pink one, but Captain Shafira stopped her. "Not all of these are safe to use—some might give me away. Here, take this one. Bayani, you can have this one, and these gems. They'll be enough to buy you passage into the city, and food if you need it."

Lintang thumbed the swirling shades of purple of her fake identity tag. A name was etched onto the flat surface.

GINGER
OF
WATNEY

Who was Ginger, and what was she doing now? Was it easy to replace stolen identity tags? Would Ginger get in trouble for having lost hers?

Lintang wanted to ask all these questions, but Captain

Shafira was already putting away her pouch and handing Bayani the sack with the lidao.

She was leaving them.

A small cry escaped Lintang's lips. She wasn't ready to say goodbye, to watch Captain Shafira walk away forever. Being in the captain's presence was safe and wonderful, and Lintang would give anything to keep her here.

"Oi!" One of the armed guards in a gray uniform marched up to them. He eyed Captain Shafira's hooded face. "You're not leaving, are you?"

Captain Shafira remained silent.

"Children aren't allowed to enter Zaiben by themselves. New rules."

"I wasn't aware," Captain Shafira said carefully.

The guard bristled. "People keep sneaking their kids in to stay with relatives, and we're overpopulated as it is."

"How dreadful," Captain Shafira said.

"I know. Just because we're the greatest city in the world doesn't mean people can saunter in and make themselves at home." He sounded as if he'd made this rant a few times.

"Absolutely," Captain Shafira said, keeping her head low so her face remained hidden. "And of course I was going in with the children. In fact"—she handed him a blood-red gemstone from her pouch — "we're in a bit of a hurry. If you wouldn't mind helping us along . . ."

"Right you are," the guard said, pocketing the stone. "This way."

Captain Shafira sighed quietly as they followed him, and said under her breath, "Plan B, then."

They reached the aqua-coated Gate Guardians. The guard announced loudly to those waiting in line that there was important business, delays weren't accept-able, these good people needed access to the bridge immediately . . .

Then, in an effort to be helpful, he grabbed Captain Shafira's pouch and pulled out a black tag. Lintang and Bayani gasped. It was lucky he hadn't looked too closely inside the pouch — he would've known immediately something was amiss with all those identity tags — but if he'd plucked out an incriminating one they'd be in trouble anyway.

Lintang held her breath as the male Gate Guard-ian examined it, and the female wrote the name on her metal sheet. Captain Shafira remained still. The Gate Guardians exchanged glances, and the male tried to peer under Captain Shafira's hood without being too obvious.

If they were caught, would Captain Shafira fight or run? And what should Lintang and Bayani do?

But after another heartbeat the Gate Guardian passed the tag back. "Purpose of visit?" he said, sounding as though he'd asked the question of at least a hundred other people today.

Lintang released her breath in a whoosh. The man in the gray uniform winked at them and strode back to his spot before the gate.

"Leisure," Captain Shafira said.

The female Gate Guardian carved the captain's answer into the metal sheet before taking note of Lintang and Bayani's tags too.

"How long are you staying?" the man said.

"Just for today."

"We are not accepting new citizens into Zaiben," the man droned. "You may not stay longer than your expected time, and you may not leave your children here. Do you understand?"

"Yes."

The man held out his hand. "Entry into Zaiben for one adult and two children is one apatite or the equal thereof."

Captain Shafira dug into her pouch and handed over a pale blue gem. The man dropped it into a crate behind him, which was already filled with sparkling crystals, then waved impatiently for the next person in line.

Lintang sagged, but she didn't have time to be relieved. Captain Shafira bumped her through the dragon's jaw to get her moving and thanked the gray-uniformed man on their way.

"Don't speak yet," Captain Shafira said in a low voice. "Sound travels through here."

It was true—their footsteps bounced off the walls, joining the beat of others farther down the tunnel. The long skeleton of the dragon was embedded in the stone, illuminated by strange crystals that were blazing white, each with a single crack through the middle.

"What are those?" Lintang said, pointing at them.

"Didn't I just tell you not to speak?"

"Yes, but—"

"They're merry lights," Captain Shafira said with a defeated sigh. "Made from merrimite crystal. When you crack one, it stays lit for twelve years. *Now* can you stay quiet?"

Lintang nodded.

The tunnel went on for much longer than it had appeared to on the outside, but maybe that was because she didn't feel comfortable walking beneath the spine of a dragon. Even when the body tapered into a tail, it went on and on.

One of the gray-uniformed guards from the front

entrance—not their friendly helper—hurried past them at a half jog. He almost knocked Lintang over in his haste to get through the tunnel.

"Ow!" she cried, rubbing her injured arm, but he didn't turn to say sorry. She glared after him. "That was rude."

"That's vigils for you," Captain Shafira said. "They uphold the law, so they think they can do whatever they want. And if you didn't notice, they'll do anything for gems."

Lintang's arm finally stopped throbbing as natural light appeared in the distance. She quickened her pace to get there faster. Cool air brushed her face.

She stepped out of the tunnel and stared.

Nothing from her life in Desa could have prepared her for this. The world had become lined with stone gray and was bustling with colorfully-clothed people. Noise and smoky air and a combination of sounds hit her all at once. It looked as though it had just rained. Drizzle still misted around them.

There was an open space right at the mouth of the tunnel, similar to the market square back at home, but at the same time nothing like it. People, so many people, hurried across the space. Some looked as if they might've come from places where the *Winda*'s crew had been born; others were Vierzan. Those with skin as pale as Avalon's had hair that was flame-red or straw-yellow or anything in between.

Everyone's clothes were wonderful. Dresses, cloaks, pants, and robes, with frills and bows, all made of material Lintang had never seen before. The air stank of smoke, but the people around them were perfumed like flowers, so floral bursts interrupted the stench.

Instead of trees, great metal poles with twisted branches dotted the roads. Their "fruit" were actually merry lights illuminating the gloom. High above them, lines crisscrossed like webs between buildings, where hanging lanterns glowed red, blue, and green.

"Oh," Lintang said, breathless.

"Parliament House isn't far," Captain Shafira said. She didn't look out of place with her cloak. Many people wore cloaks and coats with hoods and carried umbrellas made of peculiar stretchy fabric.

"Are you coming with us?" Bayani said.

Captain Shafira started forward. "I might as well take you to the building, now that I'm here."

Lintang sent a silent prayer of thanks to the Gods. Just a little longer with her captain, that was all she wanted.

The three of them walked through the puddly square and down the street. Beyond, buildings made of brick and stone rose into the clouds, some wider than the entire center of Desa. Smoke belched out of fat pipes in the roofs. Steel doors sat in grand archways, and large hourglasses hung from the walls.

The paths were cobbled with small stones, and on them rolled steel landcrafts, like the wooden toys in the schoolroom at home, with smoke streaming behind. A nearby man wound a crank at the front of one to start the engine.

The drizzle got heavier, and colorful umbrellas erupted around them. There was so much to see, yet as they walked all Lintang wanted to do was look at Captain Shafira. The captain moved through the crowd with her hood up, like a shadow of sea-green in the rainbows.

Lintang pulled the hood of her own coat up as they walked across roads and down alleyways and past buildings with heavy iron spikes for fences. When they reached another market square, Parliament House was easy to spot. It stood slick white against the gray, with pillars and merry lights and rows of windows and a beautiful arched entrance. Three sculptures stood at the front —Mratzi with her ribbons, Patiki with her basket, Niti with his hands cupped.

All of them were headless.

Lintang stopped.

"What is it?" Captain Shafira said.

"What's wrong with the sculptures?"

"Vierzans hate the Gods, didn't you know?"

"What?" Bayani said. "Why?"

"They think the Gods sent mythies to wipe humans out," Captain Shafira said. "Now they refuse to pray or build temples or leave offerings. The governors even hired hunters specifically to kill mythies." She placed a hand on Lintang's good shoulder. "If this bothers you, you're not going to like what's inside."

"Why not?"

"You'll see soon enough." She turned to Bayani. "Are you ready to go in? Do you know what you need to say?"

Bayani drew a deep breath and nodded.

Lintang stiffened. She'd thought all she wanted was a little more time, but no, it wasn't enough. She didn't want to say goodbye to Captain Shafira, not ever.

"Safe travels, Lintang," Captain Shafira said.

Lintang wanted to throw herself at the captain's feet and beg her not to leave.

"I—" she said, desperately trying to think of something, anything, to make Captain Shafira stay longer.

Before she could finish, two gray-uniformed vigils approached. "Identification, please."

Captain Shafira dug into her pouch to retrieve an

identity tag. One of the vigils snatched the pouch and tipped its contents into his palm. "Well, well," he said, sifting through the numerous tags.

"This is it," said the other vigil, pointing at one of the black tags.

Lintang tightened her grip on her sack. With only clothes in it, it wouldn't do much if she clobbered a vigil in the face with it, but maybe she would surprise them enough to let Captain Shafira escape.

She didn't get a chance to attack, though. A man stalked over, his sky-blue coat whipping around his boots. With his dark, feathery curls and hooked nose, he looked like a hawk. He wasn't Vierzan. In fact, he almost looked like he was from—

"Good hour," he said. "I'm Governor Karnezis." He eyed the numerous identity tags. "We have a problem."

"So it seems," said Captain Shafira. She didn't sound worried.

The vigil passed him the black tag. He examined it with a frown.

"Did you know," he said, "that this is the long-lost tag of Ambassador Farah of Jalakta? The *murdered* Ambassador Farah of Jalakta?"

Six more vigils came out of Parliament House. Lintang edged closer to Captain Shafira and Bayani, still clutching her sack.

Governor Karnezis turned the tag in his long fingers. "It was stolen by none other than the pirate queen."

"Goodness." There was amusement in Captain Shafira's voice. "Lucky I found it."

The vigil drew their swords. One pointed his blade at Captain Shafira's neck. "Lower your hood."

"Plan C it is," Captain Shafira said, so quietly Lintang barely heard.

She moved slowly, slipping her hood down and revealing her braids. The jewels in her hair shone in the merry lights.

Governor Karnezis smiled in satisfaction as one of the vigils snatched Captain Shafira's sword from its sheath. "Shafira of Allay, you're under arrest."

"Again," Captain Shafira added helpfully.

Lintang jerked forward. "No!"

Governor Karnezis glanced at her. His smugness became curiosity. "Why exactly, pirate queen, are you traveling with children?"

"I needed to get past the sea guardian's territory, so I took them."

"They're Islanders?" Governor Karnezis spun Lintang

to check the back of her neck. "Interesting." He turned Lintang around again but didn't let go of her arm. At least it wasn't the one with the injury. "What's your name?"

"Lintang from—" Lintang said, then stopped short, remembering what Dee and Farah the clamshell had said about not giving people too much information. "Er . . . the Twin Islands."

"The kids could be working for her," a vigil said.

Captain Shafira eyed the sparkling orange jewels on Governor Karnezis's rings and pin and on the chain around his neck. "You have a lot more sunstones than the last time we met, Karnezis." She raised an eyebrow. "Been to Allay recently?"

Governor Karnezis's grip tightened around Lintang's arm. "Wouldn't you like to know?" To the vigil, he said, "Take them away."

"Wait!" Lintang said, tugging against him. "We have to tell you something. The mythies are human—look in that sack!"

A muscle in Captain Shafira's jaw twitched. Uh-oh. Had she said the wrong thing again?

A vigil snatched the sack from Bayani.

"What's inside?" Governor Karnezis said.

"I think it's a toad, Governor." The vigil reached in. "And a piece of bark—oh!" He ripped his hand out as if he'd been bitten. The lidao launched at his face. "A mythie! Kill it!"

"No!" Lintang said, but the vigil swung their swords as the lidao bounded from step to step. "Stop! Wait! It's a person—just give it some Curall!"

No one listened to her. Captain Shafira sighed as the vigil around her stabbed and scrambled in a chaotic mess. It was almost as if they were frightened of the thing. But that was ridiculous—the lidao was harmless. The villagers of Desa dealt with mythies like it every day.

One of the vigils squealed as the lidao hopped onto his shoe. "It touched me, it touched me! What powers does it have? Am I cursed?"

Captain Shafira massaged the bridge of her nose. Bayani stood beside her, watching the entire thing as if he couldn't believe what he was seeing.

"Don't be a child," Governor Karnezis said, pulling the tail of his coat out of the way as the lidao leaped toward him. "Just kill the thing!"

The lidao hopped through a gap between legs and started into the market square. It took a heartbeat or two for the crowd to see the mythie, but one person let out a scream and others quickly followed. People fled as if they were being chased by a dragon.

"You four, after it!" Governor Karnezis said. "You two, seize the pirate queen!"

Captain Shafira turned to Lintang as two vigils grabbed her arms. "You sure know how to create chaos. Can I at least trust you not to tell him where my necklace is?"

"Your necklace?" Governor Karnezis spun to Captain Shafira, a hungry look on his hawkish face. "You don't have it on you?" His gaze roamed her neck. "No. Interesting." His attention turned to Lintang. "But you know where it is?"

What in Patiki's name was Captain Shafira thinking? Why had she mentioned the necklace at all?

Lintang looked at her, lost for words, but Captain Shafira quirked an eyebrow and Lintang realized her captain had done it on purpose. Whatever was about to happen, it was part of some plan.

"Take the pirate queen and the boy to the holding cell," Governor Karnezis said to the remaining four vigils. He sneered at Captain Shafira. "Are you going to come quietly, or do we risk these children's lives with a fight?"

"Oh, I'll come quietly. I think your vigils have had enough excitement for today."

Governor Karnezis curled his lip. "Put her in the dragon cage."

Her eyes sparkled. "The *dragon cage*? How scared should I be? As scared as your people over a category-one mythie?"

The vigil shoved her down the steps and marched her and Bayani through the frantic crowds.

"Make me proud, Lintang," she said over her shoulder.

Lintang stared after her, panic gripping her throat. What did that mean? What was she supposed to do?

The lidao had disappeared in the madness. The vigils chasing it had spread out to search.

Governor Karnezis turned to Lintang, still gripping her arm. "So, young lady. It sounds as though you and I need to talk."

The Governor

LINTANG SAT ON A LONG COUCH, made not of wicker and rattan like the ones in Desa, but of soft, squashy material. Her sack of belongings lay beside her, looking dirty and out of place. She was in what Governor Karnezis had called the "foyer" of Parliament House. She bounced her heels, trying desperately to study the portraits around the room rather than let her gaze drift upward.

Mythies, dead and stuffed, floated above her on thin, clear ropes. They were all perfectly preserved, as real as the ones still out there.

A small green dragon slithered at the top. A kraken, its tentacles held aloft, swam in the air beneath it. There were several Caletromian mermaids, their faces twisted into the grotesque expressions Lintang had seen before she'd almost been drowned. A human-size fey with wings like a flutterbee's stretched out its clawed hands to throttle imaginary prey. There were other creatures too, ones Lintang had never seen before. They all swayed in the cold breeze like a gruesome collection of wind chimes.

She touched the comforting lump of Xiang's hidden pouch. She missed her sword, but darts were better than nothing.

Make me proud, Lintang.

Captain Shafira's words rang in her ears, but what was the plan? Lintang could hardly attack Parliament House with a few darts. Was the captain expecting her to break them out of prison? Run back to the ship and fetch the other crew members? How was she to know?

The squat table before her held a platter of crumbs from her earlier meal. Dried fruits and juicy dumplings and food she'd never seen before had disappeared into her nervous stomach as she waited for Governor Karnezis to return.

Important-looking people in colorful coats marched through the foyer, leaving muddy tracks on the white tiles and plush rugs. Two women warmed their hands by a crackling fireplace, and a man who must've been some sort of servant offered them water in cups made of crystal.

Rain pattered on the arched windows. Lintang watched it grow heavier, thinking, thinking, thinking.

Make me proud, Lintang.

At last Governor Karnezis returned.

Lintang stood. She'd faced a malam rasha, a sea serpent, and Nyasamdra herself. She wouldn't be scared, not of him.

"My apologies," he said. "There were some forms I had to fill out. Metalwork, you know how it is." He smiled. "You can take your coat off. It's warm enough in here with the fireplaces."

"No, thank you."

An understanding nod. "Very well. Come into my office."

She frowned, suspicious of his kindness, and followed him down a grand corridor with more portraits and bright merry lights. It felt cheery despite the gloom outside. The smoke of the fireplace disappeared, replaced with the faint scent of something familiar.

Burning mollowood. The realization gave her a sudden pang of homesickness.

They passed a lot of doors, but it was only at the end of the corridor that Governor Karnezis opened one, revealing a hexagonal room with dark wooden paneling and gold columns. Lintang stared at the couches and bookshelves and giant hourglass before she noticed the governor waving for her to sit opposite his desk.

She sank down into a hard-backed chair and ran her fingers along its glossy arms.

He gestured to a collection of teacups and a pot on the desk, all inlaid with gold. "Would you like a sai blossom tea? Fresh from Kaneko Brown."

She shook her head.

"Shame. It's lovely." He poured one for himself. Fragrant steam wafted between them.

"So," he said, setting the pot down. "You've been traveling with the pirate queen."

She stared at the steam, considering her words. She didn't know what she could and couldn't say. What would get Captain Shafira into trouble, and what was safe to reveal?

Make me proud, Lintang.

"She needed us to get past Nyasamdra," she said, remembering that Captain Shafira had already mentioned it.

Governor Karnezis touched his cup to his lips. "Both of you? Why would she take a boy? There are sirens out there. In fact, there's a nest of sirens off the coast of Vierz right now—I just hired a hunter for them this morning."

"You can't kill them!"

He set the cup down, surprised at her outburst. "Whyever not?"

"The mythies—they're human. Sick humans. You just have to give them some Curall—"

"Ah." He picked up his cup again. "That was a terrible prank you played with the lidao. Cruel and childish."

"It wasn't—"

"There are laws against bringing mythies into this city, do you understand? No, don't explain. I know exactly what you were trying to do. It was a ploy to get Curall. Captain Shafira must need some for herself." He sipped his tea. "Whether or not you were aware of her ruse is another matter. You are just a child, after all."

Lintang bristled. A child? She'd probably faced more dangerous things this past season than he'd seen in his entire life.

"It wasn't a trick," she said. "It's the truth. I saw it. I saw a pixie turn into a human."

Governor Karnezis nodded, watching her. He didn't speak again, and she knew he didn't believe her.

Was this what Captain Shafira meant when she asked Lintang to make her proud? Was it Lintang's job to convince the governors of the truth? But how could she do that, without the lidao?

Governor Karnezis set his cup down. "Perhaps, before we go any further, I should explain who I am."

He turned his head, showing the back of his neck. A shiny scale glinted in the merry lights.

Lintang stared at it. "You're an Islander?" She had wondered about his birthplace when they'd first met but would never have believed it possible that he was from the Twin Islands.

"Yes," he said, turning back. "I'm like you."

"How did you become a governor?"

"Long ago I was chosen to guide a Vierzan ship past Nyasamdra's waters. I was wearing green that day—a poor oversight. The ship was capsized. I was the only survivor. Afterward, I came here to join the parliament and be part of the fight against mythies."

"*You* were the Islander wearing green? I heard you died too."

Governor Karnezis laughed. "We Islanders aren't so easily drowned. The Gods made sure of that."

Lintang narrowed her eyes. "Vierzans hate the Gods."

Governor Karnezis stood, opening a hidden door in the paneling. Behind it was a scattering of fresh burble-berries, a jug of water, and smoldering mollowood, its smoke curling in the small space.

"You forget," he said. "I'm not Vierzan."

Lintang stared at the offerings. The sight and smell made her heart lurch in her throat.

"You know what I miss most about the Twin Islands?" he said, shutting the door again. It blended seamlessly into the wall. "The heat. You could never imagine missing it, could you? But it's so cold here. I miss the sun. The beach. The afternoon storms. You know the scent of the forest before rain?" He inhaled, as if he could smell it, and released the breath in a rush. "That's what I miss."

Lintang missed it too. "Why don't you go back, then?"

He returned to his seat. "Because I can do so much good here. Much more than I could ever do on the Twin Islands. It's a sacrifice, to stay away, but it's for a worthwhile cause. I want to make this world strong. United. I want people to be safe." He leaned forward, suddenly intent. "Which is why I have to stop the pirate queen."

"You don't have to stop her," Lintang said. "She's innocent."

"How do you know that?"

"I've talked to her; I've traveled with her. She's a good person. She's—" *A Goddess.* Lintang bit the words down. He'd think she was silly if she said that.

Governor Karnezis watched her carefully. "She stole the crown of Allay, do you know that? That necklace is worth more than you'll ever comprehend."

"She needed proof that the Zulttania is dead."

"That's her story. But is the Zulttania actually dead, Lintang? Are you absolutely, positively sure?"

Lintang set her jaw. "If the captain says so, then it's true."

"Here's another question," Governor Karnezis said, clasping his hands on his desk. "Does it matter?"

Lintang stared at him blankly.

"The Zulttania is the reason Allay's borders are closed," he said. "The Zulttania stopped Allay from joining the United Regions. We could almost be an entire world united—peace and treaties and migration from continent to island to continent again—if not for a single stubborn ruler and a troublesome pirate." He took a cloth from his desk drawer and wiped the leaves from his teacup. "I've been speaking with the Zulttania's council. They've agreed to allow trading with the United Regions on a small island in the Biabi Sea. This is a step forward, don't you see? And the pirate queen is trying to stop it."

"The Zulttania's council framed her!"

"We don't know that. All we have is the word of a thief and a murderer."

"What do you mean, a murderer?"

Governor Karnezis lifted an eyebrow. "So she hasn't told you everything." He got to his feet. "Let's go for a walk. I have my own story to tell."

Reward

THE ROOFTOP SMELLED OF WET STONE.
In the market square below, the chaos from the lidao had died down. Lintang hoped the poor mythie had escaped. People bustled beneath the merry lights as the gloomy day grew darker. Was it evening already?

Lintang stared at the endless forest of buildings. Clouds drifted above, so close she felt she could almost reach up and scrape her fingertips across them.

Governor Karnezis leaned on the wall to breathe in the city air. "Have you heard of Ambassador Farah of Jalakta?"

"You mean the name from the identity tag you found on Captain Shafira?"

Governor Karnezis nodded. "She and her entire family were tortured and killed by the pirate queen."

Lintang pressed her lips together in a thin line. "I don't believe it."

"It's what happened, whether you choose to believe it or not. Afterward, the pirate queen burned their house to the ground. She was found watching the flames with their blood still on her hands. The servants told us later she'd been staying with the family for many months. Apparently she'd rowed all the way to Jalakta from Allay after stealing the necklace, which is quite a feat. Impossible, some say, but she's been known to do impossible things. The family must've discovered the necklace, and she'd had to kill them before they turned her in."

"It's not true," Lintang said stubbornly.

"If it's not true, why was she seen covered in their blood? Why does she have Ambassador Farah's identity tag?"

"There's an explanation. I know there is." When Governor Karnezis frowned, she said, "I know what it's like to have people not believe you. Captain Shafira's telling the truth."

A frustrated laugh passed Governor Karnezis's lips. "You're wrong to put so much faith in her."

"No, I'm not."

He sank onto his elbows, leaning hard on the wall. As he did, a series of short, sharp bangs echoed across the square. Lintang jumped as smoke billowed from the opposite building. "What's going on?"

A low horn echoed three times. The people below moved quicker, like millipedes swarming before rain.

Governor Karnezis didn't even flinch. "You see?" he said quietly, watching the smoke climb into the clouds above. "Fire, just like at Ambassador Farah's house."

"Are you saying Captain Shafira did that?"

"We can never contain her, even in the dragon cage." He sighed. "She's somehow escaped." He glanced sideways at Lintang. "There's a reward for the return of that necklace, you know."

Lintang couldn't tear her gaze from the smoke. Captain Shafira was breaking out of prison with Bayani. She'd be here soon to rescue Lintang.

"A large reward," Governor Karnezis continued. "Mountain upon mountain of gemstones. The Zulttania's council want it back."

Lintang hardly heard him. "What am I going to do with a bunch of shiny rocks?"

He gestured around them. "You could build a house this big. Hire servants to make your food, do your chores.

You could own all the land on one of the Twin Islands, if you really wanted."

Lintang finally turned to him.

"You'd be as rich as the queens of old," he said. "That ancient palace in Sundriya could be yours. Imagine living there."

Lintang's eyes widened.

"Imagine having feasts in your honor. Imagine having elegant clothes and a dozen rooms to yourself, and gardens, and horses, and people to worship you."

Lintang had seen the old palace in Sundriya. It wasn't in use anymore — there hadn't been kings and queens on the Twin Islands for centuries — but it could be repaired. She could live there, just like royalty.

Governor Karnezis leaned forward until she could smell traces of mollowood smoke on his sky-blue coat. "All you have to do is tell me where the necklace is, and everything you ever want is yours."

The fantasy vanished.

That necklace was Captain Shafira's most precious thing. It was the crown of Allay, the only proof she had that something wasn't right in her country . . . and she'd given it up. She'd handed it over to Mother, just so she could take Lintang. She could've chosen any of the village girls, but she'd picked Lintang. She'd *insisted* on Lintang. She'd believed in Lintang, even when everyone in Desa called her a liar and a troublemaker.

Captain Shafira had shown faith in Lintang when no one else had. And Lintang had let her down, again and again.

She wouldn't let her down now.

Make me proud, Lintang.

"I can't tell you," she said. "I'm sorry."

Governor Karnezis let out a long sigh. "How disappointing."

"LINTANG!"

The voice came from below. Lintang leaned over to find the market square deserted. Where had all the people gone?

But no—the place wasn't entirely empty. Captain Shafira stood at the base of the building, cupping her hands around her mouth. "Lintang, jump!"

"What?"

Captain Shafira couldn't possibly be asking her to fall three stories. She'd die.

"Lintang, please, for once, just trust me!"

Lintang sucked in a breath and braced her hands on the wall. The captain wanted trust? She'd show her trust.

"No!" Governor Karnezis said, but Lintang was

already springing over, flinching as she waited for the long drop to the bottom . . .

Except her feet landed immediately on solid ground. She staggered and glanced down. It was as if she were standing midair. There must have been a balcony of thin crystal around the rooftop, maybe to stop people from falling.

"Run!" Captain Shafira said, but Governor Karnezis reached over and grabbed Lintang's injured arm.

She screamed as white-hot pain, worse than a jellyfish sting, sizzled along the serpent-fang wound. Governor Karnezis jerked his hand away, alarmed at her reaction.

Lintang used the opportunity to stumble along the side of the building. She could barely see from the spots of pain blossoming in her vision. Behind her was a thud, and then a second, heavier set of footsteps. Governor Karnezis was chasing her.

"There'll be steps at the corner." Captain Shafira was following along below. "Be careful; don't slip down them."

Lintang reached the end of the rooftop and almost went flying. Her heel skidded down the first few steps and she landed on her behind.

"Get up, get up!"

She was still climbing to her feet when Governor

Karnezis snatched her hair. She cried out as he yanked her backwards.

"I won't let you escape, not this time." He spoke loudly, and Lintang realized he was talking to Captain Shafira, not her. He was breathing hard from the run.

Others gathered beneath the invisible staircase. It seemed Captain Shafira had had help breaking out of prison—Quahah, Eire, Mei, and Xiang stood with her and Bayani beneath the crisscrossing lines of red, blue, and green lanterns. Lintang fought to catch her breath. She had almost made it to them.

"Let her go, Karnezis," Captain Shafira said, drawing her sword.

Governor Karnezis tightened his grip on Lintang's hair. "This is the closest I've come to trapping you, Shafira. Do you think I'm going to give up my only advantage?"

Lintang gazed helplessly at the others. Bayani clenched and unclenched his fists, but he was the only one who moved. The rest of them remained still. Tense.

"Xiang?" Governor Karnezis said suddenly. "Xiang of the Elite Vigil Unit, is that you?"

Xiang held her sword aloft. Rather than answer him,

she said, "Still got that present I gave you, Lintang? Just in case?"

Lintang gasped. *The dart pouch.*

She grappled for the cord around her neck and whipped it out before Governor Karnezis could realize what she was doing. Her fingers fumbled with the drawstring. Just one dart, she needed just one dart—

But Governor Karnezis saw the pouch and clamped his free hand around her injured arm again. Scorching pain crackled through her, in her vision, across her nerves, against her throat . . .

She screamed. And screamed. It was like fire. She would've cut off her arm rather than feel it anymore.

"She's a murderer, Lintang." Governor Karnezis's voice floated into her brain from far away. "She's a criminal. Drop the pouch. Tell me where the necklace is."

She couldn't, even if she wanted to. The pain buzzed in her brain, making it impossible to remember anything.

"From Islander to Islander," Governor Karnezis said. "Come on, child. We need to work together."

Lintang stared at him through tears, keeping her gaze on his as her fingers dug into the pouch. Just one dart, just one dart . . .

Make me proud, Lintang.

She caught hold of one and sobbed in relief. The pouch dropped from her grip, leaving the single dart between her thumb and forefinger. Before Governor Karnezis could react, she twisted around and stabbed him in the hand.

He released her with a shout. She jerked forward, her arms flailing out to grab at—

Nothing. There was nothing to hold on to, and suddenly she was plummeting.

Down, down, down.

Bayani's cry echoed across the city.

She stared at the ground as it rushed up to meet her. Too fast, too fast, it was all too fast, she was going to die—

But there was a flurry of bodies, a blur of movement below, and suddenly Mei was springing off Xiang's hands, swinging onto one of the lantern lines, then flipping to another, just like she had on the rigging, and—

There.

She caught Lintang midswing. The night twirled upside down as they flipped, swung, moved with the momentum, and suddenly . . . they were on the ground.

Lintang stumbled and fell over. It felt as though she'd left her heart and stomach somewhere on the second floor. Her injured arm throbbed. She could feel blood trickling down her skin.

"Lintang? Lintang!" Bayani's voice was frantic as he dived to his knees beside her. "Are you hurt?"

Lintang clapped a hand over his face to make sure he was real. "Am I dead?"

"No," he said, pulling her hand away. "Thank the Gods, thank the Gods—"

"I'd like to think I had something to do with it," Mei said, sounding disgruntled.

"Thank you, too," Bayani said.

"Yes, thank you, Mei," Lintang said; then she hugged Bayani, because almost dying had left her with a shaky, frantic love for everyone, even if they had secrets, even if she'd been mad at them before. He was her best friend, and that was never going to change. Not now that she'd stared death in the face. Their friendship was too important to let little things get in the way.

"Well done with that sleeper," Xiang said. "I'll make a warrior of you yet."

Lintang glanced up. Governor Karnezis lay on the invisible top step, snoring.

Captain Shafira hauled her to her feet. "Come on. The square won't be evacuated for much longer."

"Where are we going?" Lintang asked.

"Where do you think, kipper?" Quahah said, offering a hand to help Bayani up. Although she was short, she was very strong. "Back to the ship."

"The *Winda*?" Lintang couldn't believe it. "We're going back to the *Winda*?"

"You've earned your place," Captain Shafira said.

Eire exhaled noisily, but no one paid her any attention.

Lintang's head spun. She was going back to the *Winda*, somehow, impossibly.

She clutched her aching arm. "What about Bayani?"

Captain Shafira untied her red kerchief from her neck. "Take off your coat." Lintang pulled off Xiang's borrowed coat, and Captain Shafira wrapped her kerchief painfully tight around Lintang's wound. When she was done, she turned to Bayani. "I don't know, Bayani. It's dangerous in Zaiben, but it's safer than being on the ship. Wouldn't you agree?"

"I want to go where Lintang is," Bayani said. He swallowed hard. "Please."

Lintang squeezed his hand. He didn't look at her.

"You can't leave him here, Captain; the governors are as mad as cackling crows," Quahah said.

Captain Shafira hesitated, studying Bayani a heartbeat longer before saying, "Right. Let's go, then." She and the others slipped off their cloaks. They were wearing vigil jackets underneath, a disguise to get them through the city safely. They had thought of everything.

"I'm really allowed to go with you?" Lintang said as they started for the empty road.

"You didn't tell him where my necklace was, did you?" Captain Shafira said.

"No, but—"

"He offered you gems, didn't he?" Mei said.

"Yes, but—"

"And you followed the captain's orders to jump off the roof, didn't you?" Xiang said.

"Yes, but—"

"Did he tell you about Ambassador Farah?" Captain Shafira said, pausing in the shadow of a building as a group of real vigils hurried past. "That I tortured and killed her and her family, and burned their house to the ground?"

"Yes, but I didn't believe him," Lintang said, determined to get the rest of her sentence out this time. "I know you'd never do anything like that."

Captain Shafira waited until the vigils were gone before leading the group out onto the street. "So you trust me. And you've proved that I can trust you. That's all I've ever asked for."

Lintang released a shaky breath. She was really going back to the *Winda*. The memory of the entire horrible day melted away until all that was left was joy, sparking in her like a beacon.

"Pelita will be thrilled to see you again," Xiang said, giggling.

Captain Shafira glanced at her sideways. "Why is that funny?"

"She's awake," said Quahah.

"So?"

"So," said Xiang with a wicked smile, "let's just say she's regained her energy."

The Ex-Pixie

"**Y**OU'RE BACK!"

Lintang braced herself as a whirlwind rushed toward her. Bayani stepped in front to take the hit, and both he and Pelita toppled onto the deck.

"Oh," Lintang said as Pelita kissed Bayani a dozen times on the cheek.

"Exactly," said Xiang, climbing out of the rowboat.

Lintang gazed around. The *Winda* was how she'd left it, familiar in the lantern light. The pulleys and masts clacked above her, the deck bobbed with the waves, and she caught a faint whiff of euco oil through the salty breeze. It was like coming home.

Pelita jumped up, giving Lintang several wet kisses on the cheek too. "I know you. You gave me gross mashed potato. Potato Girl!"

"Lintang." Bayani climbed painfully to his feet.

"Her name is Lintang." He glanced at Hewan. "Is she all right?"

"I can't imagine being a pixie for a hundred and twenty years was good for her developing brain," Hewan said.

Pelita gripped Bayani's arm and yanked him back and forth. "Niti's festival is tomorrow!"

"She's very excited about Niti's festival," Avalon said. "She's been talking about it since she woke up."

Bayani looked strangely pale in the light.

Pelita danced from Xiang to Eire to Mei to Quahah, trying to give them kisses too. They deftly avoided her, except Quahah, who was smaller than Pelita and had no way to escape unless she stabbed her with her knife. From the look on Quahah's face as Pelita tugged on the tentacles of her woolly octopus hat, she might've been considering it.

Lintang recognized the pants and shirt Pelita was wearing from Avalon's chest of old clothes. They sagged on her tiny frame.

Avalon turned to Xiang. "Did anyone recognize you?"

"Unfortunately, yes," Xiang said with a sigh. "A governor, no less."

"I suppose you couldn't stay pretend dead forever," Mei said.

They turned as Captain Shafira called for everyone to gather around.

"Lintang showed great trust in me in Zaiben," Captain Shafira said. "She's now welcome back on the *Winda*, not as a cabin girl, but as a guest, like before."

Dee cheered. Pelita released Quahah and cheered too, although she probably didn't know what she was cheering about. Yamini spun on her heel and stalked down the hatch without a word.

"What's the plan, then, Captain?" Quahah said. "Are we going to try to cure the sirens?"

Lintang gasped. "Sirens!" She'd forgotten in the chaos. "Governor Karnezis sent a hunter for them this morning."

"No one else knows the truth," Bayani said. "We have to stop them."

Eire narrowed her eyes. "We have no medicine. No point risking life."

"The hunting ship will have Curall," Captain Shafira said slowly.

Eire swung to her. "You are thinking of doing this?"

"You were happy to go after the sirens when we were killing them," Lintang said.

"Killing easy. Saving lives, not. We should leave. It is not our business to help mythies. They are predators."

"Not all of them," Bayani said, his voice rising. "Most are harmless. Gnomes and pixies and lidao."

"They probably can't think properly when they're transformed, anyway," Captain Shafira added.

Eire gestured to Pelita. "Fine, but it took girl long time to turn back. How we face sirens for long time without kill?"

"I say at least we try," Bayani said.

Captain Shafira glanced at him. "Bayani, you know this means—"

"Yes," he said. "But what's going to happen will happen no matter what. We should save the lives of those sirens if we can."

Captain Shafira stared at him for a long time. He stared back. They seemed to be having either a battle of wills or some silent conversation. Lintang's heart sank as she watched them. More secrets.

She didn't say anything, though. She'd already decided these things weren't going to get in the way of their friendship.

At last, Captain Shafira said, "All right, let's do it. Predator mythies or not, they are people in need of our help. Zazi, to the helm. Mei, the rigging. Set a course for due east. Quahah, you're on navigation. We're going to save some sirens."

Pelita cheered again, but the rest of the crew was already starting to move.

"You think we'll be able to catch up to the hunting ship?" Bayani said.

"Their captain would have to gather an all-female crew, fill out reports, top up weapon supplies . . . I'd say we have a very good chance. Hewan, get your medical kit. Lintang needs her wound restitched. Dee, Farah, organize some food for Bayani—he hasn't eaten in a while."

"Sure thing, Captain," Farah the clamshell said.

Bayani groaned. "Thank the Gods." He followed Dee down the hatch. Pelita skipped after them.

But Lintang remained. She'd finally worked out something she should've put together hours earlier.

"Farah the clamshell," she said slowly, "is Ambassador Farah."

"Yes." Captain Shafira's voice was quiet, unheard by the other crew bustling around them. "At least, in Dee's mind she is."

"Ambassador Farah was Dee's mother?"

"Many years ago, I escaped Allay on a mere rowboat. If it hadn't been for the lightning bird, the trip would've killed me." Captain Shafira drew a breath. "And if it hadn't been for Dee—Delilah of Jalakta, daughter of

Ambassador Farah—I wouldn't have recovered. The whole family took care of me. They were going to help me spread the word about the Zulttania being dead."

"What happened?" Lintang whispered as the black sails unfolded and caught a sudden gust of wind.

Captain Shafira's form disappeared momentarily in flickering shadows. "The Zulttania's council must have found out where I was staying. They sent people to kill Farah's family and burn the place down. I tried to save them . . ." She trailed off, then cleared her throat and said, "I managed to drag Dee out, but she'd already been through too much. She lost her mind."

There were so many things Lintang wanted to say, and when they all crowded in her mouth, the one that escaped was "She really thinks that clamshell is her mother."

"I don't know how she'll react if I break that fantasy," Captain Shafira said softly. "And I'm not willing to try."

Lintang stared at the hatch down which Dee had disappeared. Loud, friendly, mad, wonderful Dee—how could this have happened to her?

Captain Shafira shook her head. "I shouldn't have kept Farah's identity tag. It was a stupid mistake on my part, but I couldn't bring myself to throw it away. That's what sentimentality gets you."

Lintang thought of Governor Karnezis, of how he had been negotiating with the Zulttania's council. Of how he had talked about trade and peace and all that nonsense, when he was siding with a group of people who had slaughtered Dee's family and blamed Captain Shafira.

"Captain," she said finally, "I don't think the governors care that you're innocent."

"No," said Captain Shafira as the wind caught a sail and cast her in deep shadow. "I don't think they do either."

Once a course had been set and the helm had been secured, the rest of the crew went down for dinner. Thanks to the party who had gone ashore, they were able to have succulent slices of red meat, roasted vegetables topped with gravy, a side of herb puddings, and piping-hot tea.

Despite their conversation on the top deck, Captain Shafira made an effort to be cheerful. She told the rest of the crew how the dragon cage was made from a real dragon rib cage. She'd escaped by blowing up the bones, using bahatsi powder packed inside the hollow jewels in her hair. Lintang had never heard of bahatsi powder, and Mei explained it was a natural explosive, like a volcano or lightning. It was hard not to be jealous of Bayani, who had seen it all firsthand.

"I'm sorry you didn't get a chance to convince the governors that the mythies are human," Lintang said to him as she soaked up the last of her dinner with a slice of bread.

"It's all right. Captain Shafira believes me." Bayani nudged her. "You believe me. I trust both of you to pass the message on."

She sucked at her soggy bread. "Why can't *you* keep trying? That wasn't your only chance, you know."

"Right," he said, looking away. "Of course."

When plates had been licked clean, a cry for rouls went up, and Quahah helped Yamini set up the game.

"Want to play?" Captain Shafira said to Bayani.

He tore his gaze away from Pelita, who was teasing Twip with a nut hanging from a thread. "Shouldn't I be locked up?"

"We won't reach the reef until tomorrow night. You'll be fine."

"What if they move closer to us?" Lintang said.

"Sirens always live near a reef, and they never make nests this close to each other. We'll be safe for now." Captain Shafira gestured toward the vertical rouls boards. "Come on, Bayani, have a go."

"No, thank you," he said. "I just want to go to bed."

Captain Shafira hesitated a beat before saying, "Are you sure?"

"Yes."

"There'll be plenty of time to sleep . . . later. Stay up with us."

Bayani shook his head. "Let me rest. Please."

"All right." Captain Shafira stood. "You can have my bed."

Xiang and Mei, who were closest, turned to her.

"No, that's fine—" Bayani started, but Captain Shafira spoke over him.

"Don't be silly. Tomorrow you'll be in the cage. The least I can do is offer you my cabin. Don't worry," she said over Bayani's protests. "There are plenty of empty cabins I can sleep in tonight."

By now most of the crew had stopped talking to listen to the conversation. If Captain Shafira noticed she had an audience, she pretended not to. "Let's go. I'll put you in the cage before sunrise tomorrow."

Bayani got to his feet and followed the captain meekly from the room.

"Did she just offer her room to the kid?" Quahah said when they were gone. "Since when does the captain offer her room to *anyone*?"

Her question was met with silence at first. Then Pelita, bored with teasing Twip, jumped up and twirled on the spot. "It's because Niti's festival is tomorrow," she said, then skipped out of the mess. Her singing echoed down the corridor. *"The water will call for you, and the harvester will come, on the day of Niti's fes-ti-val."*

"What's she carrying on about?" Quahah said.

Eire snorted and put the last rouls board into place. "Girl is crazy. Not even *she* knows what she is talking about."

"The water will call for you, and the harvester will come, on the day of Niti's fes-ti-val!"

The chatter started up again, drowning out Pelita's voice, but Lintang continued to stare at the door, the words of the song echoing in her head long after Pelita was gone.

The Siren's Call

LINTANG OPENED HER EYES to find a face blinking at her.

"*Argh!*" She bolted up.

"*Argh!*" Pelita scrambled back at the same time.

"What are you doing?" Lintang cried.

"Waiting for you to wake up," Pelita said.

Lintang breathed through the zing ebbing from her nerves. "Well, don't. Wait for me outside next time."

Her arm throbbed, and she had to check that she hadn't broken the stitches again. Her circular hammock swayed from the violence of her movements. She'd been allowed to return to her original room last night.

"Today is Niti's festival," Pelita said.

Lintang had lost track of the days while on the *Winda*. Desa would be transformed, with dancing and singing and feasts and games. The adults would take their earthen jugs of water from the household shrines into the temple for a special blessing. A large fire would burn in the village center, filled with thick branches of sweet-smelling mollowood to mark the end of Mratzi's season and the beginning of Niti's. She felt strange missing it.

"*Bayani, Bayani, Bayani*," Pelita said. Her eyes were wide.

Lintang climbed out of her hammock. Bayani had slept in the captain's cabin last night. What was his secret? Why had Captain Shafira given him such special treatment?

Lintang headed for the mess with Pelita trailing after. They ate a breakfast of last night's meat, eggs, and poppy-seed bread. Pelita sat up against her so they were hip to hip and continued to say Bayani's name in sets of three between mouthfuls.

Xiang and Quahah slumped bleary-eyed into the mess. Quahah's woolly octopus hat was askew, its tentacles slung haphazardly over one another. Xiang's hair was coming out of its usual sleek bun. The two of them fell into the nearest chairs as Yamini served them breakfast and hot tea. The lanterns swayed above them.

Quahah moaned. "That light isn't helping my headache."

Xiang yawned and dropped her cheek to the palm of

her hand, her eyes closed. "Maybe we should've picked up some merry lights while we were in Zaiben. At least they have a constant glow."

"Glow," said Pelita, interrupting her own chanting. "They glowed. Three of them. *Bayani, Bayani, Bayani.*"

Quahah and Xiang looked at her. Lintang finished her breakfast. "She's been like this all morning."

"Three glows," Pelita said. "Three glowing seeds."

Quahah straightened, squinting.

"The water will call for you, and the harvester will come, on the day of Niti's festival." Pelita got up and danced around the room. "Niti's festival, Niti's festival. Today, today, today."

Xiang, who had raised her steaming mug to her lips, lowered it again. "Glowing seeds? Riddles? Has Pelita seen the propheseeds?"

Lintang stopped midchew.

"Bayani, Bayani, Bayani," Pelita sang. *"Bayani, Bayani, Bayani. Bayani, Bayani, Bayani—"*

Lintang lurched to her feet and sprinted from the room as if Mratzi herself were after her.

Lintang stopped at the foot of the steps in the carpentry room. Her lungs struggled for air.

"What's wrong?" Bayani said from inside the cage.

She stepped inside. "Is it true?" she said through gasps. "Did you see the propheseeds?"

He straightened. "How did you . . . ?"

"Pelita." The word wobbled. Her legs threatened to collapse beneath her. "So it's true? You're—" She choked and swiped her eyes. "You're going to die? For real this time?"

He didn't answer.

She inhaled sharply. "When did you see them?"

"When I was coming to convince you to go to the temple, the night Captain Shafira came to Desa." He gave a wry smile. "That was the same day you told the story of Pero and the propheseeds, remember? I couldn't believe it when they appeared."

"But . . . *the water will call for you*? That's the sirens! Why did you come aboard, again?"

"You know why. It doesn't matter whether I'm here or in Zaiben. The prophecy will come true no matter what. I just . . ." He trailed off and looked away. "I just wanted to spend my last day with you."

She couldn't swallow. Her throat felt as if it had been stuffed with cloth. "You shouldn't have left the Twin Islands in the first place. You should've gone inland. You should've run."

"I wanted to. Believe me, I was tempted. But it was

you who inspired me to be brave in the end. You and your story of Pero."

"You gnome. That's just a legend! This is real. This is *you*."

"I'm sorry."

"Don't be sorry. Think. What if we turn the prophe-seeds human again?"

"We don't have time. Niti's festival is today."

She gripped his cage bars. "There has to be something we can do."

"There's not," Bayani said. "I've spoken about it with Captain Shafira. She's been . . . kind, but truthful. I—I'm going to die today."

Lintang's forehead fell against the cold bars. "Why didn't you tell me sooner? By the Gods, Bayani, *why* do you keep hiding things from me?"

He put his hand over hers and said gently, "I don't like to worry you."

"Oh, you stupid, useless—" She sucked in a breath through her teeth and turned her hand to grip his fingers. "You owe me now, for keeping another secret. You can't die. All right? Just . . . don't."

"I don't want to." His voice was very small.

She choked back a sob and clung to his fingers as if her hold alone could keep him in this world.

He had bags under his eyes, his hair was tousled and slightly greasy, there was a rip in the shirt he'd borrowed from Avalon—maybe from his time in the Zaiben prison—and he looked so, so . . . weary. He'd been holding on to the secret of the mythies since he was sick in Sundriya. He'd been burdened by the weight of the prophecy since their last night in Desa. How had he managed not to buckle under the pressure? How had he carried it all, just so Lintang wouldn't worry?

She thought of his cry when she'd fallen from the roof of Parliament House. She thought of how frantic he'd been afterward. He'd kept secrets from her, yes, but he cared about her. He always had.

She shut her eyes and leaned her forehead against the bars. She would find a way to save him. No matter what.

Eventually Captain Shafira came in. "We're about to board a ship called the *Glory*," she said. "That means we're dealing with Captain Moon."

"Captain Moon?" Lintang sounded old and tired as she lifted her head from the bars. It was hard to believe the day was still going, with other things left to do. "The one you fought on a volcano?"

"Yes, but she's a reasonable person."

Bayani gave an incredulous laugh. "How can you say that?"

"Because you didn't hear how the fight ended. I explained my story to her, and she believed me. Well, I can't be sure she actually believed me, but she let me go, in any case. If our mythie story weren't so incredible, I'd try to explain that to her too."

"What will you do instead?"

"What we always planned to do—storm the ship, seize as much Curall as we can, and leave them adrift so we can get to the sirens first." She eyed their interlocked hands. "Is everything all right down here?"

"Lintang found out about the prophecy," Bayani said.

"Yes. Xiang and Quahah figured it out too." Captain Shafira pursed her lips. "Many of the crew aren't happy you're on board right now. But you're safest here. Wait by the cage, Lintang. This shouldn't take long. When we return with the Curall and are far enough from the *Glory*, you can come back up." She turned to leave, then glanced over her shoulder. "Do not, under *any* circumstances, let Bayani out of the cage. Do I make myself clear?"

"Yes, Captain."

"Captain!" Avalon thundered down the stairs, looking determined. "You need to put me in the cage too."

"Avalon—"

"*Please*, Captain."

"You can't both be in the cage. You might kill each other if we cross the sirens." Captain Shafira's voice softened at Avalon's expression. "It's only a precaution anyway. We're nowhere near the reef. And our agreement stands, doesn't it?"

Avalon set his jaw. "It does."

"What agreement?" Lintang said.

"One I'm not making with Bayani," Captain Shafira replied. To Avalon, she said, "Come with us to the *Glory*. We'll tie you up when we head for the reef. All right?"

Avalon nodded reluctantly, his gaze flicking to the cage before he followed her up the steps.

When they were gone, Lintang squeezed Bayani's hand. "How are you feeling?"

"A little strange, actually."

"Strange? Strange how?"

"I don't know. I—" He broke off.

She studied him. "Bayani?"

He shook his head as if clearing his thoughts. "Sorry. I'm all right. Don't leave, please."

"I won't. I'm staying right here."

They stood in silence, but not for long. He shifted his weight.

"Are you uncomfortable?" she said as he released her hand.

He shook out his fingers. "Just cramped." But then he lurched, clutching his chest.

She stiffened. "What's wrong?"

"I—," he said through gasps, "I think—the sirens—"

"But the captain said we're not near the reef."

He lurched again, then moaned and clawed at his hair.

"All right." Lintang breathed through a surge of panic. "All right, maybe we're nearer than we thought. That's fine. I'll stay here with you."

"Run." The word sounded as if it had been ripped from somewhere deep inside him.

"It'll be fine," she said. "I won't let you trick me into opening the cage or anything—"

He lunged at the bars of his cage and pulled.

"Just calm down," she said. "When the siren is medicated, you'll stop feeling . . . however you're feeling."

He tugged harder at the bars. A shadow passed across his face, as though the lantern flame had flickered.

She frowned. "Do you really think you're going to be able to—"

The metal groaned. A satisfied sigh escaped his lips. When he pulled again, the bars bent slightly.

"Oh," she said, backing away. "Oh, you shouldn't be able to do that. You can't—oh my—" She spun and ran for the steps. "Captain Shafira! We need you!"

The Mythie Guidebook Entry #96:
Siren [Kaneko Brown]

~ ~ ~ ~ ~ ~ ~ ~

The Kanekonese siren (kijo) is a sea mythie in the predator category. It is the second-largest humanoid, with seaweedlike hair and fingers, and glows bluish-green beneath the surface of the water.

Diet: Meat of any kind.

Habitat: Throughout the five seas.

Frequency: Extremely rare.

Behavior: These mythies are capable of submerging ships and killing the crew without the need for a reef. Like the common siren, it calls for males, but unlike the common siren, it gives power to its victims, making them strong and violent, unable to think of anything but getting close to the mythie. If you come across a male under the thrall of a Kanekonese siren, DO NOT ATTEMPT TO SUBDUE HIM. Step aside and allow him to continue past. Any attempt to stop him or slow his progress will trigger him to destroy all obstacles, including shipmates or loved ones.

Eradication: Unknown.

Did you know? There has been only one recorded sighting of a Kanekonese siren since the Infestation.

Danger level: 5 for males. 4 for females.

The *Glory*

⌒⌒

T HE *GLORY* LOOMED OVER THE *WINDA* like a steel monster. Sunlight glistened on bronze wheels that churned through the water. Steam rose from pipes in thick, smelly plumes.

A plank of wood bridged the two ships, and ropes weaved between railings, so that the *Winda* looked like a younger sibling clinging to its proud elder.

There was no one around. Lintang glanced at the hatch down to the galley and mess, then at the bridge that would take her to the *Glory*. If she went downstairs, she would find only Hewan, and the medic probably wouldn't be able to help against a superstrong Bayani.

No, the people who could stop him would've boarded the *Glory*.

Lintang ran across the rolling deck toward the plank. "Hellllooooo!"

The smoke cleared to reveal a figure sitting on the railing. Lintang slowed. She'd forgotten about Pelita.

"Run!" Lintang said, waving both arms.

Pelita copied her cheerfully. Lintang grabbed her wrist and dragged her onto the plank. "This isn't a game. Bayani's under the siren's spell."

"Bayani, Bayani, Bayani," Pelita sang, climbing up. She shuffled along at an agonizingly slow pace. The plank sloped steeply upward. Lintang would've pushed Pelita to go faster if the waves hadn't been smashing against both hulls with a vengeance. She wasn't afraid of heights, but with the plank wobbling and the ships heaving, she couldn't trust her balance. The heel of her boot skidded on the wet wood, and her heart felt as though it had fallen into the ocean. She clutched at Pelita to steady herself.

Pelita laughed. "This is fun!"

"If you say so," Lintang said, breathless. She checked over her shoulder but couldn't see whether Bayani was following through the swirling steam. "Keep going."

They made it to the top and climbed onto the gritty steel deck. Pelita ran across it. "Hello, everyone!"

The *Glory*'s crew was sitting against the railing, tied up in their crisp, clean uniforms. Avalon stalked before them with a sword.

Lintang grabbed Pelita. Would he be under the siren's spell too?

"What are you doing here?" he said.

She hesitated. He *sounded* normal, if a little sharper than usual. But that was to be expected during a siege, wasn't it?

Or was his briskness due to a more sinister reason?

As she studied him, a shadow passed across his face, exactly like what had happened with Bayani.

Mei jogged over. "What's going on?"

"Mei," Lintang said, stepping back, "Mei, be care—"

Avalon lunged. He wrapped his arm around Mei's throat. Pelita yelped. Lintang yanked her away.

"We need to go to the siren," Avalon said, lifting his blade in front of Mei's face.

Mei strained to pull his arm from around her neck. Her round cheeks turned pink. She opened and closed her mouth, but the action was useless. She was suffocating.

"Let her go," Lintang said, still clinging to Pelita. "Avalon, she's dying!"

"We have to go to the siren," Avalon said again. "You'll see. It's the only way—"

There was a heavy *thunk*, and he rocked. His arm slipped from Mei's neck and he collapsed to the deck, revealing Dee with one of her frypans.

Mei tumbled down too. She clutched at her throat, struggling to get her breath back. Lintang rushed to her.

Dee crouched over Avalon. "Sorry, starflower," she said, running her hand along the bump swelling on his head. "That's going to hurt tomorrow."

"He was . . . so strong," Mei wheezed.

"I know," Lintang said. "Bayani bent the bars of his cage."

Mei climbed to her feet. "We need . . . to hide. I'll . . . free them." She gestured to the bound *Glory* crew. "Dee . . . take Avalon . . . safe. Lintang . . . warn captain."

"But Bayani's on his way!"

"I'll stay here"—Mei stopped and winced—"to hold him off." Then she whispered what sounded like a prayer in her language.

Dee pulled Avalon into her arms. Lintang led Pelita toward the *Glory*'s hatch. As they passed the plank, Lintang dared a peek down.

Bayani was climbing up.

"Hurry!" Lintang cried. She yanked at Pelita to move faster. Pelita laughed wildly as they ran.

The *Glory*'s staircase was nothing like the *Winda*'s. The steps were steel grates that clanged with each footfall. When Lintang and Pelita reached the next deck, they saw that the passageways had large round windows, allowing in streams of daylight. Merry lights lined the walls. Each metal door was closed tightly. If there were sleeping quarters behind those doors, they were private and unwelcoming.

No creaking timber; no euco oil scent. The passageways twisted and turned, making it difficult for Lintang to figure out where she and Pelita had been and where they had yet to go.

At last they rounded a corner to find Eire standing outside one of the metal doors. She already had her khwando raised with the axe pointed at them. When she realized it was them, she didn't lower the weapon. "What are you doing? Silly children, you will ruin whole mission."

Lintang stopped short of the axe blade. "I need . . . Captain . . ." she said, panting. "Bayani . . . siren . . ."

Captain Shafira appeared from the room, tucking vials of Curall into her pouch. "Lintang? I told you to stay on the *Winda*."

"She thinks she is tough like adult," Eire said, scoffing. "She thinks she is ready to fight monsters."

"Monsters, monsters," Pelita said, bounding beside Lintang.

"Bayani," Lintang tried again. "Bayani's under the siren's spell."

Captain Shafira frowned. "All right, but that doesn't give you permission to leave his cage when I specifically said—"

"He bent the bars." The words tumbled over each other in her attempt to make herself heard. "He's strong. It's—"

"Xiang!" Captain Shafira hadn't even let her finish.

Xiang appeared from the room, dipping her darts in the clear Curall liquid. "What's wrong?"

"Make sure you have some sleepers," Captain Shafira said. "We have a Kanekonese siren."

Xiang's head snapped up. "Avalon?"

"Dee managed to knock him out," Lintang said.

Xiang gave a breathy, nervous laugh. "She got lucky. It's almost impossible to take down someone under the spell of a Kanekonese siren."

"She took a risk," Captain Shafira said. "She knows the agreement."

"What was it?" Lintang said.

"Avalon's given us permission to kill him if it gets too dangerous."

"What? No!"

"If he's knocked out, we should be safe. It's Bayani we need to worry about now."

"He's on his way," Lintang said.

Pelita was still bounding up and down.

"He's going to want to take control of one of the ships," Captain Shafira said. "He'll probably head to the engine room." She shoved a vial of Curall at Lintang. "Keep this."

"Should we medicate Lintang now?" Xiang said.

"No, we need as much Curall as possible against the Kanekonese siren. She can use some if there's any left over." Her expression turned grim. "If you see Bayani, let him pass; then, while his back is turned, shoot him with a sleeper. If you can't get a clear shot, leave him. You don't need to die for this. Eire, back Xiang up. Pelita and Lintang, come with me to the engine room."

She turned and jogged down the passageway, her boots thunking heavily on the grated steel deck. Lintang had nowhere else to keep the vial, so she slipped it into her boot, then hurried after the captain with Pelita skipping behind her. "Didn't you just say the engine room is where Bayani will be going? Why are *we* going there?"

"Because the engine room has a weapon. A good one." Captain Shafira slowed at a corner and checked around it. "Keep an eye out for Captain Moon. We haven't come across her yet, which means she might be preparing an ambush."

They headed along the corridor. The clanking and humming and hissing became louder.

At last they reached a steel door with a spoked wheel. Captain Shafira turned it. The door opened and steam hissed out, clearing to reveal a small metal balcony. It overlooked a room with enormous steel pipes that wormed like intestines.

Lintang had to shout to be heard over the deafening noise. "Where's the weapon?"

Captain Shafira beckoned them onto the balcony and pointed to a cleared corner of the room. Inside the space, with a tube in its mouth and steam curling from its nostrils, was a real live dragon.

The Mythie Guidebook Entry #27:
Dragon [common]

～～～～～～～～

The dragon is a reptilian sky mythie in the predator category. Its impenetrable hide, unstoppable talons, and ability to breathe fire make it almost invincible. It is a solitary creature that lives in nests made of precious stones and gold. The various dragon species are described in detail in Dragons Around the World.

Diet: Meat.

Habitat: Worldwide, mostly on small islands or empty plains.

Frequency: Moderately common.

Behavior: Dragons collect and hoard valuable objects. They are violent creatures that enjoy fighting other predator mythies and destroying towns and cities. Heavily populated areas are always in danger of a dragon attack.

Eradication: The only weapon known to be effective against dragons is another dragon's talon. Only trained professionals are permitted to attempt eradication of a dragon. All populated areas should have dragon evacuation plans. DO NOT ATTEMPT TO KILL.

Did you know? In the second year of the Bauei period, one dragon killed another in the vicinity of a United Regions military unit, which was then able to procure the UR's first set of dragon talons.

Danger level: 5

Captain Moon

THE BALCONY HAD STEPS leading into the room. Lintang and Pelita followed Captain Shafira down to the next level. The vial of Curall in Lintang's boot dug uncomfortably into her foot.

Pipes wound around them, so hot the air rippled. Lintang swiped at her sweaty forehead as they drew nearer to the dragon. Its scales glistened red in the merry lights, and its nostrils flared with each exhalation of smoke. Besides a twitching tail and the slightest tap of a claw, it didn't move. It cracked open an eye at their approach, then closed it again. The tube sticking out of its mouth sizzled.

There was a person in that body.

"Don't worry," Lintang said, hoping it could hear her through the clamor. "We'll save you."

Captain Shafira withdrew a vial of Curall from her

pouch and rolled it between her palms. "How does this work? Do you think I can just spray it, like Bayani did with Pelita? Or will the hot air turn it to steam and dilute it?"

Pelita hummed and tapped Lintang on the shoulder. Lintang ignored her.

Captain Shafira continued thinking out loud. "I could get Xiang to use one of her darts . . . but its hide's probably too thick to pierce."

"Are you really going to use the dragon as a weapon?" Lintang said, batting Pelita away as she continued to tap her shoulder.

"Yes. It takes a good long while for the Curall to take effect, which will be enough time for us to release it so it can stop the siren."

"Why can't we medicate the dragon afterward?"

"It's likely to fly away before we can."

"But what if one of them is killed?"

"It's a chance we have to take, unfortunately. Every-one's life is in danger right now." Captain Shafira exam-ined the vial again. "I'm just not sure of the best way to administer this."

"Maybe we can ask the lady behind us," Pelita said.

Lintang and Captain Shafira spun to find a Vier-zan woman in a long, sky-blue coat pointing a sword at them. Every part of her was clean and perfect. Her dark hair was pulled back, not a strand out of place despite the humidity. Her polished gold medals gleamed in the merry lights.

Captain Shafira smiled. "Nice to see you again, Captain Moon."

Captain Moon's sword didn't waver. "I gave you the benefit of the doubt that day on the volcano. I let you go." Her expression darkened. "Now I see I was wrong."

"We're not here to hurt you. We just needed to borrow some Curall." Captain Shafira held up the vial. "See?"

"Right, and what exactly were you planning to do with my dragon?"

"That's a more difficult question to answer." Captain Shafira slipped the Curall back into her pouch slowly so Captain Moon could see she wasn't reaching for a weapon. "I wanted to medicate it."

Captain Moon snorted. "That story's almost as wild as your last one."

"Look, we're heading for a Kanekonese siren. I know because I had a boy on board the *Winda*, and he's on his way to kill us."

"You don't expect me to believe you were stupid enough to take a male on board this close to sirens."

Captain Shafira shrugged.

Captain Moon waved her sword, directing them to move away from the dragon. "Let's go."

Captain Shafira snagged Pelita's arm and led her toward the steps. Lintang followed, acutely aware of the blade near her back. They walked carefully up the staircase. The steam swam around them. Lintang cursed each step as the vial of Curall jabbed into her foot.

When they reached the balcony, Captain Shafira opened the door and moved aside to let Lintang and Pelita go into the passageway first. The cool air was a welcome relief to Lintang's lungs and sweaty skin. She was about to walk out when Captain Shafira unsheathed her sword and fell upon Captain Moon.

Captain Moon had to move swiftly to block the attack. The blades met with a clang. Pelita shrieked and clung to Lintang.

Captain Moon's gaze fell on Captain Shafira's glittering black blade. Her eyes widened. "That's—"

"Yes, I found it in the end," Captain Shafira said. "Didn't I tell you?" And with a grin, she swung the sword again.

The two thrust and parried, each as skilled as the other. A few clashing blades and a clever maneuver later, they'd switched positions, so now Captain Shafira was on the staircase, with Captain Moon's back to the doorway. Lintang pulled Pelita into the passageway, feeling useless but not wanting to try anything in case she accidentally distracted Captain Shafira.

Captain Shafira spun away from Captain Moon's advancing sword, her braids whirling behind her. Captain Moon's sword clanged against the metal railing of the balcony.

Lintang's body buzzed with panic. She half wished she had her little wooden sword, just to do *something*. Pelita jumped up and down anxiously beside her.

Captain Shafira managed to kick Captain Moon's ankle, dropping her to one knee. Captain Moon blocked an attack while she was down, then stabbed forward so violently that Captain Shafira had to jump two steps down the staircase, giving Captain Moon time to get to her feet again.

"I forgot how good you are," Captain Shafira said, sounding impressed. "You've had more training than just the navy, haven't you?"

Captain Moon grunted. "There are a lot of things you don't know about me."

"I could say the same."

The swords met with a clash, again and again.

"Stop!" Lintang said. "You're on the same side!"

Clash! Clang!

"She has a point," Captain Shafira said, blocking another string of attacks. "You made that decision the last time we fought, Captain."

"That was before you took over my ship."

Lintang edged onto the balcony again. Captain Moon was clearly winning, pushing Captain Shafira farther and farther from the exit.

But then Captain Shafira's lips quirked as she reached the foot of the steps, and Lintang realized that perhaps Captain Shafira was *letting* herself be pushed away.

She was heading back to the dragon.

Pelita shifted from foot to foot, her knuckles at her lips, looking as excited as she did worried.

"It's fine," Lintang said, grinning as Captain Shafira got closer to the dragon. "It's all going to be—"

"Hello, Lintang."

Lintang whirled around to find Bayani standing at the door. He held Eire's khwando.

Lintang shoved Pelita behind her. Her stitches tugged painfully at the movement.

Bayani stepped onto the balcony. Shadows swam across his face. He kept his head low as his dark eyes stared at her from beneath their lashes, hungry, cruel, and not at all like her best friend's.

"Call for your captain." He was calm. Too calm. His grip tightened on the khwando.

Lintang's heart jumped to her throat. She couldn't speak, couldn't even think . . .

Bayani lifted the axe.

"CAPTAIN SHAFIRA!"

Her scream echoed in the engine room as she shielded Pelita and braced for the pain. Rather than an axe blade, though, something whistled past her face and clunked against the wall. She cracked open an eye.

Captain Shafira's black sword was on the balcony floor. Bayani lowered his weapon. Pelita giggled as if they were playing a game.

"You have my attention," Captain Shafira said over the machinery. Lintang risked a glance behind her. Captain Shafira was weaponless now, but Captain Moon had lowered her sword and was staring at Bayani. "What do you want?"

"I want to get to the siren."

"Fine," Captain Shafira said. "Then leave the girls alone, and you can be on your way."

Bayani didn't move. "You have a dragon. A dragon can kill my siren."

"All ship dragons are given a sleeping sickness before

departure," Captain Moon said. "It won't be going any-where."

Bayani raised an eyebrow. "Can Curall reverse a sleeping sickness?"

No answer.

He held out a hand. "Give me all your Curall."

Captain Shafira didn't hesitate. She walked past Captain Moon, across the room, up the steps, and to the balcony. "We won't keep you," she said, holding her pouch upside down and letting the vials clink to the steel floor. "Are you going to need me to steer the ship?"

"No. You might stop me. I have plenty of other, less resourceful people to choose from." He lifted his boot and smashed all the vials. Pelita laughed.

Captain Shafira's gaze caught on the khwando. "Where are Eire and Xiang?"

He ground the heel of his boot into the broken glass instead of answering.

Captain Shafira drew a breath and tried again. "How did you get Eire's weapon?"

"What, this?" He heaved the khwando from palm to palm. "Picked it up on my way through." Then he smiled, and it was a terrible, frightening smile.

Captain Shafira didn't speak.

Bayani stepped out of the engine room. "Stay," he said, then closed the door, and with the sounds of the spoked wheel turning, it locked into place.

Captain Shafira pushed it. It didn't budge.

"So," said Captain Moon, starting up the staircase, "we really are dealing with a Kanekonese siren."

Captain Shafira turned to her. "Tell me there's another way out of here."

"The pipes lead to the ocean; you'd never get back onto the ship by going through them. Other than that door, there's no exit."

Captain Shafira pushed it again. "We have to get out."

Captain Moon's boots clanged loudly on the steps. "I haven't faced a Kanekonese siren before, but I've had some training. We're not going to do anything against the boy's orders, or we're all dead."

"Um," said Lintang.

"We're dead if we reach the siren anyway," Captain Shafira said. "It'll drag this ship under, taking us with it."

Captain Moon reached the balcony. "Why in Patiki's name did you have a boy on board? Even with regular sirens it's dangerous to take a male—"

"This is absolutely not the time to lecture me." Captain Shafira kicked the door. "Just get us out of here."

"Um—" said Lintang again, but Captain Moon cut her off.

"I told you, there isn't another way out."

"What kind of ship doesn't have multiple exits in the engine room?"

"Does *your* ship have multiple exits in the engine room?"

Lintang tried again. "Um—"

"The *Winda* doesn't have an engine room. It's a sailing ship."

"You still have that old thing? Move with the times, Captain Shafira. Sailing ships are for slaves to the elements—"

"EXCUSE ME, POTATO GIRL WOULD LIKE TO SAY SOMETHING."

They all turned to Pelita, who nodded at Lintang. "Go ahead."

Lintang slipped off her boot and said, "I have another Curall, if you're interested?"

The Job Offer

$\mathcal{A}$FTER CAPTAIN MOON UNSHACKLED the dragon, Captain Shafira sprayed the Curall against its nostrils. "Hopefully that'll do it," she said, tossing the vial aside and stepping away. "The sleeping sickness should wear off in a grain or two."

"Oh . . . good . . ." Lintang said, eyeing the dragon's chest as it moved up and down.

"The dragon can break the door, but it'll need a target," Captain Moon said.

Captain Shafira turned for the staircase. "I'll do it."

"No." Captain Moon stopped her. "The dragon knows and despises me. It'll go after me first."

"Wakey, wakey," Pelita said, and they glanced at the dragon to find its eyes blinking open.

Captain Shafira pushed Lintang and Pelita away. "Hide."

The two of them ran to the corner, finding a spot behind some pipes.

"Why do you have children with you?" Captain Moon said as she started across the room.

"Long story," Captain Shafira said. "And don't you dare start lecturing me again!"

The dragon wobbled to its feet. Lintang peeked between pipes, trying to see through the steam. The dragon's front leg gave way and it fell again, hitting the metal floor.

"Poor thing," Lintang whispered.

"I'll go help it," said Pelita, starting forward.

Lintang lunged to grab Pelita's baggy shirt.

The dragon raised its snout, its nostrils flaring as it sniffed the room.

"Hey!" Captain Moon shouted from the balcony. "Remember me?"

The dragon whipped around. Its eyes narrowed to slits. No longer did it look like a stumbling, weak thing. The Curall was doing its job.

Pelita clapped. "Well done, dragon!"

Lintang clamped a hand over Pelita's mouth. Too late. Pelita giggled behind her palm.

"Keep quiet, you two!" Captain Moon said. "Dragon, over here. Over here!"

But the dragon slithered toward Lintang and Pelita, sniffing them out in the steam. Lintang mentally measured the distance between them and the staircase. They might be able to make it, if the dragon was still drowsy.

"Pelita," she said as the dragon picked up its pace, "do you want to play a game?"

"Yay!"

"First one to the staircase wins. Ready?" The dragon had one last pipe to weave around—they could go the other way and steal an extra heartbeat. "Go!"

They sprinted for the staircase. Behind them the dragon roared, its talons scraping the metal deck as it gave chase.

"Run, run, run!" Lintang screamed, but she needn't have. Pelita sped across the room as fast as when she was a pixie.

The dragon's warm breath drenched Lintang's back. She winced, waiting for the pounce, waiting to be knocked to the floor and devoured, but there was a battle cry behind her and a scrabbling sound. She risked a peek over her shoulder.

Captain Shafira had thrown herself at the dragon and sent it off track. It scrambled to right itself as Captain Shafira leaped to her feet and raced after Lintang. "Don't slow down!"

Pelita was already at the foot of the staircase, jumping on the spot. "I won, I won!"

Lintang reached her, but Captain Shafira's arms came around them both, hurling them sideways to the hot floor. Pain zinged up Lintang's wound. A breeze whipped above as the dragon soared overhead. It kept going, heading for Captain Moon.

"That's right," Captain Moon said. "Come and get me!"

It snapped at her head. She ducked, and its snout clanged against the door. It swiped at her. She spun out of the way. Its talons sliced through the bottom of the solid door as easily as a knife through fish flesh. Light from the passageway streamed in.

"That's not good enough," Captain Shafira said. "You need it to destroy the door completely."

Captain Moon grunted, using her sword to keep back the dragon's snapping jaw. Sweat dripped from her face. Her perfect hair had come loose. Her coat now had three large rips across the front. "I'm working on it."

Captain Shafira pulled Lintang and Pelita to their feet. "Are you two all right?"

"This is great!" Pelita said.

Lintang couldn't tear her gaze from the battle. The

dragon slashed at Captain Moon, ripping more holes in the door and just missing her each time.

"That will do," Captain Shafira said as the door finally crumpled. She jogged to the other side of the room, where the dragon had been shackled, and rattled the chains.

The dragon's head jerked up.

Captain Shafira banged the chains against the wall. "Freedom's on the other side. Don't you want to get out of here?"

The dragon spread its wings and launched from the balcony. Its tail just missed Captain Moon on its way down.

Lintang ushered Pelita up the staircase. There was enough space in the door to get into the passageway, but Lintang hesitated, watching the dragon land in front of Captain Shafira. Steam drifted over, blocking them for a moment; then bright light spilled into the room. The dragon had ripped through the wall. Lintang stood on her toes, trying to see around the pipes. There was a moment of shadow as the dragon flew out of the ship. Fresh air billowed in, swirling the steam.

But where was Captain Shafira?

"Come on, what are you waiting for?"

There she was, already halfway across the room. Lintang grinned, relief flooding her. Of course Captain Shafira was all right. She was unkillable.

Captain Moon stooped to pick up the black sword from the balcony. "I'm impressed."

"Back at you," Captain Shafira said, reaching the top of the staircase. She took her sword from Captain Moon and sheathed it. "Come on."

The four of them sprinted down the passageway. "You'll be adrift without a dragon powering the ship," Captain Shafira said. "When we're done I'll send someone to get you."

"That's all right. We can send a message to Kaneko Brown for help."

"Just like our last encounter, eh?"

Captain Moon groaned. "Don't remind me."

They climbed the first set of stairs.

"I know you're good," Captain Moon said, "but what makes you think you're going to win against a Kanekonese siren?"

"We have to. We're the only ones who know the truth about the mythies."

"What truth?" Captain Moon said, but Lintang was no longer paying attention. Horror surged through her.

Captain Shafira was right. If the Kanekonese siren killed them all, no one else would know mythies were human. Innocent people would continue to die.

They started down the next passageway. Spots had appeared before Lintang's eyes, and tiny spears attacked her lungs. Pelita kept up with the captains easily. She was even humming as she ran.

"No," Captain Shafira said to a question Captain Moon had asked while Lintang was busy fighting for breath. "I'm the last one you should be worried about." Impossibly, she picked up her pace. "My crew, on the other hand . . ."

Lintang jolted to a stop.

Captain Shafira only made it a few more steps before she realized Lintang wasn't following, and stopped too. "What are you . . . ?"

"Bayani," Lintang said. She had to wheeze the word. She clutched her aching lungs. "Bayani . . . He's going to die . . . today."

Her heart throbbed, and not from the run. It was already happening. He was under the siren's spell. Even if Captain Shafira won, even if they saved the siren, Bayani wasn't going to make it.

Pelita and Captain Moon waited, chests heaving, faces red.

Captain Shafira didn't move. "I'll do everything I can, but I can't promise I'll be able to save him. I'm sorry."

Lintang slapped a hand over her eyes. Not even the Goddess could help him now.

She heard footsteps, and when she uncovered her eyes, Captain Shafira was standing before her.

"I have come across a lot of horrific things in my travels," Captain Shafira said, "but this is the worst. Bayani—" She broke off. Breathed deep. Tried again. "Bayani is one of the best people I've ever met. It's not fair, what's happening to him. And for him to die under my care . . . I hate it. I hate it so much, I want to find Mratzi and take her on myself."

Lintang curled her hands into fists. "Me too."

Captain Shafira gripped her shoulders. "But we can't." When Lintang opened her mouth to argue, she said firmly, "We *can't*. We don't have the power to stop a mythie like the propheseeds, and I—I'm worried you're going to try something silly to save him. I'm worried you're going to die under my care too."

"But—"

"Promise me," Captain Shafira said. "Promise me you won't risk your life to save him."

Lintang had to grit her teeth against more tears. She couldn't promise that, not even to the Goddess.

Captain Shafira smiled, but it was a sad smile. "Lintang. You're brave, and loyal, and imaginative, and everything I look for in a shipmate. I want you to be a crew member of the *Winda*, and you can't do that if you're dead."

Lintang's breath stuck in her chest. "Y–you want me?"

"I do. I promised your mother to return you to Desa, and I will. But I never said anything about not taking you away again."

A traitorous tear slipped down Lintang's cheek. "Really?"

"Really," Captain Shafira said. Her expression turned grim. "But if you want to be invited onto my ship, it means not giving up your life to save Bayani. It means letting today play out how it's supposed to."

"You mean letting him die."

"If that's what the prophecy means, then yes," Captain Shafira said. "You need to let Bayani die."

Mythie Guidebook Information Page: Origins

～～～～～～～～

Documented reports around the world speak of shooting stars that appeared before the Infestation, which marked the end of the Chihin period and the beginning of the Bauei period. The shooting stars are widely understood to be the arrival of the new creatures to our world, in the form of what we commonly call "mythies." These creatures have been part of our myths and legends since the beginning of humanity, and there is speculation over whether the Gods were inspired by our creations or whether we foresaw the introduction of the mythies throughout our various cultures.

One question we must ask is why? Why would the Three Gods send predatory, parasitic beasts to our world in such a violent fashion? Why do the mythical creatures seem to focus so much on humans, both as prey and as hosts to their young (see section on reproduction)?

Mythie hunters and scholars of mythology agree that the introduction of these aggressive species seems to be a threat by the Gods toward humanity. One governor of the United Regions went on record to say he believed the mythies were sent to this world specifically to wipe out humans for good.

While this may be an alarming theory, other experts won't go as far as that. Everyone concurs, however, that the Three Gods — Niti, Patiki, and Mratzi — have a lot to answer for.

Sacrifice

THEY MADE A DETOUR to the *Glory*'s medic's office. Eire and Xiang weren't there.

"Did you have crew stationed here?" Captain Moon said as Captain Shafira stopped at the doorway.

Captain Shafira didn't answer.

"No bodies is good," Captain Moon said. "No bodies means he didn't kill them."

Captain Shafira scanned the room. Lintang peeked in too. The place had already been ransacked during their earlier search for Curall, with cupboards broken, drawers open, and boxes strewn about. There was no blood, at least.

"Maybe they've gone back to your ship," Captain Moon said.

Captain Shafira still didn't speak.

Lintang touched her arm. Every grain of sand that

fell through the hourglass was time away from Bayani. "Captain? We need to get to the *Winda*."

Captain Shafira jerked at the touch. "Right," she said, the silence leaving her. "Let's go. If Bayani's cut the tethering ropes, we'll have to figure out another way aboard."

They climbed to the top deck, into the wind and sun. There was less steam than before. The ship no longer had anything powering it.

Captain Moon's crew were untied and standing at attention around the perimeter of the deck. They were staring toward the stern but turned when Captain Moon marched forward. There was a *shiiing* of swords as they saw Captain Shafira.

"Arms away," Captain Moon said. "First mate, report."

A woman stepped forward as the others reluctantly returned their swords to their sheaths. "A spellbound male has boarded the pirate ship. He instructed us to remain here, and as per K-S Protocol One we followed his orders. Our dragon escaped shortly after and headed east."

"And the *Winda*'s crew?" Captain Moon said.

"The invading crew returned to their own ship with the spellbound male and a second, unconscious male."

Captain Shafira advanced. The crew braced themselves but didn't draw their weapons again. "Does that include the Vierzan and Phaizen women?"

The first mate glanced at Captain Moon before answering. "My attention was on the boy and the dragon. I wasn't taking note of—"

"Never mind." Captain Shafira turned to the *Winda*. It was still against the *Glory*, sails raised, bobbing gently. "I'll find them myself."

Lintang and Pelita followed her to the plank joining the ships.

"Why has he left everything?" Lintang said. "Why hasn't he set sail?"

Her third question remained unasked: *Is he already dead?*

But no—when she looked across she saw Bayani standing on the bridge with the spear side of the khwando pointed at Zazi's neck. The rest of the deck was empty. The only movement was the flapping of Zazi's sarong.

"Wait." Captain Moon hurried up to them. "We should have a plan of attack. I could—"

"The best thing you can do is medicate the siren if you see it," Captain Shafira said.

"Medicate," Captain Moon said. "You want us to . . . medicate the siren."

"Right. You'll see."

"But what about the dragon?" Lintang said. "It's flown away."

"It'll be back," Captain Shafira said grimly. "Dragons can never resist a siren."

She used her sword to cut the tethering ropes, and shuffling down the plank toward the *Winda,* they left Captain Moon behind. Pelita hummed to herself. The two ships knocked against each other, then separated. Lintang almost lost her balance as the plank wobbled. Captain Shafira reached out to catch her. Overhead, the lightning bird shrieked, its shadow passing over Lintang.

"We're coming across, Bayani," Captain Shafira said when they were close to the *Winda.* "Don't hurt Zazi. We aren't here to stop you from getting to the siren."

"By all means, join us," Bayani said. "I don't expect you'll stop me, considering the siren's heading here instead. I can feel it."

Captain Shafira reached the railing and helped Lintang and Pelita onto the deck.

"Where are the others?" she said when they were safely aboard.

Bayani laughed. "In the mess."

"All of them?"

He smiled that frightening smile. "Pelita," he said, "why don't you collect everyone?"

Lintang wanted to stop her, but Captain Shafira shook her head. Pelita skipped down the hatch.

"What if it's a trap?" Lintang whispered.

"Then it's too late anyway. Just don't move. Don't do anything sudden. He'll kill Zazi if he thinks we're trying to stop him."

Fear crept into Lintang's throat, stealing her voice. She nodded instead of answering.

It was hard to believe that Bayani, quiet, kind Bayani, was the person they were so afraid of.

The plank of wood joining the two ships toppled into the water. The *Glory* drifted away. Captain Moon stood on her deck, watching them. The steam had almost cleared completely.

Lintang drew a breath of salty air. "How are you feeling, Bayani?"

"Amazing." He fixed his gaze on the ocean. "The siren's almost here."

"I'm back!" Pelita ran up the steps, brandishing Lintang's wooden sword.

Lintang gasped and turned to Bayani, but he only smirked at the weapon and watched the others climb up.

First came Dee clutching Farah the clamshell, then Mei, Quahah, Yamini, Eire . . .

At last Hewan stumped up, helping Xiang, whose arm was in a splint. Captain Shafira's breath rushed from her lungs as if she hadn't exhaled since finding the medic's office empty.

"Sorry, Captain," Xiang said when she reached the top. "He caught my dart in *midair.*"

Captain Shafira's lips quirked. "You're alive. I forgive you. Where's Avalon?"

"I've tied him up, but he's still unconscious," Dee said, running an anxious hand over her bald head. "Twip's with him, so he's not alone."

Captain Shafira surveyed her crew. "They're alive," she said under her breath. "All of them. That's unexpected." Her attention fell to Bayani. "He's showing restraint."

"Is that a good thing?" Lintang said.

"Under the spell of a Kanekonese siren, it's supposed to be impossible. Xiang tried to stop him, and he didn't kill her."

Pelita skipped between crew members, passing Lintang the wooden sword on her way. She was the only one who dared to move.

"This is nice, Dee," Farah the clamshell said. "We so rarely take breaks to enjoy the sun."

"Are you all right, Zazi?" Quahah said.

Zazi's gaze fell to the spear point at her neck. "I've had better days."

"What are we doing out here?" Xiang said.

Bayani laughed. *"Enjoying the sun."*

The ship lurched starboard. Everyone staggered. Lintang fell hard against the railing, almost losing her grip on her sword. She stared into the water. It glowed bluish green, brighter than Nyasamdra. Something was down there. Something big, almost as big as Nyasamdra, and shaped like a long-haired human.

"Here, Captain!"

Xiang gestured to seaweedy tendrils tugging at the railing.

Fingers. They were the siren's *fingers.*

"Where are the dragon talon harpoons?" Captain Shafira said.

Xiang smashed at the fingers with her good fist. "Bayani threw them overboard."

Everyone else scrambled to hold on as the ship continued to tilt. The *Winda* was almost horizontal at this stage. The wall was now a floor. Pelita scampered along it, laughing. Eire's khwando rolled down the slope of the deck, and Eire raced to catch it before it fell in the water.

Captain Shafira pried at the siren's fingers. They wouldn't budge. "Xiang, tell me you have your darts."

Xiang dug into the pouch around her neck. "They won't penetrate the skin."

"It's worth a try."

"Help me with my blowpipe—I can't do it with one hand."

While Captain Shafira undid Xiang's bun, Lintang searched for Bayani. He was crouched on the railing of the bridge, staring at the glowing water. It looked as though he was about to jump in.

Zazi had escaped in the chaos and was carefully sliding down the steps away from him.

"Bayani!" Lintang cried.

Either he didn't hear, or he was ignoring her.

She ran along the sideways wall, squeezing past the others as they tried to climb higher. Ropes had fallen free from the masts, giving them something to hold on to.

Mei helped Hewan, and Quahah had Pelita by the wrist to haul her up. Captain Shafira didn't stop Lintang —she was too busy helping Xiang. Eire hacked at the glowing fingers with the axe of her khwando.

Lintang had almost reached the point directly below the bridge when someone yanked her back.

"What are you doing?" Yamini said. "Leave him alone. He'll kill us all!"

"He's my best friend," Lintang said.

"Not right now he isn't."

"Yes, he is!"

"You think you're some invincible hero, but you're not. You're way out of your depth. Let it go, or you'll end up dead."

Bayani moved to throw himself at the siren.

"No!" Lintang said. "Bayani, don't jump!"

His gaze snapped to her. "Why? Are you going to stop me?"

"Lintang, don't—"

"Yes!" Lintang yelled.

Yamini let out a low moan. "He's going to kill you," she said. "You're on your own." Then she turned and ran.

Bayani jumped down, landing between Lintang and the other crew members. Shadows continued to flicker across his face.

She raised her sword and backed away. He strode forward, keeping a short distance between them.

"Don't do this," she said, but they were just words,

useless words falling from her mouth, her brain too numb with fright to come up with anything worthwhile. How could she stop this? How could she save him?

She gripped her sword so hard her hands ached. "Fight it." More useless words. "Come on, Bayani. You're strong."

"Yes," he said. "I am. Finally." He wrenched the wooden blade out of her hand and snapped it in half. She gasped as he tossed it overboard. The two pieces bobbed on the waves.

"This isn't some festival dance," he said, and she recognized the words she'd said to him in the classroom in Desa.

He advanced. She stumbled away. She felt exposed, off balance without anything to protect her. He had bent the cage bars with his bare hands. She wasn't going to win this fight.

The railing started to curve upward. It was too steep —every time she stepped back, she slid forward again. Toward him.

He stopped before her.

"The siren wants me to kill you," he said quietly. "And I can. I broke Xiang's arm without any trouble. I can snap your neck before you even feel my hands at your throat."

Lintang barely heard him over her pulse roaring in her ears. He took one last step toward her. She flinched, raising her arms in a useless attempt to shield herself.

He stopped.

She waited. He didn't move again. His fists bunched at his sides. His whole body shook.

Slowly, she lowered her arms. "Are you . . . fighting the siren's spell?"

A choke fell from his lips. Sweat from effort sheened on his face. The shadows across his features retreated. Still, he didn't move.

Lintang's jaw dropped. "How are you doing that?"

"Lin . . . tang . . ." He couldn't seem to unclench his teeth to speak. "I'm going to jump. Don't . . . don't come after me."

It was Bayani again, *her* Bayani. She reached for him.

"Don't!" He wrenched from her touch, the shadows swarming once again, and with what might've been the last traces of his willpower, he turned and threw himself into the water.

A shriek escaped her. He was already submerged. He was sinking. No—swimming. He was swimming down toward the siren.

She cried for help. No one noticed—Captain Shafira, Eire, and Xiang were still straining to break the siren's grip, and Yamini and the other crew had made it farther up the deck.

She stared at the bubbles between the glow. Bayani had gone.

No.

No.

She leaned back against the deck, gasping.

Nothing could stop the prophecy.

Bayani had told her not to go after him.

Captain Shafira had offered her a place on the Winda.

She kicked off her boots and stepped onto the sideways railing. Her dream life was in her grasp, and she was going to give it up for a prophecy that couldn't be broken. She must have been as crazy as Pelita.

She drew a deep breath.

And dived.

Transformation

THE SEA WRAPPED AROUND HER like a blanket. Bubbles rushed past her skin. The siren glowed in the water, its hair drifting around its face, hypnotic to watch. Its hands pulled at the *Winda*, but a tendril of its hair clung to Bayani, pinning his arms to his sides. He struggled, so at least he was alive. For now.

The water will call for you,
And the harvester will come.

The chant was caught in her head like a flutterbee in a net.

Bayani, Bayani, Bayani.

A mess of bubbles escaped his mouth. His face was screwed up in pain.

She kicked harder. She would break every rule in the world if it meant she could save him.

But then a hot light burst through her chest. She jerked to a stop. Something was happening. Something bad.

Or was it good?

She felt full, somehow. As though she had been carrying a bucket inside her all this time, and it had only just overflowed.

Gold caught her eye. She held up her hands. They were glowing.

The heat in her chest increased until it was scorching. She was barely able to keep the scream at bay.

Her head slumped back and she stared at the surface, at the sunlight and the blue sky —

And the stars. She could see the stars.

Shooting stars.

They crashed into Ytzuam, through a field of unplanted seeds. The curtain between the two worlds billowed, and the impact of the shooting stars scattered seeds throughout her world.

She thrashed, trying to contain the pain, trying to work out what she was seeing. She was having a vision, but who — or what — was showing it to her?

She saw a man unwittingly absorb one of the star seeds; then he burst apart as a gnome sprang from him.

Another human killed the gnome, absorbing the

star, and that man became a selkie, smooth and gray as it glided through the water.

Then another human, into a Caletromian mermaid . . .

One of the Caletromian mermaids who had died in her presence. The same Caletromian mermaid whose infection she now carried.

The scorching feeling spread into her arms and legs and *no*, it wasn't an infection. It was life.

Life.

The mythies weren't a sickness. They were creation. She held within her an extra star, which filled her with life until it overflowed and turned her into a creature from her own stories.

She curled into a ball as the scorch grew unbearable. She could feel the mythie inside her, coiling, ferocious, powerful.

Monstrous.

The Mythie Guidebook Entry #68:
Lanme Vanyan

∞∞∞∞∞∞∞

Lanme Vanyan is a sea and sky mythie in the predator category. She is a combination of humanoid, serpentine, and avian, with a snakelike tail and fangs and the wings of a talross. There has yet to be a confirmed sighting of her.

Diet: Unknown.

Habitat: Usually oceanic, although it is said she occasionally ventures to land.

Frequency: Single entity.

Behavior: This mythie will fight any challenger. A show of strength is all it takes for Lanme Vanyan to attack.

Eradication: Unknown.

Did you know? According to stories collected all over the world, every legendary warrior who has gone up against Lanme Vanyan has been ruthlessly slaughtered.

Danger level: 6

Mother of Monsters

LANME VANYAN SNARLED. A glowing siren floated before her. The siren was her enemy.

Everything was her enemy.

Lanme was the mother of monsters, the warrior queen. The creature in front of her must be destroyed.

Her dark hair drifted around her face. Her tail uncurled as she prepared to move. She would fight this siren to the death.

A shadow amid the glow caught her attention. A human boy floated within the siren's tendril-like hair. He wasn't moving. She paused, watching his body drift toward the surface.

Save him.

She didn't know where the voice had come from. She hesitated, torn between the desire to obey the voice and the desire to rip the human to shreds, but something throbbed through her—panic or something else, she didn't know—so she streaked down. She sliced through the siren's hair as if it were nothing but jellyfish tentacles and wrapped her arms around the boy. He was small and light in her grip. With a flick of her tail she sped to the surface, bursting out to find herself face-to-face with the underside of a capsized ship.

Her wings unfolded, shaking water from their feathers and lifting her higher into the air. The boy shuddered and coughed in her arms. He vomited water as she carried him over the side of the ship. A sail had fallen from its place and tangled into a sling. It was a safe place for him.

She took great care placing the boy in the sail. He sat up, wheezing. "Lintang. Lintang!"

She didn't know that word. She left him and flew over the deck of the ship to deal with the siren.

"LANME VANYAN!"

The scream came from below. She stopped midflight and spun to find a scattering of humans along the sideways deck.

"Where in the name of Mratzi did that thing come from? Eire, go! Mei, help her. Xiang and I will deal with the siren."

Lanme searched for the owner of the voice. It had

sparked something in her, a recognition, a warm feeling. She knew she liked this human, the way she'd known to save the boy.

A different human scrambled across the rigging toward her, like a spider on a web. Lanme curled her tail, preparing to attack.

"Mei, wait!" Another voice, this one harsh. The owner had a weapon with an axe and spear on either end. She hauled herself up to the rigging, a vicious smile on her face and a string of fangs around her neck. It must have been the human called Eire.

The human Mei paused. Lanme flicked out her forked tongue. Mei smelled of fear. It would be a simple kill.

The boy above tried to croak something to them— *Wait, it's Lintang*—but his lungs were still recovering, and their human ears were weak.

They would not stop. Nor would she.

She lunged for Eire, but Mei leaped, snagging a loose rope. Mei soared around Lanme and the rope caught on Lanme's throat. Lanme jerked back.

Eire pounced, raising her axe. She sailed through the air while Lanme was still trapped, and for a heartbeat it looked as if Eire might succeed where so many others had failed: she might defeat the mother of monsters.

But then, with a shriek, an elegant black bird soared between them. Eire shouted as the bird passed in a flurry of feathers. The axe flew from Eire's hand, missing Lanme's head by a breath, and splintered the deck behind them.

Lanme wrenched the rope off her neck. A bird had saved her life. Unacceptable.

"Stupid creature!" Eire cried to the bird as it flew away. "What are you doing?"

Lanme snarled. Mei scrambled up the rigging, away from her. Eire did the opposite. She released a powerful cry and sprang forward. Lanme slashed at her, but Eire used a broken rope from the rigging to swing away from the attack and snatch her weapon back. She whirled and jabbed the spear end at Lanme. Lanme barely dodged it. Again and again Eire came for her, knocking away any counterattacks, using the rigging to swing and duck and block. Lanme bared her fangs and flew higher, out of reach. She had no interest in games. She would deal with the human after she'd destroyed the siren.

She scanned the water. There was another ship nearby, this one made of steel. The blue-uniformed humans had a large crossbow out, loaded with a dragon talon harpoon. With a snap, the harpoon pierced the siren's hand. A flurry of bubbles raced to the surface as it screamed beneath the water.

Fools. Did they think they would kill the siren with a simple harpoon? Lanme would sink both ships and destroy the siren. Enemies, all of them.

The siren released the wooden ship, the movement so violent it rocked the hull. Eire and Mei clung to the rigging as the other humans slid across the deck. The ship tilted upright slowly, slowly, until it was sitting on the water as it was meant to.

The boy cried out. Lanme whipped around to find him toppling from the tangled sail. She sped to catch him before he hit the water again. He thudded into her arms with an *oof*.

"It's got Bayani!" Mei scrambled down the rigging. "Captain, we need more weapons, we need—"

"I've got it!" Eire raised her axe.

"No!"

There was that voice again. The voice that made Lanme warm.

The owner was a woman with hair like ropes. She stood at the railing, staring at Lanme. Her gaze was on the boy tucked safely in Lanme's hold, but it slid to Lanme's arm. Lanme looked down too. Her skin had a streak through it, as though she had been wounded. She bristled. Who had dared injure her?

"It's Lintang!" The human sounded wild. Almost . . . frightened? "Hold your weapon, Eire, don't attack, it's Lintang!" She ran across the deck toward Lanme. "I should've known. Lintang, I'm sorry, come here, we'll medicate you—"

Lanme beat her wings and lifted into the air, curling her tail in coils. The sun warmed her back as she cast a shadow across the deck and the rope-haired woman.

The woman slowed. "Xiang!"

Another human with a strapped arm put a pipe in her mouth and blew.

Lanme jerked as something pierced her abdomen. The boy in her arms gasped. She kept a tight hold of him and swooped for her attacker.

"No!" The rope-haired woman jumped in front of Xiang and raised her sword. "We were curing you. It's going to be fine, Lintang."

Lanme growled at them. The boy wriggled from her arms and stumbled onto the ship. "What about the siren?" he said. "I can't feel its spell—"

The rope-haired human kept her sword trained on Lanme in a defiant display of aggression. Had Lanme not already decided she liked the woman, she would have ripped her to pieces.

"Captain Moon hit it with a dragon talon dipped in Curall," the woman said. "Injecting the stuff should mean it'll work quicker."

"I hope so," said Xiang, eyeing Lanme.

Lanme didn't want to deal with these humans any longer. She liked the boy, and she liked the rope-haired woman. They were not her enemies.

A shadow passed overhead. A dragon swooped toward the ship.

Lanme bared her teeth in a sneer. The humans might not have made good opponents, but a dragon certainly would.

Battle of Three

T HE DRAGON ROARED, rearing into the sky. Its long neck curved as it prepared to unleash its fire.

Lanme's insides burned. She was the champion of monsters. No creature should dare challenge her.

She sprang, clamping her hands on the dragon's shoulders. It tried to toss her aside, but she held on and slashed at its wings. They twisted in the air like a whirlwind. The dragon snorted flames in her face. It was nothing but a warm breeze, but it was a threat, and she didn't tolerate threats. She moved to sink her fangs into its neck.

"Lintang! Lintang, please don't kill it!"

She hesitated. The boy was calling her.

They were in the schoolroom, both of them barely six years old, heat rising from the earthen floor—they sat together, an insect chirruping nearby, her arm against his warm back as they drew crooked Vierzan letters on slates—she leaned over his shoulder to copy his work and he smelled of straw from the gaya farm—

She shook off the vision and used the momentum of her tail to fling the dragon away. It flew through the sky, past the metal ship and off into the distance. Her heart pounded rapidly as she recovered from the strange images. They had provoked things in her. Tender, delicate emotions that would not do for a warrior.

She needed to fight. Fortunately, there was still a challenger waiting below. She folded her wings and dropped into the ocean. The silky water embraced her.

The siren was trying to take hold of the ship again. Its long, glowing arms reached for the hull as its hair wafted around its face.

Lanme zipped toward it and bit it beneath the arm. The siren yanked back, its face twisting into a snarl. It turned, its movements slow in the deep ocean, and reached for her instead. Lanme weaved easily out of its grasp.

It swatted hard at the water, causing a change of currents that spun her momentarily away. Sea debris and streams of sunlight whirled past her eyes.

While she was regaining her bearings, the siren

reached for the ship again. Lanme reoriented herself with a sudden lurch of perplexing panic.

Not the Winda.

She sped toward the siren. With a flick, she wrapped her tail around the siren's wrist and yanked it down. The siren tried to crush her with its free hand. She bit its fingers. Bubbles hissed from its mouth, but it didn't pull back. Instead, it pushed Lanme down, down against its arm as if it were going to squash her like a fly.

She strained the muscles in her tail to push back. One of her coils unwrapped from its wrist. Then another. And another. Soon she was free, and she slipped away just before being flattened.

A shadow rippled over them. The dragon had returned. Shouts echoed from the ship, dulled by the water, but enough to compel her to react. The crew needed her.

She dodged another swipe from the siren and spiraled up. The siren's hand followed her out of the water. While the hand was still exposed, the dragon veered around and breathed fire onto it.

The siren ducked back into the water. One challenger subdued, for now.

The dragon swooped toward Lanme. She sped to

meet it. This time when they collided, she had less strength and dropped toward the water.

Impossible. She was Lanme Vanyan, the most ferocious creature to exist in this world. She could not be defeated, certainly not by a mere dragon.

And yet she had trouble holding her position. Her tail sank into the ocean.

What was happening?

"Lintang, hold on! You're about to turn back, but the dragon should too. Just keep going a little longer."

The voice ignited another onslaught of images—

She stood alone in the mess after dinner, knife in hand, determined to hit the motionless rouls board, but the knife flew too far to the side—Captain Shafira emerged from the doorway, offering to show her how to aim, her braids smelling of unknown blossoms, her laugh like sunshine on water—

She pushed the vision away and strained to keep the dragon from shoving her deeper into the water.

She was losing. It was too strong. Why, why, why?

She put her head down and pushed as hard as she could. Her wings beat frantically.

The dragon snapped at her. She flinched. This time she could feel the heat from its jaws properly. It seemed to realize this and opened its mouth to roar at her.

A familiar screech echoed across the sky. In a brilliant

flash, the black bird from before plummeted toward them. The dragon snapped at it. The bird weaved away, then came back to keep the dragon's attention from Lanme.

But the dragon hadn't forgotten to push her down. She was still sinking.

And she was glowing.

"Yay, Lintang!"

A little girl burst from the body of a pixie—

"Who are you?" "P-Pelita."

"The mythies are humans."

She *was* human.

Her entire tail was submerged now. The crew of the *Winda* shouted, but their words were a buzz.

She sank to her belly. Her wings drooped. The dragon kept pushing her down, even as it snapped at the lightning bird. Every time the dragon flapped its wings, it forced her a notch lower. She gasped, straining to hold on.

"Lintang!" Captain Shafira's voice pierced the haze. "Your captain is giving you an order. Win. Do you hear me? *Win!*"

Lanme screamed into the dragon's face and pushed with more strength than she knew she had. With one final shove, she let go and flipped back into the ocean. She whipped her tail into the air, wrapped it around the dragon, and slammed it onto the waves. The dragon shuddered with the impact, then floated, stunned.

Her tail uncurled just as there was an explosion of pain in her chest, as if someone had shoved a hot steel rod through her. She burst to the surface and screamed and screamed. Salt water splashed into her mouth. Her tiny, human mouth.

She was Lintang again.

People on the *Winda* called her name.

"Bayani!" she cried. "Captain Shafira! I'm here! I'm—"

Something wrapped around her waist. A glowing strand of the siren's hair.

Lintang didn't even get a chance to cry out again. The siren yanked her underwater. She went down, down, down.

This wasn't like the time with the Caletromian mermaids. This was fast and violent and terrifying. The water became so cold it burned. The blue sky got farther away, until it disappeared altogether, and still she went down.

She opened her mouth in a silent scream as a brilliant white light scorched her eyes and something sharp gripped her arm; then the white and the cold and the terror disappeared into nothing.

• • •

A familiar larder, lit by a flaming wooden torch. Lintang, almost five, stood before it with her mouth open. She had never been allowed to look in the larder before.

"There are many rules about storing food, Lintang." Mother put a hand on her shoulder. "One day you'll need to know that everything belongs in a certain place, just like the people of the village."

Lintang wandered in and peered into a large pot filled with grains. She looked at the hanging meat, and smelled the dried herbs, and felt the soft flour.

"There's a lot of things in here, Mummy. I don't think I can remember it all."

Mother laughed. "I know you will. Do you know why?"

"No. Why?"

Mother leaned down, her belly full with Lintang's new brother or sister, and placed her hands on either side of Lintang's face. Her gray-green eyes shone with promise. "Because you're clever, and capable, and my little girl. My most precious thing."

My most precious thing.

My most precious thing.

Home

FOR THE SECOND TIME in her life, Lintang opened her eyes to find herself in the captain's cabin. This time, Captain Shafira was already there.

"Finally." Captain Shafira got off her chair and sat on the end of the bed.

Lintang blinked at the morning sun streaming through the window. "What . . . ?"

"You're safe now. And hopefully well rested—you slept an entire day and night."

Lintang moved to shield her eyes from the brightness, but a sharp stinging stopped her. In addition to the bandages on her arm from her earlier stitches, there were now heavy bindings around her shoulder.

"The price of being rescued," Captain Shafira said.

A chill drenched Lintang's insides. It all came back to her: the dragon, the siren, the deep, deep ocean—

"Who could possibly have dragged me back to the surface from so far down?"

Captain Shafira's lips twitched. "I wonder whether you'd believe me."

The rest of the day came back to Lintang, and she cried out. "The mythies! It's not an infection—it's a star. A second seed from Ytzuam. The stars are jumping from person to person each time a mythie dies—"

"I know."

Lintang cut off. "You know? How could you know?"

"Bayani told me."

Someone knocked on the door, and Bayani poked his head in. "Is she—? Oh. Awake. Hello."

Lintang propped herself up on her non-sore arm and stared at him. He was here.

Alive.

"Bayani?"

Pelita peeked in from behind him. "I'm here too!"

Lintang glanced at Captain Shafira. "You said I slept all night. Does that mean . . . ?"

"That Niti's festival is over? Why, yes, it does."

"But . . . but . . . how?"

"Good question," Captain Shafira said. "Come in, you two, and close the door."

Bayani and Pelita did as they were told and moved

closer to the bed. Pelita skipped right up to Lintang and kissed her on the cheek, but Bayani hovered by the desk, looking uncertain.

Lintang sat up. She was wrapped in her golden sarong from Desa. A vague memory captured her, of her pretty velvet dress tearing as Lanme Vanyan burst from her body.

She stared at Bayani. "The propheseeds . . . they said you would die."

"No, they said the harvester would come, not that she would take me."

"So you saw her?"

He hesitated. "She was there, yes."

"What happened?"

"I—I asked her to let me live, and she said I could."

Lintang's eyes widened. "You convinced the Goddess of Death to let you live? How did you do that?"

"I don't know." He didn't look at her. "I just asked."

Lintang and Captain Shafira shared a glance. Lintang had the feeling they were thinking the same thing.

"Almost everyone must ask Mratzi for more time," she said. "Why are you getting such special treatment?"

"Maybe it was because you saved me in time." A grin tugged at his lips. "Even as Lanme Vanyan, you were a hero."

"You mean I was dangerous," Lintang said, her stomach growing cold again. "Is everyone else safe? Xiang, Mei, Eire—they all fought me . . ."

"They'll be fine," Captain Shafira said.

Lintang fingered the blanket, remembering her battle with the first mate. "Eire almost beat me."

"When it comes to fighting beasts, Eire's the best," Captain Shafira said. "That's why we need her."

"You don't need her anymore. You can just cure mythies now."

"No, Lintang. I stand by my agreement with her." At Lintang's groan, Captain Shafira added, "I live in a world where most people think I'm a criminal and a liar. My promises are the only thing I have. I respect Eire as my first mate, and so should you."

Obviously Captain Shafira didn't know how Eire treated Avalon.

Wait—*Avalon*.

Lintang gasped. "Is Avalon all right?"

"He'll be okay," Captain Shafira said. "He's suffering from a headache, but he'll heal."

Lintang sagged, the surge of panic ebbing from her body. "Thank the Gods." To think he'd given the others permission to kill him if he got too dangerous! She was going to have to have a word with that boy later.

"And what about Captain Moon?" she said.

"She's sent a message to Kaneko Brown for help. Someone will be picking her up soon. She's promised to explain everything to the governors when she returns to Zaiben."

Pelita danced over to the desk and pawed through one of the jars of gems. Bayani watched her warily.

"Did you manage to save the dragon and the siren?" Lintang said.

"Yes, thanks to you. The *Glory*'s medic is taking care of them."

Lintang stared out the window at the endless ocean. "So . . . where are *we* going?"

"Back to the Twin Islands. I have to return you to your family." Captain Shafira frowned at Lintang's bandages. "Your mother will be furious with me for not bringing you back in one piece."

Lintang drew an unsteady breath. She had disobeyed Captain Shafira's orders by diving in after Bayani. Did this mean she was no longer invited to be a crew member?

"Are you all right?" Bayani said.

Lintang didn't know how to answer. She had turned into Lanme Vanyan, faced a Kanekonese siren, fought a dragon, almost drowned twice, battled a sea serpent, worked as a cabin girl . . . and yet even after all that, the thought of leaving the *Winda* forever was impossible to bear.

Captain Shafira glanced at Bayani and Pelita. "Give us a grain. I need to speak to Lintang alone. And tell Yamini to bring up some food and water."

"Stay close," Lintang said as Bayani opened the door.

Pelita grinned over her shoulder. "We're on a ship. We can't go very far." Then she twirled out onto the deck, humming.

Bayani smiled at Lintang and closed the door behind them.

"He's still hiding something from us," Captain Shafira said, voice low. "How many secrets does that boy have?"

"Enough to fill the sky," Lintang muttered. She didn't care about Bayani's secrets right now. She wanted to know what her punishment was.

Captain Shafira must've figured out what Lintang was thinking, because she returned to her chair and said, "I meant what I told you before. I want you to be a crew member."

Lintang glanced up. "Really?"

"You think I didn't notice what you did yesterday? You were everything I could have hoped for and more."

"But I disobeyed your orders. *Again.* I jumped in after Bayani. And on the *Glory* you said—"

"I know what I said." Captain Shafira leaned forward, with her elbows on her knees. "My instructions were 'Don't give up your life to save him.' And you didn't. You let the day play out how it was supposed to. You were brave, and loyal, and selfless." She shrugged. "How could I not offer you a place here?"

Lintang's insides shone as bright as merry lights. She couldn't keep from smiling.

"So the plan is to return you to Desa, pick up my necklace, and repair the ship, and then we can go again. Sound good?"

Lintang hesitated. Captain Shafira noticed at once.

"What's the matter?"

"When you say *go* . . ."

Hollowness swallowed the rest of her sentence. She would see Desa for one fleeting breath, and then . . . was that it? Would Captain Shafira take her away forever?

She had dreamed of her mother while sleeping. It had left an ache in her, that same empty feeling as before, and this time it hadn't quite gone away. She wasn't sure she'd be able to leave home without knowing if she'd ever see her family again.

Captain Shafira studied her thoughtfully. "How about you spend some time in Desa before I take you away? I'll come back on Patiki's festival—that will give you over half a season with your family."

"So you'll go without me?" Panic clawed at Lintang's chest. She didn't want to leave her family behind, but she didn't want to miss out on traveling with Captain Shafira either. It was like being torn between two homes. "You'll definitely come back, won't you?"

"I promise," Captain Shafira said.

Lintang squeezed the blanket. A promise from Captain Shafira was as good as a promise from the Gods.

She breathed deep. All these conflicting emotions were making her insides jittery.

"What about Governor Karnezis?" she said. "Will he try to find me?"

"I doubt it. He won't bother looking for you when he could be sending ships after the *Winda*."

Lintang released the blanket. "I think he wants your Zulttania's council to stay in power. He said they've agreed to trade on an island in the Biabi Sea. He wants them to join the UR."

Captain Shafira nodded. It was some time before she said, "I'm going to have to go back to Allay. I have to tell my people the truth."

Allay. The forbidden island. Lintang had never in her

wildest fantasies imagined she'd have the opportunity to see it.

"Can I come?"

Captain Shafira smiled. "I wouldn't dream of going without you." She leaned over and dug something from beneath the desk. "By the way, I fished this out for you. I don't suppose it's any good now, but all the same . . ."

She dropped two pieces of wood on Lintang's lap —the remains of Lintang's sword.

Lintang picked up the hilt and snapped blade to inspect them under the sunlight. They looked like nothing but a broken child's toy.

The thought made her eyes prickle.

"You were pretty good with that thing," Captain Shafira said. "Xiang was impressed. She wants to teach you with real swords next time you're on board."

Lintang tore her gaze away from the three carved moons on the hilt to stare at her. "Really?"

"Absolutely." Captain Shafira kicked her boot up on the frame of the bed and rolled one of her braids between her fingertips. "You belong on the *Winda*, Lintang. Know how I know?"

Lintang stroked the warped wood of her sword. She *belonged* here. She liked the sound of that. "How?"

"When the siren pulled you under, the lightning bird dragged you all the way to the surface again."

"Keelee saved me?"

"Sure did. The lightning bird is your protector now too."

Lintang hesitated. "But . . . it's a mythie. Aren't you going to medicate it?"

An odd expression crossed Captain Shafira's face, although it was gone too quickly to read.

"Xiang tried to hit it with a dart dipped in Curall. She's got excellent aim, but it dodged every attempt. It seems it would rather protect us than turn human."

Yamini knocked on the door with a platter of food and a flagon of water, halting their conversation. She placed the things on the desk, then stalked out, all but slamming the door behind her.

Lintang picked at a bowl of unfamiliar berries that must've come from Vierz. Despite Yamini's attitude now, she'd tried to stop Lintang from going to Bayani while he was under the siren's spell. Did that mean Yamini actually cared about her? Or had she done it for some other purpose?

"I can't work out whether Yamini likes me or hates me," Lintang said at last.

Captain Shafira unscrewed the cap from the flagon. "It's complicated. She is upset because I forgave you, while she'll never be anything other than a cabin girl."

The first berry was sour; the next was sweet. The two tastes tingled on Lintang's tongue as a strange feeling of sympathy washed through her. Having Captain Shafira's disapproval, with no chance of redemption, would've been awful.

"You won't forgive her?" she said.

"She was offered gems to betray me, just like you were. But she took the offer."

Lintang stopped midchew, her sympathy for Yamini disappearing.

Yamini had *betrayed* Captain Shafira?

"She grew up differently than you," Captain Shafira said, seeing Lintang's expression. "She lived on the streets of Zaiben, forced to steal to eat. Gems mean more to her than they do to you."

"How could you let her back on the ship?" Lintang cried. "How do you know she won't turn on you again?"

"When she realized what she'd done, she was very sorry. She begged to come back, even if she had to spend the rest of her life as a cabin girl. I relented." Captain Shafira sighed. "I think she expects I'll give her a pardon one day, and she'll be allowed to be a proper crew member again. That wasn't the agreement. I'll have to talk to her."

Lintang scowled. To think she'd actually started to feel sorry for Yamini.

"Eat," Captain Shafira said, standing. "I have to check on things. You can come out when you've finished."

She left, and Lintang gulped down her food, barely tasting it. She set the plate on the desk, downed the flagon of water, and hurried out of the room, clutching her broken sword pieces. The salty air was fresh against her skin. It reminded her how much she loved being here, even if she had to live with a traitor like Yamini.

The first person she saw was Avalon, who was lounging on a chair near the mainmast. He was giving instructions to Zazi and Dee as they carried a plank of wood to a splintered piece of the deck. His head was bandaged, and Twip was on his shoulder. Hewan hovered nearby, begging him to go back to bed. He ignored her and raised a hand when he saw Lintang. Despite his injuries, he looked happier than she'd ever seen him.

Zazi nodded to Lintang, then yelled as the plank thunked to the deck. Dee had dropped her side to pull Farah the clamshell from her belt and wave at the same time.

From the rigging, Mei called a hello between flips.

Lintang reached the bow and hugged her broken sword to her chest. The ship cut through the waves, as powerful and proud as it had ever been.

Keelee screeched, circling above.

"Thank you!" Lintang said to it.

She lifted her face to the wind. She'd done it. She'd impressed Captain Shafira, just like she'd said she would. She was allowed to stay.

Bayani joined her. "I'm sorry I snapped your sword."

Lintang laughed. "To be fair, you also did the impossible and fought a Kanekonese siren's spell to save me. I think we're even."

He propped his elbows on the railing. "I still can't believe I managed to resist it. The spell worked fine on Avalon."

"Mmm." She glanced at him. "Maybe there's something about you. Something special."

"Or," he said, "maybe the people who wrote *The Mythie Guidebook* need to remember we're not all like them." He eyed her broken sword. "Avalon might be able to fix that."

"No, it's all right." She took one last look at the hilt with its three carved moons in one hand and the chipped and worn blade in the other, then tossed them both overboard. The wind caught them, letting them fly, before they sank into the white foam. "I'll be getting a real sword next time."

"Next time?"

"I've been invited onto the *Winda* as a proper crew member."

"Really?" Bayani said. "That's great! Congratulations!"

"I'll be going home for one more season, though, to tell the village all the new stories I have."

He nudged her. "Good, because I'm not ready to say goodbye to you yet."

"You could always ask to come with us. I'm sure Captain Shafira won't mind having someone who can communicate with the Gods on board."

He didn't answer.

She licked salt from her lips and studied him. "How did you know the 'infection' was a second star?"

"Mratzi showed me when I was drowning," he said, looking at her in surprise. "How did *you* know?"

"The second star gave me visions of where it had been. Was it really all an accident? The shooting stars, the scattered seeds . . . ?"

"Yes. It was really, truly an accident. The Gods tried to warn us, but they'd never involved themselves with the living world before. We were just crops to them.

They didn't know our languages, or our cultures, or anything."

"But they can talk to you."

A long pause. Then, "Yes, they can talk to me."

"How, Bayani? How are you so special?"

He gazed out at the ocean for a long, long time. So long, in fact, she wondered whether he'd heard her. Then he said, "Mratzi showed me something when I was underwater. Something . . . impossible. I need time to figure it out."

She sighed. "I'm never going to get the whole truth from you, am I?"

"You will, I promise. One day."

"Mmm." She wasn't sure she believed him. But she wasn't going to let his secrets get in the way of their friendship—she had made that decision already.

She stared down at the water. It rushed toward them, breaking in two when it hit the prow. Looking at the water was different after being a mythie. The ocean had felt comfortable then, sort of like a home.

"What happened to Lanme Vanyan?" she said after a silence.

Bayani looked at her. "She was you."

"Yes, but . . ." Lintang examined her hands. "Where is that body now? Where is the second star?"

"Extinguished," Bayani said. "The extra seed is gone forever, thanks to the Curall."

"But I was a giant snake woman with wings. Where did that all go?"

"I don't know," Bayani said. "Inside you, I guess. She was the mythical version of you. Having that second star just . . . brought her out."

Lintang curled her fingers against her chest. So the extra star had been an enhancement of who she already was, or, perhaps, the adult she would be one day.

The mother of monsters. The warrior queen. What a thing to live up to.

Pelita bounded over to them. "What are we talking about?"

Bayani and Lintang exchanged a hesitant glance. "Home," Bayani said after a pause.

Pelita grabbed his arm, then Lintang's good one. "Home is wherever you two are."

"I like that," Bayani said.

"Me too," Lintang said. "Maybe you could both become crew members with me."

"Yay!" Pelita said.

Lintang laughed and turned to face the ship. She took in the wooden deck, the splintered mast, the billowing black sails, the bridge, and the people. Captain Shafira was at the helm, staring off into the distance. Xiang, still in her splint, argued with Eire about something while Quahah watched in amusement.

Lintang smiled. She would be going home for a while, and that made her happy. But the *Winda* was home now too. Captain Shafira would return for her at the beginning of the planting season, and after that . . . well.

She would make her own legends.

Acknowledgments

I'd like to thank Anne Hoppe, Rachael Stein, and everyone at Clarion Books for bringing Lintang to the U.S. I'm thrilled you love this story as much as I do.

Thank you to Zoe Walton, Cristina Briones, and the rest of the fabulous team at Penguin Random House Australia for your support and enthusiasm in bringing this book to life. Special thanks to Lindsey Hodder for plucking me from the slush!

Molly Ker Hawn, my agent, thank you for swooping in and rescuing me in the nick of time, just like a superhero. Thank you also for your kindness and patience over the years. I've appreciated our correspondence more than you could know.

I would never have met my editor if it weren't for SCBWI Australia West. Thank you to everyone who works so hard in this organization, and special thanks to Cristy Burne for being absolutely amazing.

Emma Burchett, Jennifer Liu, and Helen Pemberton —my cheerleaders—thank you so much for all the positivity over the years. *supertacklehugs*

My lovely year fives of 2016! Thank you so much for listening to early drafts of this book, for giving feedback, for being so incredibly enthusiastic. Your excitement made this whole process a wonderful dream.

Thanks to my family and friends for putting up with the lifelong brain strangeness that comes with being a writer. Vivienne Chan, let's do brunch.

Marissa Meyer, I owe you so much. You were there for me in my dawning days as a writer and have continued to be a supportive and positive presence in my life. Your encouraging emails were sometimes the only thing that kept me going. Thank you, thank you, thank you.

Finally, Marguerite Klup.

Marguerite. What can I say? How can I possibly express my deep gratitude for being there with me since we were fifteen, for reading every word I've ever written, for loving even my worst work with all that you have? How can I thank you for the praise, support, dedication, and long hours you've put toward my dream? You are the bestest of best friends. I wouldn't be here without you.

DATE DUE

			PRINTED IN U.S.A.